ASSASSIN'S HONOR

Something in his peripheral vision made him whirl around to the right. He pulled the trigger in the same instant he felt a stab of pain slash into his lower abdomen and his right leg. The guard he shot died instantly, but he knew he was just as dead now. It would just take longer. He attempted to get into a firing position, but fire lanced through his entire body. Gritting his teeth against a scream, he rolled onto his stomach, tearing his already-shredded stomach even more. He could now make out the thudding of boots approaching over the alarm, and it began to dawn on him that he just might fail for the first time in his life. He tried desperately to raise his weapon as an avalanche of sound exploded into the room and several guards rushed in and blazed away.

As the energy beams sliced him in half, he consoled himself with a final thought that at least it had been death that had beaten him. . . .

After all, everyone loses then.

MECHWARRIOR

IMMINENT
CRISIS

Randall N. Bills

A ROC BOOK

To my father, Jay Pope Bills.
In a world filled with misguided, disappointing,
and disposable heroes,
thanks for being *my* hero.

ROC
Published by New American Library, a division of
Penguin Putnam Inc., 375 Hudson Street,
New York, New York 10014, U.S.A.
Penguin Books Ltd, 80 Strand,
London WC2R 0RL, England
Penguin Books Australia Ltd, Ringwood,
Victoria, Australia
Penguin Books Canada Ltd, 10 Alcorn Avenue,
Toronto, Ontario, Canada M4V 3B2
Penguin Books (N.Z.) Ltd, 182–190 Wairau Road,
Auckland 10, New Zealand

Penguin Books Ltd, Registered Offices:
Harmondsworth, Middlesex, England

First published by Roc, an imprint of New American Library,
a division of Penguin Putnam Inc.

First Printing, March 2002
10 9 8 7 6 5 4 3 2 1

Copyright © FASA Corporation, 2002
All rights reserved

Series Editor: Donna Ippolito
Cover art: Ed Cox
Cover design: Ray Lundgren
Mechanical Drawings: FASA Art Department

ACKNOWLEDGMENTS

To Jason, Kathy, and Finn Hardy. Though our paths may have parted, our friendship will continue to grow across the distance. See you soon!

To Dan "Flake" Grendell. As I sit writing this, with half-filled moving boxes around me, I know ours is a friendship that can survive whatever fate throws our way. Thanks for the help on the assassin scene!

To Loren and Heather Coleman. Thanks for making the move the least painful of our lives and opening up your home and family to ours. Such friendships are rare and precious, and we thank you!

To Loren Coleman. Thanks for constantly extending a helping hand as I made the big leap!

To Rich Cencarik, Rich Darr, Brian Golightly, Ben Rome, Kenneth Peters, and Chris Johnson. Thanks for the katana and sentiment. May your own blades never shatter!

To the authors of the FedCom civil war novels: Loren Coleman, Blaine Pardoe, and Thomas Gressman as well as Chris Hartford, Bryan Nystul, Christoffer "Bones" Trossen, and Dan "Flake" Grendell, who may not have written a novel, but whose "behind the scenes" work and ideas helped to flesh out the picture from which we drew our individual strokes. Thanks for the great experience and the impetus to improve my own writing.

To FASA Corporation and all those who made it what it was for twenty years. It may be gone, but it will live on in us.

Much to my chagrin, thanks to Donna Ippolito, for putting up with me as those deadlines kept slipping. As usual, she's taken my at times incoherent thoughts and shown me how to turn them into a good novel. Thanks!

Finally, to my wonderful wife, Tara, and my son, Bryn, who make it all worthwhile.

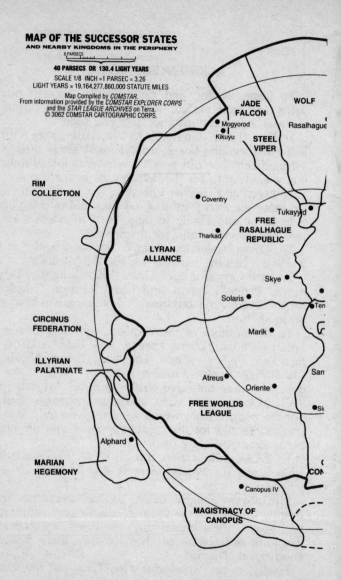

MAP OF THE SUCCESSOR STATES

AND NEARBY KINGDOMS IN THE PERIPHERY

8 PARSECS

40 PARSECS OR 130.4 LIGHT YEARS

SCALE 1/8 INCH =1 PARSEC = 3.26
LIGHT YEARS = 19,164,277,860,000 STATUTE MILES

Map Compiled by COMSTAR.
From information provided by the COMSTAR EXPLORER CORPS
and the STAR LEAGUE ARCHIVES on Terra.
© 3062 COMSTAR CARTOGRAPHIC CORPS.

JADE
FALCON

WOLF

Mogyorod

Rasalhague

Kikuyu

STEEL
VIPER

RIM
COLLECTION

Coventry

Tukayyid

FREE
RASALHAGUE
REPUBLIC

Tharkad

LYRAN
ALLIANCE

Skye

Solaris

Ten

CIRCINUS
FEDERATION

Marik

ILLYRIAN
PALATINATE

Sar

Atreus

Oriente

FREE WORLDS
LEAGUE

Sia

Alphard

MARIAN
HEGEMONY

C
CON

Canopus IV

MAGISTRACY OF
CANOPUS

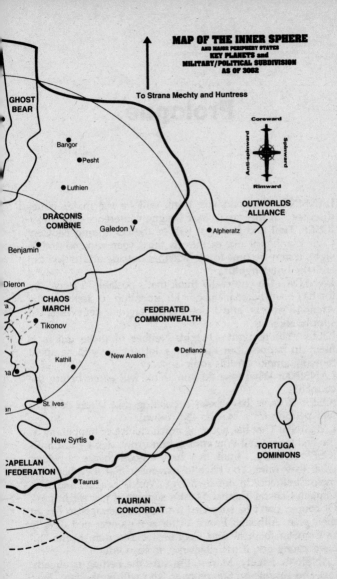

MAP OF THE INNER SPHERE
AND MAJOR PERIPHERY STATES
KEY PLANETS and
MILITARY/POLITICAL SUBDIVISION
AS OF 3062

To Strana Mechty and Huntress

Coreward

Anti-spinward

Spinward

Rimward

GHOST
BEAR

Bangor

Pesht

Luthien

DRACONIS
COMBINE

Galedon V

Benjamin

Dieron

CHAOS
MARCH

Tikonov

Kathil

New Avalon

St. Ives

New Syrtis

CAPELLAN
CONFEDERATION

Taurus

TAURIAN
CONCORDAT

OUTWORLDS
ALLIANCE

Alpheratz

FEDERATED
COMMONWEALTH

Defiance

TORTUGA
DOMINIONS

Prologue

LANSING: What do you think will be the major issues discussed at this year's Star League conference, Martin?

JOSEF: First and foremost will be the continuing FedCom Civil War. As it moves into its third year with no end in sight, it may be time to see whether outside arbitration can end the bitter fighting.

LANSING: Do you really think that's possible? Prince Victor has been adamant about his intention to dethrone the Archon-Princess, and I don't think anyone believes she'll simply abdicate.

JOSEF: You're right, Dwight. Neither of those things is likely to happen, but I'm sure a lot of time will be spent blowing smoke on this topic anyway.

LANSING: What else do you think will come before the council?

JOSEF: Rumors have been circulating that Word of Blake will petition for a seat on the council.

LANSING: That has about as much chance of happening as the Fed Com Civil War ending tomorrow, don't you think?

JOSEF: Actually, I think they have a good chance of getting what they want. You have to remember that they have immense influence in our own Free Worlds League, and with Captain-General Thomas Marik's support, it just might pass. Of course, don't be surprised if ComStar attempts to thwart their plan. Although Prince Victor is no longer tied directly to ComStar, both he and Coordinator Theodore Kurita still have strong ties, if not allegiance, to the Order.

LANSING: Finally, Martin, I'm sure the betting is already fast and furious on Solaris over who will be the new First Lord. Who is your first pick?

JOSEF: Well, Dwight, after closely studying the voting members and their alliances, I don't see how Archon-Princess Katherine Steiner-Davion can miss becoming next First Lord of the Star League.
—Chief correspondent Dwight Lansing interviewing senior political correspondent Martin Josef for the holovid newsmagazine *The Real Deal*, Free Worlds League, 4 November 3064

Royal Palace
Dormuth, Marik
Marik Commonwealth
Free Worlds League
4 November 3064

George Michael Hasek, Duke of New Syrtis, Field Marshal and Minister of the Capellan March, stopped at the entrance to the large hall, a little short of breath in the higher gravity of Marik. Or maybe it was a sudden case of nerves. He knew what he had to do, but if he failed, it could be political suicide. He couldn't let that happen to his people.

He studied the faces of those milling around in a chamber that looked far too utilitarian for a royal ballroom. They were the elite of the elite, the rulers of the Great Houses of the Inner Sphere, along with many lesser nobles and high-ranking military officials of every stripe, not to mention a smattering of Word of Blake personnel and the few ComStar individuals allowed for courtesy's sake. Even Periphery delegations from the Magistracy of Canopus and the Taurian Concordat were present. Watching them, George couldn't help thinking that only the Clans were missing from the illustrious gathering. He smiled, thinking that would be like a pack of wolves loose among the lambs.

Of course, no Clansman would ever be invited to the third meeting of the Star League Council of Lords, which opened today. George was equally uninvited, and that was the reason he was entering by the passage reserved for functionaries and minor aides rather than through the official entrance on the other side.

Drawing himself up to his full height, he stepped into the room, which was like entering a world of bright plumage, pheromonal perfumes, and subtle cockfights. All around him were the false smiles and inane chatter of nobles and military men who cared more about furthering their own power and prestige than their responsibilities to their people. Though he was a part of this world three times over, being with these types always made him feel like he needed a shower. Smiling and chatting politely the whole time, they would gladly slit each other's throats.

He scanned the room, seeking the person he'd traveled some four hundred and fifty light years to see. She spotted him at the same moment. Dressed in the pristine white she favored was his liege-lord, Archon-Princess Katherine Morgan Steiner-Davion. She stood among a group of her lackeys, and for an instant George saw her as a crystal spike, diamond hard. If he wasn't careful, he would impale himself on her, like a Combine samurai falling onto his own blade. When their eyes met at over two dozen paces, her expression froze briefly, and he had no doubt that her metaphorical dagger was unsheathed. The way her eyes flicked over him from head to toe left no doubt about the deadliness of her threat.

Pushing through the crowd, he strode toward her. He and Katherine had been tiptoeing around each other for two long years, each trying not to step across the final line, as troops under George's nominal command fought troops loyal only to her. Yet, a part of him still did not want to believe that she had abrogated her duty to her people. Perhaps she would still offer him an olive branch. Perhaps there was some way to bridge the terrible gap that yawned between them.

It was true that he had defied her in the Chaos March and on Kathil, and that he had taken to wearing the old uniform of the Federated Suns. But he had not come out against her and for Victor in the civil war. That had to count for something.

George revered his father, a man unwavering in support of the Davions, but he believed his first responsibility was to the people of the Capellan March. He was their defender and their champion. If Katherine and Victor wanted to spend their days battling each other instead of attending to the welfare of their people, how could he support either one of them?

Another two paces and Katherine's expression transformed into one of joy, like someone receiving an unexpected but welcome guest after many years' absence. For those who knew what to look for, the ice in her eyes only glittered more treacherously. He steeled himself for a confrontation that could turn more terrible than any 'Mech battle, then swept into the midst of her circle of Lyran nobles.

"Archon-Princess, I request an audience," he said, bowing formally, his expression arranged into one of polite courtesy.

Katherine Steiner-Davion folded her hands gracefully at her waist and smiled sweetly at those around her, as though begging their pardon. Not one of her group was a military man, yet most wore accoutrements that mimicked military medals, a fact that George found galling. These sycophants arrayed themselves in pseudo-military decorations that mocked the courageous men and women who protected their worthless hides.

"Gentlemen," she said, her words coated in enough sugar to choke a man, "it would seem that I have an unexpected visit from one of my field marshals. I beg your forgiveness and hope that I will have a chance to continue our important discussion at a later time." Her words, combined with her tone and gestures, turned George into the country bumpkin military commander interrupting his betters. With a flurry of sneering smiles, the courtiers voiced their empty platitudes and left.

He waited until they were out of earshot, then plunged right in. "Archon-Princess, I must ask why you've not responded to any of my communiqués over the last ten months," he said.

"My Duke," she began, "I realize you've just finished a long and tiring interstellar voyage, but so have many others in this room, and yet they manage to maintain their civility."

"Is that why you belittled me in front of those Lyran nobles?"

"Come, come George," she said smoothly. "We both

know how the game is played. I've been out of Lyran space for a long time, and I can't show more favor to one of my field marshals wearing the uniform of the Federated Suns than to them. We both know your worth to me. Anyway, please, George, this is not the time or the place for such a discussion."

Her surreptitious glance around the hall told him volumes. She did not want this conversation out in the open, so if he could keep her here, she might just give him what he wanted. Something to prove she was still worthy of her throne.

"What better time than now, Archon-Princess? You have ignored me for far too long. I'm still your field marshal and your duke, and I believe you owe me and my people some answers."

She paused as though to consider, all the while seeming to preen for an audience, though the nearest possible observer was more than five meters away—and looking in the other direction. George could hardly believe his eyes. Was this what she had become? Had she worked so hard to create a false image for the public that she could no longer turn it off? The thought saddened him, but only strengthened his resolve.

"My Duke—George—I do owe you and your people some answers. However, you must realize the strain my brother's horrible actions have placed on our realm and on my time. You, of all people, should know how many long hours are spent each day trying to stop the madness. If you can but wait until I return home from the conference, I'll make it a priority to answer all of your requests."

That not only failed to answer his question, but implied that she assigned him the same priority as any ruler of a single planet. Annoyed and frustrated, he decided to push harder. "But Archon-Princess, what have you been doing? Two years have passed, and yet forces declaring their loyalty to you—forces that should be under my purview—continue to fight against my March. Continue to kill military personnel in my March. Continue to kill civilians in my March."

He hadn't raised his voice, but his tone had taken on

an intensity he hadn't intended. "I can understand your actions when it comes to those units who espouse Victor's cause, but when your forces attack units loyal to me, what am I supposed to think?"

She sighed wearily as though his questions were physically painful, then looked over his shoulder as though suddenly recognizing someone.

"George," she said quickly, "perhaps you would like to walk with me. I hear that the Arboretum attached to the Royal Palace is a wonder." With that, she turned and began to walk sedately toward the ballroom's southern exit.

He hesitated, knowing that he might lose some of his advantage by leaving the hall, but she was already a few steps ahead of him. Out of the corner of his eye, he spotted Jerrard Cranston heading his way through the crowd. That settled it. George had no intention of speaking with either Victor or his lackey. Today was not the day for that battle.

After leaving the ballroom, he and Katherine walked for several minutes without speaking. Just when he was trying to decide whether or not to finally break the silence, she did it for him.

"I appreciate your position," she said, "and your devotion to *my* March that you safeguard is admirable." The emphasis rubbed George wrong, but he did not interrupt. "But why have you come here, George? You barge uninvited into the Star League council, and though you say you do not support Victor in any way, you come dressed in the uniform of the old Federated Suns for all the Inner Sphere to see. Don't you think that casts some doubt on your sincerity?"

"I am here, Archon-Princess, to speak with several individuals in my capacity as *your* field marshal," he retorted, "and I also wanted a chance to speak with you personally. As for this uniform, I wear it because it's time to stop maintaining the charade that there is a Federated Commonwealth. It died the day you enacted the emergency clause in the Alliance Treaty and pulled the Lyran half out. That is not to say I criticize you for those actions, as it did spare the Alliance citizens the horror of an invasion that the Commonwealth citizens had to bear." A slight shift in her shoulders indicated that she felt his subtle thrust against her leaving so many Fed-Com citizens to die.

"However, I do not wear it to support Prince Victor or to undermine your authority. I wear it because I am a realist, regardless of the civil war tearing our realm apart." As he finished speaking even he wasn't sure whether the words were true or simply the ones she needed to hear. At times like these, he wished for the clean fight of 'Mech combat, when the raised barrel of an enemy's PPC left no doubt what he or she intended to do.

She gazed at him sidelong as they continued toward what he assumed was the location of the Arboretum. She was truly beautiful, he thought. He might almost have courted her once—before her actions revealed the rottenness of her core. Oh, how his mother would have loved that, he thought ruefully.

"George, why don't you sit at my delegation's table during the conference?" she asked suddenly. "I'd prefer that you wore a Commonwealth uniform, but I can actually use your explanation to my advantage. It would show that you don't support Victor. Afterward, you could go about the rest of your business. Yes, I think that would work very well, don't you?"

George couldn't believe what he was hearing. Not only was she ignoring his repeated requests for answers, but she seemed to care only about using him to further her position on the council.

The Star League council be damned, he cursed silently. What about our homeland? What does this Star League conference do for the Federated Commonwealth but increase your political standing with our enemies while our civilians bleed?

At that moment, it began to dawn on him that she would never extend him an olive branch because she couldn't even see the need for it. Bracing himself, he forged on. "I'm sorry, Highness, but I will not sit at your table. You did not invite me here as part of your delegation, so I do not feel obliged to attend. I've other work I came to do, and once that is finished, I will leave."

His words should have elicited some reaction from her—any reaction—but neither her face nor her body betrayed the slightest emotion. Suddenly, George was terrified by what he had done. He had just rebuffed his own liege-lord, a woman who could order troops onto his soil. When she spoke, the words came out soft as silk, with no hint of the steel he knew to be hidden there.

"Well, then, my Duke, let me remind you that you *are* a field marshal in the military of the Armed Forces of the Federated Commonwealth, and as far as I'm aware, the AFFC has not been issued new uniforms. As such, you *are* defying the chain of command and, hence, defying me. Since you've just said you think I've a right to stop those who defy me, what am I to do? Additionally, you complain about troops loyal to me fighting troops you say are attempting to stay neutral, and yet those troops fight back. If they are yours to command, why have they not stood down? So, I ask again, George, what do you think I should do?"

He stopped in his tracks, forcing her to halt too if she wanted to hear his response. He saw the situation with utter clarity. He had come here with the hope of reconciliation, to see if something could be salvaged between him and Katherine. Instead, she'd thrown her rank in his face and ignored his concerns, which were one and the same with the well-being of the very people she'd sworn to protect.

"I can ask the same of you, Archon," he said, gratified to see the spark of anger in her eyes at the shortening of her rank. "What am I supposed to do? I owe you my loyalty, as do the troops under my command, but in return for that loyalty, you have a duty to me, to the men and women who serve under me, to the citizens of the Capellan March. If you've failed in that duty, what am I supposed to do?" Though her skin was pale and flawless as ever, he knew the gauntlet of his words had caught her a ringing blow to the cheek. The gauntlet lay at her feet, waiting to be picked up.

"I cannot answer that question for you, Duke Hasek,"

Katherine said. Her voice was cold as she drew herself up into the regal monarch she was. "The decisions you make must come from where you believe your honor and duty lie. Just remember that the ultimate consequences of your decisions will be on your head. And those consequences will affect the very people you claim to protect and accuse me of ignoring. Now, if you'll excuse me, I think I will postpone that walk in the Aboretum." She began to walk away, then turned for a single parting shot. "Perhaps in the near future I'll walk with you in your own Garden of Roses, George dear. I hear they are very beautiful."

As she returned toward the ballroom, he almost glanced down to see whether the gauntlet was still there or whether she had picked it up. He watched her retreating form, thinking about her final comment. It had been so innocent, yet it could just as easily have been a veiled threat of an assault on New Syrtis because of what he'd done and said today. Once more, doubts assailed him. He thought of something else she'd said, and he knew she was right. The people of New Syrtis would pay for his actions, as people across the Capellan March were already paying. He looked down at his hands, wondering how he would ever wash them clean of the blood.

He'd done what he thought was best for the people of the Capellan March, but he couldn't be sure it was the right thing. Reared since childhood in a duke's household, he fully embraced feudalism as the best possible government. Yet, he had just defied his liege lord, throwing his honor and his duty to the winds. Though he was now fully convinced that Katherine *had* failed in her duty to the people of both the Federated Suns and even the Lyran Alliance, and so had renounced her right to the throne, he could not help a twinge of conscience.

No matter how much he wanted to deny it, there was a word for the path on which he'd just set his feet. They called it treason.

wanted ACs, why not go for rotaries? I love my Ultra autocannon, but oh, what I could do with even one of those RACs."

Grayson gave a quick laugh. "Well, you're right about one thing. This *Templar* is definitely the finest ride I've ever had. I don't know why General Richards approved my request, but you won't hear me argue."

For perhaps the hundredth time, he looked with satisfaction around the cockpit of his brand-new 'Mech. Everything—from his primary and secondary screens to his targeting joysticks and foot pedals for controlling the 'Mech's speed and direction— gleamed as only a machine that had just walked off the assembly line could. Even the smell of paint and cleaning agents was sweet.

Grayson had piloted various 'Mechs during his ten years in the military, but all had been vintage models, some even hundreds of years old. Permeated with the grime, sweat, and fear-filled stench of myriad other warriors, they had seemed familiar, like old friends of the family.

The *Templar*, on the other hand, had only recently begun to roll off the assembly lines of Kallon Industries on Wernke. Massing eighty-five tons of weapons, metal, and myomer, the assault-class machine was a walking behemoth to put the fear of god into any enemy. The *Templar* was also the Federated Suns' first attempt at building an OmniMech. More versatile than a standard BattleMech and first developed by the Clans, Omnis boasted modular technology that let them change their weapons load-out in mere minutes.

"Yeah, yeah. It's a great 'Mech, but what in the name of Kerensky made you pass up the chance for an RAC?" Jonathan demanded.

"I tested the rotaries, Jon, but their jamming rate is unacceptable. I didn't want to risk losing one of my main weapon systems, no matter how impressive their rate of fire. As for the gauss, well, let's just say I'm trying something new today."

Grayson smiled to himself, knowing Jonathan would never understand how any MechWarrior could pass up a chance to field a rotary autocannon, one of the most powerful weapons a 'Mech could mount. Well, he would soon find out.

"New and stupid," Jonathan said.

"New and different," Grayson shot back.

"I said new and stupid."

This time, Grayson laughed out loud. Even Jonathan Tomlinson couldn't make him mad today.

Titans stalked the world, throwing thunderbolts to vanquish their enemies and proclaim their mastery of all they surveyed. Except that these giants were clothed in metal and piloted by humans, with all of their faults, frailties, and misconceptions. And that was exactly what Grayson was counting on. With their backs to a frost-covered canyon, the Swift Foxes were about to be cornered by the Snow Cobras—cornered and devoured.

"Cobra One, I confirm contact bearing one-one-zero," one of his men reported.

"Confirm," Grayson said. "Enemy is directly ahead.

Outriders, increase speed." A chorus of affirmatives echoed the order.

Grayson knew that the key to beating the Davion Light Guards was to neutralize their speed. The Guards regiment consisted almost exclusively of medium and light 'Mech designs, which allowed them to maneuver out of almost any trap with enviable ease. The Eighth had taken to calling them greased foxes, after the greased-pig contest played in almost every rural community in the known universe—a derogatory term the Guards had begun to flaunt with pride. They were undefeated till now, but Grayson told himself that all would change today.

Having dogged the Guards for the better part of two straight days, his company had finally maneuvered them toward a box canyon. With his assault 'Mechs positioned at the tip of an inverted V, they would deliver enough firepower to pin the Guards down, while his light and fast machines would swing out from the wings of the formation to close the door. Once the enemy was trapped, the heavier machines could wade in toe-to-toe against the lighter Guard 'Mechs.

Another minute passed in a white blur as the sides of the frost-covered canyon loomed larger. The Guards streamed toward the opening, desperate to keep the Fusiliers' superior firepower at range. Then, the first of their 'Mechs to reach the canyon entrance seemed to stall in confusion, perhaps uncertain of the terrain. Compared to the Fusiliers, who knew the region inside and out, the Guards had been on New Syrtis less than a year.

The distance between the two forces quickly cycled down to less than two kilometers, and still the Guards did not move. Grayson could see a Guard *Fireball*, one of the fastest 'Mech designs ever produced, vanish into the lengthening shadows of the canyon. Racing along at a speed of over one hundred-eighty kilometers per hour, its feet spit up blooms of snow as it dashed off to scout the terrain.

That still wouldn't be enough, Grayson thought. Not nearly enough. Many of the Guard 'Mechs were finally turning toward the onrushing Fusiliers, seeming uncertain of whether to fight or flee.

The decision was made for them.

As the distance clicked down to less than seven hundred-fifty meters, Jonathan triggered his autocannon, and a barrage of hypervelocity, uranium-tipped shells shot out on three-meter tongues of flame from their twenty-millimeter barrels. At this speed and distance, the rounds over-shot the enemy 'Mechs, digging furrows in the snow and chopping holes in the underlying ice. Undaunted, Jonathan kept the lead flying, tracking the stream of shells across the ground and into the leg of a *Garm*, which immediately fell backward.

"What the hell," Grayson heard Jon mumble. There was no way his fire could have taken the *Garm* down so quickly. The only advantage of small autocannon like his *JagerMech*'s was their range; their damage was minimal, at best. Whether it was the ice or the surprise at getting hit that took the *Garm* down, it quickly regained its feet. Even as it rose, it returned fire with a spread of long-range missiles. Their sooty contrails stained the azure sky.

The Guards had begun to spread out, waiting for the *Fireball*'s return before committing to the uncertain safety of the canyon. Grayson had to give them their due. His company outweighed them two-to-one in pure tonnage, which was enough to make any MechWarrior sweat. And yet they stood their ground, digging in to hold off the onrush.

As the distance fell to six hundred-ninety meters, azure whips of man-made lightning crisscrossed the sky in both directions. The fire from one of the PPCs belonged to the *Caesar* of Subaltern Dennis Jenks, to Grayson's left, but it merely flashed ice into water vapor, carving a long furrow as it did. The return fire, from a *Jackal*, found its mark, washing cobalt flame across Subaltern Adela Tonkovic's *Quickdraw*, to Grayson's right. More than a half-ton of armor flashed instantly into metallic mist that fell spitting and hissing into the snow at her feet. Either the Guardsman was a master gunner to hit at that distance or the 'Mech was a 55 variant, which incorporated the latest targeting and tracking system available to front-line troops. In either case, Grayson hoped this wasn't a harbinger of things to come.

"I can't believe they're not breaking," Jonathan said, the rumbling of his autocannons filtering through the link.

"Are you serious? These are the Davion Light Guards we're talking about," Leftenant Jack Mantas chimed in. Mantas's *Banshee*, to the left and slightly behind Grayson, was the only 'Mech in the entire company slower than the *Templar*, and he was having a hard time keeping up with the formation. "If you ask me, their lead lance is about to smash into us to give the rest of the unit a chance to get away. That *Fireball* is going to come back any minute to let them know they're trapped."

Jack had barely spoken when the *Fireball* appeared from the depths of the canyon. The Guards instantly exploded into action, showing both their experience and their skill. Sure enough, the lead lance charged directly into the teeth of the advancing Fusiliers. Grayson ID'd General Jessica Quarles's *Hatchetman*— a new 6D variant—as well as a *Centurion*, an *Enforcer* III, and a brand-new *Osiris*, still painted in the gray base coat it received on the factory floor. Meanwhile, the other lances scattered to either side in an effort to elude the wings of the Fusilier formation now sweeping in.

"I think I owe you a Timbiqui Dark, Jack," Grayson said, though he knew the fight was far from over.

"I'll take you up on that offer tonight, sir!" Jack called back.

With the *Templar*'s inexorable forward advance and the Guard lead lance now moving toward him, Grayson's own weapons were in range at less than five hundred-forty meters. Grasping a joystick in each hand, he brought his cross hairs onto Quarles's *Hatchetman*, which was in mid-jump, launching through the air on a contrail of super-heated plasma. Grayson's crosshairs burned gold with a solid lock, and he triggered his targeting-interlock system to fire a stream of rounds from both his forty-millimeter autocannon.

With his target at max-range and in mid-jump, and his own 'Mech moving at maximum speed, he would surely have missed the shot any other time. But he'd stacked the deck. Though he hadn't even lifted the *Templar*'s autocannon arms, the shell-streams bent slightly toward the target, slamming into the center torso of the jumping *Hatchetman*, pulverizing armor. The *Hatchetman* listed slightly to the left in the air, beginning to rotate along its axis. In a feat that spoke of her piloting skill, Quarles spread her arms wide to catch air resistance and bring her slowly tumbling 'Mech under control. Then she brought both legs into a crouch, hitting the ground in a sidewise roll through the snow. Though she landed hard in a geyser of snow and ice, the *Hatchetman* exploded back onto its feet, despite the loss of more than a ton of armor.

"Blake's blood!" Jonathan shouted. "What the hell was that?"

Grayson allowed himself a savage grin. His ace in the hole had worked just as he'd hoped. "That, my friend, is New Avalon Institute of Science technology at its finest," he said, loud enough for his throat mic to pick up. "Ever hear of precision autocannon ammunition?"

"Are you kidding? Sure, I have. I read the trade manuals, but I thought it was still in field trials."

"Not anymore. The Fusiliers received their first shipment earlier this month."

"Unbelievable. I almost didn't believe the NAIS claims. They always exaggerate everything. But damn!"

"Yeah," Grayson said. "Hot damn." Another wonder of new technology, and he was using it for perhaps the first time in all of the Capellan March. Precision ammunition was "smart" autocannon submunition that incorporated advanced targeting circuitry and a modified, self-propelled gyrojet shell whose microbursts allowed the shell to auto-correct in flight toward a target. The shells were only effective against a moving target and, because of their size, they drastically reduced the amount of ammunition his *Templar* could carry.

For various reasons, none of the more advanced autocannon like the ultra, rotary, or LB-X classes could use precision ammunition. If you wanted to field the new ammo, it was back to the autocannon that had been used on battlefields for centuries. Grayson figured he'd just proved that the trade-off was worth it. Seeing how well it worked, he couldn't wait to test some of the other submunitions that had arrived. Of course, his other ace in the hole was also straight off the NAIS research engine.

At the time of the original Clan invasion, their technology was far superior to anything fielded by the armies of the Inner Sphere. One of their most potent pieces of high-tech weaponry was an advanced targeting system that tied into a 'Mech's direct-fire weapons, providing an accuracy that Inner Sphere 'Mechs could not duplicate. After twelve years of research, the boys at NAIS had again proven why they were the best advanced-weapons research and development team in the Inner Sphere. They had developed a similar targeting computer, albeit with a slightly lower rate of efficiency than its Clan counterpart, but Grayson wasn't complaining. He knew his own skills and was damn proud of what he could do in a 'Mech. But he also knew of almost no one who could have made such a shot.

Weapons fire continued to fly, but it was almost anti-climactic from that point on. Though a Guard *Raptor* and a *Hellspawn* had broken out on the right-hand side, their comrades were trapped in a slowly tightening noose. An intense fusillade of fire knocked the *Garm* back onto the ground for good, quickly followed by the *Jackal* and two other 'Mechs that seemed to disappear under a barrage of laser and autocannon fire before Grayson could even identify them. His own losses were minimal, with only Lef-tenant Peterson's *Men Shen* down for the count.

Though Quarles's *Hatchetman* had managed to wade in among Grayson's troops and had been the one to cut the head off the *Men Shen* with a blow from her depleted uranium-tipped hatchet, the forty-five-ton machine didn't have a chance against several 'Mechs twice its weight. The *Hatchetman*'s sudden stillness made Grayson glance quickly at a secondary screen to verify what he already knew—the *Hatchetman* had just powered down.

"Yield," the general's weary voice said over the shared frequency. "All troops power down and yield. It seems the Cobras have finally found their bite."

As the scenario ended, Grayson's viewscreen fully pixilated for a moment and then solidified, showing a scene of subtle but important differences. What had been damaged armor now showed only as splotches of paint, while severed 'Mech limbs were back in place. 'Mechs that had previously been vaporized by the explosion of their fusion engines slowly regained their feet, none the worse for wear.

Grayson couldn't help but laugh out loud at Quarles's final comment. She probably thought her words had cut, but not this time. The Eight Syrtis Fusiliers had finally beaten the Guards.

2

JOHANSEN: From the very beginning, the Archon has been ruthless in suppressing those who oppose her, regardless of what the mewling media has portrayed. She's a political animal and knows very well how to manipulate the masses.

SMYTH: Oh please, Dr. Johansen. Are we supposed to believe that the Archon-Princess has hood-winked an entire Great House—no, two Great Houses—for years?

JOHANSEN: No, not completely, or there'd be no war. However, she's managed to convince enough people long enough to keep herself in power. There are only two major thorns in her side at the moment, and one of those has dared defy her to her face. Mark my words, in the next few months, you'll see an attack directly on New Syrtis.

SMYTH: That's preposterous! Why would the Archon-Princess attack Duke Hasek? She has no reason to do so. In fact, I much admire the man for keeping New Syrtis out of the fighting.

JOHANSEN: And you wonder why I think you're blind! Have we ever seen a statement from Duke Hasek condemning the troops under his command for continuing to oppose troops loyal to Katherine? If nothing else, the charnel house of Kathil should demonstrate to anyone not blinded by media glitz and the Archon's façade that Duke Hasek has his own agenda, one that does not support the Archon. He may not have declared for Prince Victor directly, but in her eyes, if you're not with her, you're against her. Fighting will come to New Syrtis, Mrs. Smyth. It is only a matter of time.

—Dr. Deryl Johansen, political correspondent for the Federated News Services, and Jessica Smyth, Sub-Minister of the Kestrel Administrative Area, on *The Steffelbus Group*, Kestrel, Federated Suns, 10 May 3065

Headquarters, Eighth Syrtis Fusiliers
Saso, New Syrtis
Capellan March
Federated Suns
19 May 3065

> *. . . And night and night*
> *The virgin comes*
> *A sea of blue swallows*
> *The light of the sun . . .*

As the words of the song penetrated Grayson's concentration, he frowned and grabbed the remote to silence the local radio station. He always listened to music whenever it was time to attack the mounds of paperwork that went with his job, but it was getting harder to find any he liked. Usually, he tuned into the latest underground station, catching the newest music before it was rubber-stamped for mass-market consumption. Increasingly, though, he simply couldn't stand to listen.

No matter how disguised the lyrics, the music invariably seemed to take sides in the civil war. Millions of people had already died—one of them a person he'd loved with all his heart—yet Grayson could still not make up his mind about which side was in the right.

His concentration broken, he gazed idly around his tiny, windowless office. On one wall hung two holos of his family and one of his Warrior's Hall graduation class. A detailed topographical map of New Syrtis covered another wall, and the other two were lined with bookshelves containing everything from Sun Tzu's *The Art of War* to Ian Davion's *The Strategy of Deception*. One whole shelf was devoted to the rules and regulations of the Syrtis Fusiliers. The only other objects in the room were Grayson's desk, which was buried in hardcopy, and two chairs, one of which he currently occupied.

Grayson knew that the Capellan March would officially enter the fight before long. He was also sure that George Hasek would align himself with Victor Davion, for both personal and political reasons. Yet, Katherine Steiner-Davion sat on the throne of both Tharkad and New Avalon, the lawful ruler of the whole Federated Commonwealth. Despite all that had happened, he still couldn't get past the idea that had been ingrained and trained into him: to oppose the rightful ruler was treason.

With a sigh, he tried again to concentrate, and simply could not. Rubbing his eyes, he leaned back in his chair, hoping to clear his head of the questions conjured by the music—questions he'd been asking himself ever since the war began, demanding answers he still did not have. When a knock on the door sounded, he welcomed the interruption.

"Enter," he said.

The door opened to admit a bone-thin man with a sharp nose and piercing blue eyes, who Grayson always teased about being so skinny he could have hidden behind a broom handle. Yet, the man's most distinguishing feature was his long blond hair, which he wore in a single braid down to the small of his back. It made him an odd sight on a military base, and his uniform—a one-piece suit of snow-white, with a sky-blue stripe running down the trousers to the white and blue of his half-boots—added to the strangeness.

It was unlike any uniform in any military unit Grayson had ever heard of, but Colonel Chad Dean, commander of the mercenary Vanguard Legion, was unlike any person he'd ever known. Which was, of course, how Chad managed to get away with that hair and that uniform. Some Fusiliers had mocked him at first, but they quit laughing after going up against Chad in combat exercises. In the war-torn era of the thirty-first century, skill on the field was all that mattered.

"Chad," he said, his pleasure washing away the last of his gloomy thoughts. Standing up, he quickly walked around the desk and gave his friend a bearhug. Chad's unit had recently returned from a stint in the equatorial region of New Syrtis, doing guard duty on some supply depots located on a chain of tropical islands.

"I see you still insist on trying to kill me every time we meet," Chad grumbled.

Grayson laughed. His friend had a streak of sarcastic humor similar to Jonathan Tomlinson's, but his deadpan delivery often made it sound like he wasn't joking. In this case, Grayson knew that Chad wasn't referring to the bear hug but to Grayson's own shaved head, a stark contrast to Chad's luxurious locks.

"I'm just glad to see you again," he said.

"Oh is that all?" Chad let a slight smile crease a face that almost never let its guard down.

"How was it?" Grayson asked. A lot of soldiers liked being sent down to the Hothouse, where things were generally quiet and the weather was warm.

"Dull and too hot. Can't believe I'm actually saying that, but after a year and a half on this glacier, stomping my 'Mech through the jungle had me losing weight almost by the minute. Amazing how much you can sweat and still live."

"You, lose weight? You'd have to drop bone mass if you wanted to do that."

"I'll have to try that the next time I get fat like you."

Grayson's attempt at a look of wounded pride failed miserably.

In one of his quicksilver changes of topic, Chad managed to lower the temperature of the room without even batting an eye. "Heard the latest from Kathil?"

"Yeah," Grayson said.

"What do you think?"

Grayson's hands balled into fists so tight he could feel his fingernails digging into his flesh. "Oh, it's a great victory for our side, right? Down with the tyrant, hurrah the taste of freedom and all that." The fighting on Kathil had become infamous. The first real shots of the civil war had been fired on that world, and the fighting had dragged on for a year and a half. Now the planet was safely back in the fold of the Capellan March, but thousands had died or been injured in the brutal struggle.

"It still hurts, doesn't it?" Chad said. It wasn't a question.

"How can it not? We threw snowballs at each other when we were eleven. Went to the same schools. Attended Warrior's Hall together, and then we both got billets in the Fusiliers. We loved each other like the brother and sister neither one of us ever had. She was a tracker—so what? If not for Andrea, I probably would've been like most MechWarriors, utterly arrogant and unwilling to admit how important our armor assets can be. And now, nine months later, I still wish I'd proposed to Andrea when I had the chance."

Chad didn't say anything for a few moments. "With her assigned to the Sixth, you two wouldn't have had much time together."

"Better than nothing," Grayson said, running one hand over his shaved head. "Which is all I've got now." Andrea Jacobsen and her unit were destroyed while trying to rescue the Fifth Davion Guards from a trap in which the Fifth was also destroyed.

"It would only have caused more pain," Chad said softly.

"How could it? I can't imagine the pain being more than it was . . . is."

Chad was silent for another moment. "And yet you don't hate?" he asked.

Grayson shook his head. "That would be like spitting on her memory. She was a soldier and she did her duty, but neither of us was ever convinced a civil war would solve anything."

"I just can't figure out how you don't make this whole thing personal after losing your girl to the Lyrans. You think the Light Guards aren't going to take it personally that the Fifth Davion Guards were destroyed in the final push to take Kathil last month?"

"Yeah, I'm surprised we haven't heard General Quarles's screams yet," he said. "She usually lets everyone know what's bothering her."

They both paused, each expecting the other to laugh. But there was really nothing funny. The death of such a large and prestigious unit was no joking matter.

"How many units does that make?" Chad asked, serious again.

Like every soldier in the Capellan March—if not in the entire civil war—Grayson had closely watched the seemingly endless battle for Kathil. Perhaps the second-most important planet in the entire Federated Suns, it was home to one of the largest JumpShip manufacturing facilities in the Inner Sphere—and without JumpShips, interstellar travel would not be possible. Both sides had thrown one unit after another into the meat grinder, each attempting to gain the upper hand and secure the world for their benefit.

He counted off the numbers with an upraised finger for each unit lost. "The Second NAIS Cadet Cadre was wiped out during the initial fighting. The Kathil CMM bought it during Wave One. The Eighth Fed-Com RCT was destroyed in Wave Two. The First Capellan Dragoons and the Eighth Donegal Guards RCT went down in Wave Three. From the reports I saw, the Second Chisholm's Raiders RCT and the Fifth Davion Guards RCT got wiped out in the most recent fighting."

Chad shook his head sadly. "And the Sixth is as close to being destroyed as you can be and still maintain cohesion. If the First Federated Suns Armored Cavalry hadn't arrived in January to bail out the Sixth, the Raiders would likely be holding the planet instead of us."

"It's a travesty," Grayson said.

Chad raised his eyebrows in a show of irony. "That sounds almost like treason."

Grayson laughed bitterly. "Strange words coming from a mercenary." He and Chad had talked and argued endlessly about the civil war. The Vanguard Legion was known for its animosity toward the Lyran Alliance, and Chad had no problem figuring out where he stood in this war.

"I'm just repeating what you've been telling me for so long."

"It's not treason to hate what occurred there," Grayson said. "When was the last time you saw so many units fight until they were destroyed? Even during the Clan invasion, most units fought the good fight and then withdrew to fight another day. Five full RCTs fought on Kathil, and now there's not even enough left to form a single regiment!"

"Come on," Chad said sharply. "Open your eyes. This is civil war! This isn't about conquering someone else's territory. It's about protecting worlds and people that both sides believe they should defend. It's been the same through ten millennia of human history, and it's not about to change now. Every soldier who made planetfall on Kathil knew how important that world was for whoever could take it. And we took it."

"Did we?" Grayson snapped. "Who is we? The Armored Cavalry is firmly committed to Victor, and they're fresh troops compared to the Sixth, which spent the last year and a half losing personnel faster than water. Is Kathil a Capellan March world again, or simply a world Victor can now use to win back his power?"

Chad shrugged like he didn't get it. "Isn't that the same thing?"

"No, I don't think it is. It's true that Katherine was underhanded in taking over Victor's throne, and that's a legitimate grievance. But I don't know what's going on with him anymore. Sometimes I wonder if he traded in his Davion birthright for a samurai sword or a ComStar cloak and dagger. I've never once questioned my loyalty to Duke Hasek, and he's never given me cause to. Victor, on the other hand . . ."

A brooding silence fell over the room. Chad stepped closer and laid one hand gently on Grayson's shoulder, giving it a reassuring squeeze.

"It's getting time for you to make up your mind, Gray. Or someone else will be making it up for you. It won't be long before the war comes home to New Syrtis."

The hair stood up on the back of Grayson's neck. Chad was right. New Syrtis was a March capital, and it was nothing short of a miracle that George Hasek had kept it neutral till now. Soon they would all be forced to choose.

3

With four Alliance Province capitals under Prince Victor's control, many pundits are wondering whether Victor will try to cut the Archon-Princess off from Skye, the fifth and final Alliance province capital not currently under his control. It would be a stunning blow to her in the Alliance, where she should have her strongest support. With Skye's history of determined resistance against any incursions, it is doubtful that even Prince Victor can summon the forces necessary to conquer the ever freedom-loving people of Skye.

—Holoclip from *News at the Top of the Hour*, Tharkad, Donegal Broadcasting Company, Lyran Alliance, 4 June 3065

Warrior's Hall
Near Saso, New Syrtis
Capellan March
Federated Suns
5 June 3065

It was graduation day at the Warrior's Hall, the Capellan March's top military academy, and a new set of recruits was about to enter service. The Hall of Ceremonies was packed, the acrid tang of sweating bodies mixing with plumes of smoke and clouds of perfume in a way that had Grayson on the verge a violent sneeze. He held back in honor of the occasion, his gaze playing over the room. The scene brought back good memories, and the anxious young faces of the cadets awaiting graduation reminded him of his own not-so-distant past.

As those recollections began to bubble up, a face he did not want to confront hove into view. Her chocolate-brown eyes and short, curly brown hair framed a face more tomboyish than beautiful, but he had always thought her magnificent. Unwilling to visit such territory today, Grayson thrust the image and its memories aside.

It wasn't just fond memories that had brought him here tonight. The regiments of the Syrtis Fusiliers often recruited the top graduates of the Warrior's Hall to fill vacant billets in their ranks. Grayson had his eye on Cadet Williamson, who he hoped to acquire for a spot in Force Lance, Second Company. Standing at the back of the hall with the Eighth's two other battalion commanders, he looked out across the sea of people: cadets in the front rows, relatives and friends in the back rows. Top honors had already been bestowed and graduation certificates handed out. All that remained was a short speech by Duke George Hasek.

On cue, the duke appeared from a door at the far right of the stage and walked smartly to the podium. A military man born and bred, he simply would not look right in anything but a uniform. Today, he was in his element. Gazing out across the sea of faces, he projected quiet confidence combined with undeniable strength.

Grayson noticed both cadets and officers straightening their backs to affect an even more disciplined demeanor. As for the ladies, even the married ones were acting like a flock of startled birds. Their fans snapped and their ostentatious hats jiggled as their heads bobbed to and fro in whispers to their neighbors. It reminded him of some avian courtship dance, with plumage spread wide. Who could blame them, though? With the exception of Tancred Sandoval, George Hasek was arguably the most eligible bachelor in the entire Federated Suns.

Clearing his throat, the duke brought instant silence to the hall.

"Warriors," he began, "today you graduate, answering the call of honor and duty to serve the Federated Suns, just as so many others before you have heeded the call to protect what we have built across the seven-and-a-half-century history of our great House. However, this day brings a need like none we have known for hundreds of years. For wolves do not merely bay at our gate but have found their way in among us. What's worse, they are not Capellans or Kuritans, or even pirates from the Periphery. No, they are our own people, our own comrades. Most of you have watched as New Syrtis was spared the disease that has crippled our beloved State. Yet, you have brothers, sisters, cousins, and friends on other worlds who have not been so fortunate. The pain and anguish has been felt by us all."

He paused for a moment and closed his eyes, as though experiencing the pain of the thousands, perhaps tens of thousands, who had already lost their lives or their loved ones to the war. From anyone else, Grayson might have thought it cheap theatrics, but not from George Hasek. As the silence continued, he noticed tears streaming down the faces of more than one civilian in the audience.

Opening his eyes, the duke continued in a voice heavy with emotion. "Today is a day to leave behind the things of youth and to pick up the mantle of adulthood. Soon, we must all be prepared to take our stand. I have pledged to protect the Capellan March and the Federated Suns, and today I reaffirm that oath. Looking at you, the future of the Capellan March sitting before me, I am confident that we will prevail. Congratulations and welcome to the ranks of our military!"

With that, he gave the assembled warriors a smart salute, then turned from the podium and strode from the hall by the same door he'd come in. Grayson could almost sense the beating hearts of every person present as the shock of the duke's speech registered on almost two hundred souls. Glancing around, he saw looks of astonishment that he was sure mirrored his own. Not only was this the shortest speech ever given at a graduation ceremony, but it was like nothing any of them had been expecting.

Something had changed for the duke to be so blunt, but no one knew what.

Almost thirty full seconds passed without a sound

or movement in the entire hall, then came an explosion of noise as everyone began to talk at once.

"What the hell?" Grayson said, leaning toward Major Geoff Pitcher, commander of Second Battalion.

Geoff looked equally shocked. "Do you think this has something to do with Kathil? The duke still hasn't made any official announcement. Maybe he figures Katrina is going to come for New Syrtis now that we've taken Kathil back."

Grayson shrugged. "You got me—"

"Please, ladies and gentlemen, some decorum. Attention!" a voice said loudly, cutting through the conversational buzz like a laser through armor. The grizzled features of Leftenant General William Hasek, commandant of the Warrior's Hall, immediately had every warrior in the room snapping to attention and silence. The old man had been teaching at the academy for over three decades. His commanding presence silenced the civilians as well.

"I know that the duke's comments have raised many questions," he said. "However, ours is not to question, but to heed. As members of the Armed Forces of the Federated Suns, we know our duty. You civilians should know yours as well. Cadets, it has been my distinct honor to lead you to this point in your lives. Today, I name you warriors and ask that you uphold our legacy. Dismissed."

With those words, the ceremony ended. Family members, held at bay during the three-hour ceremony, attempted to rush forward and embrace their newly graduated son, daughter, brother, sister, cousin, nephew, niece, or friend. Grayson noticed a distinct air of alacrity surrounding some of the cadets the way it did all the regular servicemen around him. He tried to tag each of those cadets' faces and names. They were the type of soldiers he wanted in his command. They'd understood the implications of what was said here tonight.

He thought of the references to the Armed Forces of the Federated Suns. What happened to the Armed Forces of the Federated Commonwealth? Yes, most of the troops in the Capellan March had begun to wear a uniform more closely aligned with the traditional uniform of the old AFFS in a silent protest against Katherine. But this? Was it an official proclamation against the FedCom and the Archon-Princess?

Geoff raised his eyebrows. "Armed Forces of the Federated Suns, eh?" He shook his head in disbelief. "Do you think the duke is finally taking an official stand?"

"I'm not sure. Could just be the commandant putting his own spin on things."

"Except that the duke is going to hear about this. Just 'cause the general is George's cousin doesn't mean he won't be in hot water for this."

"You've got a point." Suddenly a new thought hit Grayson. "Maybe this is simply another way for the duke to remain neutral, while letting his troops know the direction in which he's moving. It still gives him deniability with Katherine."

Looking around, Grayson could see that the crowd was not breaking up, but was simply shifting as various cadets attempted to speak surreptitiously with their classmates, while not alarming the civilians. He nodded once to Geoff and pushed into the crowd. None of the civilians would know who he was, and most of the cadets were so engrossed in their conversations that they failed to notice the presence of a superior officer. Which was fine by him. He wanted to hear their words uninhibited by his presence.

We're going to war! I know we are. What else could it mean?

About time we take that whore off the throne.

So, we're just going to side with Victor. Who says he's any better than Katherine?

I don't care what you say, we're not going to war. Who would attack New Syrtis? The Archon-Princess?

We should just stay out of it. Is it really our war? Who cares who sits on New Avalon's throne? If the duke has to go his own—

That last was suddenly cut short when the three graduates involved in the conversation suddenly realized that a leftenant colonel was standing right next to them. Three sets of perfectly timed salutes and snapped-to attentions made Grayson realize he would hear nothing more from them.

Throwing a casual salute, he walked on, thinking about what he'd heard. There seemed to be as many ideas about what was going to happen, or what should happen, as there were cadets. That last conversation was particularly troubling. It was one thing to declare war against the throne—though he still was not completely comfortable with that idea—but it was something else to talk about the duke taking the Capellan March in a new direction. It had been centuries since the Duke of New Syrtis had been a prince, equal in almost all things to the First Prince on New Avalon. Could George Hasek actually be heading in that direction?

Moving aimlessly, almost restlessly among the crowd, it dawned on him that everyone around him was as confused as he was. No one knew what was going on and that began to scare him. Seeing the confusion, he actually began to hope that the duke *was* making a decision. One way or another, it was time for action. Right? Better to jump in than be caught unprepared. Right? But which way to jump? Could you take action and yet not take sides?

At that moment, Grayson simply could not say.

4

With the arrival of the Gray Death Legion on Hesperus, there can be no doubt that Katherine Steiner-Davion sees an enemy on the horizon and has moved to protect her largest supply of BattleMechs. Lori Kolmar-Carlyle is also Baroness von Glengarry, and she would never move to this posting without a direct command from her liege, Katherine herself. Does Katherine's intelligence suggest that Prince Victor is moving to secure the final Alliance province capital? If so, he may have bitten off more than he can chew. There are also rumblings that Skye—as so many times in the past—has begun to agitate for total independence from the Alliance.

Even now, our sources report a significant increase in the activities and combat readiness of Hesperus II's defenders. And if Skye is moving to secede, what has finally given the rebels the confidence to act?

—Pirate broadcast by the People for Unity,
Tharkad, 23 July 3065

The Cave
Saso, New Syrtis
Capellan March
Federated Suns
22 July 3065

Known as the Cave, the Regional Military Headquarters of the Capellan March was aptly named. Carved from a limestone cavern far beneath the planet's surface, it dated back two hundred years to Damien Hasek, who had ordered its construction upon being named Duke of New Syrtis in 2829. Streaked with yellow, brown, and red mineral deposits, the bare rock walls were still visible, making the place as beautiful as it was impregnable. Though most of the stalactites and stalagmites had been cleared during the chamber's original construction, many still hung around the outer edges, silent sentinels that had watched over the activities of this place for more than two hundred years.

Near the capital city of Saso but some two kilometers underground, the Cave was impervious to almost any type of attack, including orbital bombardment. The five separate exits, along with the dozens of marked tunnels, allowed for instant retreat should the unthinkable come to pass. It was the military cerebellum and nerve center for the entire Capellan March, whose one hundred forty-one inhabited star systems were protected by forty 'Mech regiments, five times that many armor regiments, and ten times that many infantry regiments. The March sat between two foreign borders that, together, stretched over seven hundred light years of interstellar space. In a civil war, with every planet potentially poised on the brink of violence, those borders increased exponentially.

"Could you possibly fit any more brass in here?" Geoff murmured, sidling up to Grayson, who, in the crush, had dropped the sealed envelope handed to him and every officer as he or she entered. Swearing, he shouldered several officers out of the way to retrieve it.

"If George Hasek could, he would. It would mean we had more forces on planet," he said.

In the center of this claustrophobic vault, which measured roughly thirty meters on a side, sat a holographic table, an unassuming piece of equipment that could project images up to five meters in diameter, allowing everyone present an unobstructed view. Right now, an image of the entire Federated Suns hung in the air—all five hundred-plus star systems—with borders delineating the Crucis, Capellan, and Draconis Marches, along with the further subdivisions of Combat Theaters, Operation Areas, Polymorphous Defense Zones, and Combat Regions.

Worlds with a significant military presence were coded, and each of those worlds displayed a color representing the political disposition of the planetary forces: yellow for Victor, blue for Katherine, and gray if neutral. Any planet that had active fighting was highlighted in red; there were a lot of red circles floating in the air.

Seated in two half-circles around the holotable, comm technicians manned banks of computer consoles tied into the New Syrtis hyperpulse generator station. With the information streaming in from nearby star systems via HPG, they kept the map continually updated.

In between those computer banks and the holotable were the commanders of every 'Mech regiment on planet: the Davion Light Guards, the Eighth Syrtis

Fusiliers, the Vanguard Legion, and the New Syrtis Capellan March Militia. Also present were the commanding officers of each aerospace, armor, and infantry brigade attached to the Guards and the Fusiliers, the planet's two Regimental Combat Teams.

Representing the Eighth were Duke Hasek, Major General Deborah Palu, and the RCT's four brigade commanders. Also present were Major General Tia Caruthers and the commanding officers of the New Syrtis CMM. Grayson saw Chad Dean among that crowd of dark-green clad soldiers, and his tall, fair-haired frame looked like a sunflower in a weed patch. Though some officers seemed to snub him, they were generally armor or infantry officers. The Legion had neither, fielding 'Mechs exclusively.

Noticeably absent were the top brass of the Davion Light Guards.

The rest of the room, which rose at a slight angle from the center bowl, was filled with each 'Mech regiment's battalion commanders and the armor and infantry regimental commanders. Including the various technicians present, that brought the number up to eighty individuals, almost sixty of them brass. A dozen flat-screen table monitors occupied the rest of the room, allowing anyone to view information up close or to add their own comments with a light stylus. It was a gathering like nothing Grayson had ever witnessed. The Davion Guard officers, however, were nowhere in sight.

"Where are the Guards?" Grayson murmured to Geoff.

"I'm not sure. I would've thought that—"

A sudden commotion at one of the entrances brought Grayson's and everyone else's head around. Four Light Guardsmen began to make their way down through the gathered officers, and a hush fell over the cavern. There seemed no end of surprises of late.

Only recently stationed on New Syrtis, the Davion Light Guards had been adamant about declaring their neutrality in the civil war, though everyone knew that the unit's commanding officer, Hauptmann General Jon Buchvold, was a political appointee of the Archon-Princess. While the rest of the units on planet began to adopt the older Federated Suns ranks and uniform, the Guards had remained steadfast in using the Federated Commonwealth uniform and ranking system. Though this had not caused problems at first, in the last month, there had been incidents of personnel from other regiments butting heads with Guardsman over it.

Today, though, the four Light Guard officers making their way toward the duke were wearing Federated Suns uniforms. Was this the reason he had called such a large gathering of officers—to let everyone know that the Guards were firmly on the Fed Suns side? A show of solidarity to boost everyone's morale?

That certainly made sense, Grayson thought, but he wondered what had caused the sudden change of heart. Was this the final signal the duke had been waiting for? The event that meant the time of waiting was over?

As the four officers reached George Hasek, they

saluted. The duke gave each a firm handshake, followed by a few words that were inaudible to the rest of the crowd. Then he slowly turned to address the assembly of officers, his voice now loud enough to reach the last ranks.

"Officers of New Syrtis, may I present to you Marshal Jessica Quarles, the new commanding officer of the Davion Light Guards, as well as Light Commodore Athena Davion-Ross, Major General Jacob Drathers, and Major General Angela Voss. I'm sure you all recognize them, but today they come before you more our comrades in arms than ever before."

Surprised murmurs swept the room, but there were also a few hurrahs and some applause that started at the far side of the cavern and soon swept the Cave with its enthusiasm. Grayson wasn't exactly sure what to think, but it was a relief to know that even the remote possibility of fighting between troops on planet had been eliminated.

Holding up his hands for silence, the duke went on. "Let me speak plainly. Jon Buckvold was taken into custody three days ago by members of the Guards, and is accused of dereliction of duty and endangerment of personnel. A tribunal composed exclusively of Guardsmen will convene in the next week to begin preliminary hearings to determine the necessity of a full court martial."

His words reminded everyone present of what was at stake. Yes, the Davion Guards were now firmly committed to New Syrtis, but it had required the removal of their commanding officer to do so. Whether the charges were trumped-up or real was inconsequential. The fact remained that a personal appointee of the Archon-Princess had been removed, and there would be consequences.

Grayson noted that the duke never once said that the Guards had taken this course of action at his behest. The Davion Guards had arrested the general, the Guards would try the general, and if necessary, the Guards would court martial the general.

George Hasek again raised his hand for silence. "Officers of New Syrtis, I believe the time has come when we can no longer ignore the inevitable. I know my words and actions over the last months have caused some confusion, and though that was not my purpose, it was necessary. Now I must put aside all posturing. You have all proven that your loyalty to the Capellan March and myself is unquestioned. You have also proven your dedication to the Federated Suns and what it stands for.

"I make no excuses, for I need none. I have called this meeting to make sure that you do understand what will transpire shortly. I am convinced, as is General Richards, that New Syrtis will come under attack by forces loyal to Katherine Steiner-Davion before the end of the year."

The duke paused, a look like surprise on his face. Perhaps he had been expecting shouts of alarm or consternation, but his commanders continued to receive his words with attentive silence. Combined with the duke's words and actions of the preceding months, not to mention the stunning reversal of the Guards' long-held political stance, his statement was almost anti-climactic.

Looking around at the faces of the men and women who controlled the lives of over ten thousand soldiers and more than a hundred thousand civilians on planet, Grayson was momentarily overcome with sorrow. They calmly awaited the fight. More, many of them were looking forward to the fight. For some of them, sitting on the sidelines had been a curse. Their brothers in arms across a thousand light years were declaring for one side or the other, and 'Mechs were marching to the drums of war, while New Syrtis had done nothing for almost two years. Was he the only one who thought of the last twenty months as a blessing? Blood would soon flow like a river flooding its banks, but what he saw on the faces of many around him was *finally*!

Realizing he hadn't been listening for some minutes, Grayson missed the last of the duke's speech. Slightly mortified, he glanced around to see pride and determination mirrored on almost eighty faces. Only one or two others flickered with doubt.

Clearing her throat, Major General Deborah Palu, senior officer of the Fusiliers and overall commander of the on-planet forces, took the duke's place and began to speak. "Men, as you've no doubt surmised, the envelope each of you holds is the plan for the defense of New Syrtis. Open it now."

As the sound of dozens of envelopes being torn open echoed through the room, a voice close to the front spoke up. "Sir, I realize that this attack is based on the best intelligence we have, but how are enemy forces going to get past the *Covenant*? The ship could probably withstand an attack by even three or four

Fox-class corvettes." The *Covenant*-class WarShip of the same name maintained orbit around New Syrtis and was one of the reasons why Katherine had yet to strike at the world.

Craning his head to see, Grayson saw that the voice belonged to Colonel Meda Brown, recently promoted to command of the 384th Federation Mechanized Infantry Regiment. From the withering look Deborah Palu gave her, she almost seemed to regret recommending the promotion.

"*Colonel*, if you had reviewed the document first, you would already know the answer." The emphasis Palu placed on her rank made Brown flinch. "However, since you've brought it up, I'll clarify for those who can't read. As you know, the fighting on Kathil ended earlier this year, with the shipyards and the world now firmly in our hands. What almost no one knows, and we ourselves have only recently learned, is that a remnant of the Second Chisholm's Raiders was able to secure the McKenna Shipyards long enough to take control of both the FCS *Andrew Davion* and the FCS *Hanse Davion*. They immediately jumped out of the system and have not been seen since."

Several low whistles floated through the room, while Palu gazed impassively at the assembled officers. "I'm no expert in naval warfare, but I think one *Avalon*-class cruiser would be a match for the *Covenant*, much less two." Not a soul dared contradict her, nor did they need to. Putting an *Avalon* against the *Covenant* would be akin to Grayson's *Templar* attacking a *JagerMech*. Hardly a fight.

"Now, as I said previously, open your envelopes. You have exactly five minutes for a preliminary review, and then I want suggestions on the fly. We've been sitting on this rock for eighteen months, crosstraining with all on-planet forces for the last six. You better not need any more time than that."

So, this was it, Grayson thought. The floodgates were opening wider, and war would engulf New Syrtis in blood and death as it had so many other worlds for light years in every direction.

5

Jason Hasek Proving Grounds
Near Saso, New Syrtis
Capellan March
Federated Suns
2 September 3065

Leaning against the leg of his *Templar,* Grayson swirled the fluid in his spare canteen. Sweat ran down his face and dripped across the bridge of his sunglasses, prickling his scalp where a few days' growth of hair was desperately trying to scratch out life on his shaved head. Though the day was almost balmy for a glacier, the slight northwest wind sent tiny shivers down his spine and made him wish he'd done a better job of mopping himself off. This was no time to catch a cold. At least he'd had the good sense to throw on his jump suit. He shivered involuntarily again at the very idea of standing out in this weather—fine though it might be for this time of year—clad only in traditional MechWarrior garb of cooling vest, shorts, and combat boots.

At the sound of crunching feet, he looked over his shoulder to see his command lance walking toward him from where they had locked down their own 'Mechs. The heat his *Templar* had generated during the latest exercise sent up plumes of steam as the hot metal bled heat into the cold air. It made his lance mates look as if they were walking through a wall of fog. That was nothing new, of course. With the intensified training of the last few months, it felt like all he did was walk through a continual fog haze anyway.

Jonathan Tomlinson walked over. "Ah, the nectar of the gods," he said, holding out a small, collapsible metal cup to Grayson.

Grayson smiled, uncapped the canteen, and poured out a quick shot of the slushy liquid. Dennis Jenks also grinned while holding out an identical cup.

"Adela," Grayson said, swirling the canteen roughly so the sound of sloshing liquid could be heard.

Though she always refused, he always offered. He respected her wishes, but this was Snow Cobra tradition.

She flashed her beautiful smile but shook her head.

"Ah, gorgeous, I'll figure a way to get you yet," Jonathan said.

"First, I'd rather drink aviation fuel than a Cobra sour," she fired back. "Second, you've been trying long enough and where's that gotten you?"

Dennis hooted while everyone else chuckled.

"Oh, that hurt. That really hurt, Adela," Jonathan said.

"Well, the least you could do is try and have a hurt look on your face when you say it."

"Or at least a hurt voice," Dennis put in.

Jonathan held up his hands as if to ward off an attack. "Hey, I'm trying. Gimme a break. Anyway, I was talking about the Cobra sour, not me. Poor drink just got insulted."

There followed more laughter as two glasses and a canteen—along with Adela's canteen of water—were raised in a toast. She never partook, but she respected the unit's traditions.

"To the strike of the Cobras," four voices intoned as one, and then the three men knocked back their shots. Grayson felt his eyes water at the shock of bitterness, while Jonathan let go a growl of satisfaction.

The Cobra sour, based on a drink older than space travel, was at heart a whiskey sour without the sugar. It was supposed to consist of two fingers of bourbon, one tablespoon of fresh lime juice, one of lemon juice, and a cup of crushed ice. In the field, however, you made do with what you had. The bourbon was easy, but the lime and lemon juice were powdered extract, and the crushed ice was a handful of chipped ice. After it was sloshed around in a canteen, you either had a drink the Eighth had used for toasting for a century or more—no one could even remember when or why the tradition had started—or a liquid for scouring grime off your 'Mech. Grayson had never tried the latter, though he'd heard it worked just fine.

A soft thumping sound intruded and quickly became the ponderous vibration of 'Mech footfalls. Glancing out from under the *Templar*'s legs, Grayson and the others could see the approaching silhouette of a *Hatamoto-Chi*. It was Chad Dean's 'Mech.

It was still odd to see a design so closely tied with the Draconis Combine walking across the glaciers of New Syrtis. Perhaps even more so because for centuries the Combine rulers were famous for their dislike of mercenaries, their code of bushido at odds with the soldiers they called lucrewarriors. Though their "death to mercenaries" policy had softened under Coordinator Theodore Kurita, mercenaries were still few and far between under the Dragon's banner. So, for a mercenary to pilot a *Hatamoto-Chi* was strange indeed.

Even queerer, the entire command lance of the Vanguard Legion was composed of traditional Combine designs: two *Hatamoto-Chis*, a *Grand Dragon*, and a *Mauler*. Grayson had never gotten the complete story out of Chad—who liked his secrets a little *too* much—but he knew it had to do with the Legion's previous contract with the Combine to help search for the location of the distant Clan homeworlds. In one of the great ironies of history, it was the act of a Clan traitor that finally revealed the coordinates and the route.

The *Hatamoto-Chi* halted a short distance away as Chad locked the 'Mech down. His three lancemates pulled alongside and began their own shut-down process. Within moments, a hatch on the side of the *Hatamoto-Chi*'s head—which resembled the traditional *kabuto* helmet of a samurai—swung open while a long chain-ladder unrolled and dangled to the ground. Clad in a jumpsuit, Chad shimmied out of his cockpit and rapidly began to descend the ladder. Years of practice let him easily skirt the hot launch tubes of the Streak-type six-pack short-range missiles in the torso. Grayson had never heard of the HTM-2T variant until he'd seen Chad's, but he'd been posted on the Capellan border so long that he hadn't needed to keep up with Combine tech.

"I see our erstwhile companions have arrived," Dennis said.

Jonathan nodded. "Yeah, after the drubbing they gave us, I'm surprised they waited this long to begin their heckling."

"When was the last time they 'heckled' us?" Grayson demanded. "They've beaten us in roughly half these exercises, and I haven't heard them say a single word against us."

"Colonel Dean doesn't need words. He just gives you his look, and you know the rest of us mortals are beneath his notice," Adela said.

Jonathan and Dennis nodded agreement, but Grayson wondered if his unit was over-reacting to the fact that a merc unit was giving as good as it got. It looked like the Combine wasn't the only place that could be unfriendly to mercs.

He shrugged slightly. "Chad Dean's a good friend, and the Legion is a crack unit you'll be glad to have on our side when the hatchet falls."

"Do we really think the Archon-Princess will attack?" Adela asked.

"Oh, come on," Jonathan cut in. "When are you going to open your eyes, girl? That witch wants absolute rule over the Federated Suns and the Lyran Alliance, and as long as George Hasek sits on the throne of New Syrtis, she'll never have it."

Adela winced slightly, as did Grayson. The civil war had been raging for almost two years, with the forces under Duke Hasek nominally considered "rebels" by the crown, but it still felt wrong to speak so disrespectfully of Katherine. She was their rightful liege lord, and the power and authority inherent in her birth passed from her, through Duke Hasek to them, his men at arms. It had been that way for centuries, and to oppose her still didn't sit right with many soldiers, no matter how much their rational minds might argue for it.

"And don't give me any lip about the witch thing," Jonathan said. "We're rebels, remember? Or are we just training for the hell of it? The duke expects this planet to be attacked, and that's what all this training is for, right?" He looked around angrily, his previous good humor evaporating like ice before a hot spring sun. With a disgusted shake of his head, he turned and walked away.

An uncomfortable silence descended. It wasn't the first argument like this since the duke's bombshell, but it was the first to leave such a bitter taste. Grayson knew he should be leading by example, showing his troops the direction their thinking should take. But he still had his own doubts. Sure, the duke had them preparing for the worst-case scenario, but it wasn't to invade another world or to directly attack Katherine's supporters. It wasn't really choosing sides to prepare to defend your homeworld if attacked, was it? After all, what if some overzealous unit decided to simply hand the Archon-Princess the prize of New Syrtis? She wouldn't have ordered the attack, but it would still have occurred. Then, it would be completely justifiable to defend the world.

So why didn't he speak? Call Jonathan back and demand a retraction? Was he afraid to find out how far down the path of "choosing sides" some of his people had traveled? If so, he wasn't fit to be commander of Third Battalion.

Before he could do anything, the soft crunch of boots against snow and ice announced the arrival of the Legion's command lance. Because the Legion's warriors hated the Lyrans, similar arguments with them had recently degenerated into a shouting match, with Adela defending the Archon and Jonathan cursing Katherine, while Grayson tried to walk a middle ground between.

"Ho, Chad," he said as his friend walked up to join the group.

"Hey, Grayson." A chorus of hellos and congratulations ensued, and the talk immediately went to the latest exercise and how the Legion had defeated the Fusiliers. With the hot topic of civil war safely stowed for now, even Jonathan rejoined the group, happy to throw in his two cents about how he had carried the day, regardless of the Eighth's loss.

Listening to the talk, Grayson was pleased at the rapport that had developed between the two units, just as the Eighth had been cementing a similar bond with the Guards. Yet, the unanswered questions of loyalty and "sides" still boiled just beneath the surface. Soon, very soon, they would all be asked to decide. Would Adela really be able to fire upon her countrymen? Would Jonathan be infected by the hatred of the Legion and kill as many Lyran loyalists as he could find?

As for Grayson, would he ever feel right in his heart about a decision either way?

6

Through the heroic efforts of General Adam Steiner, the Jade Falcon attacks on Alliance worlds during the latter half of 3064 were finally contained by January of this year. Though some believe the Falcons' wings have been clipped, given half a chance, they will surely attack again. The longer this civil war drags on, the more it pulls forces away from defending the border with the Jade Falcons, the more vulnerable we are to further rapacious attacks.

We must also ask whether it is only the Falcons we have to fear. What's to stop Clan Wolf from attempting a strike through the thin line of the Jade Falcon zone at the belly of the Pandora Theater? Combined with a renewed assault by the Falcons through either the Arc-Royal Defense Zone or through the coreward edge of the Melissia Theater, a new Clan invasion could carve out another massive slice of our Great House, without ever crossing the Tukayyid truce line. Can anyone forget that the Truce of Tukayyid expires in a mere twenty months?

—from *The Clan Menace*, a special report, Donegal Broadcasting Company, Donegal, Lyran Alliance, 19 September 3065

Hasek Ancestral Palace
Saso, New Syrtis
Capellan March
Federated Suns
20 September 3065

"**W**hy does every conversation we have end like this?" George Hasek asked. Though he kept his voice down, he didn't hide his frustration. "I've got an impending attack on this world that we'll be lucky to repel, thousands of civilians who I should be protecting dying, and this is all you can talk about?" He breathed in deeply, trying to calm his anger.

"And what else should I talk about?" his mother asked. "You won't listen to reason, so my only choice is to bring up the subject whenever I can. You think I don't know the strain you're under? Unless you've suddenly acquired a case of amnesia, you'll remember that I *was* in the military for years, not to mention at Morgan's side for decades." Kym Sorenson-Hasek was also keeping her voice down, but she was no less adamant.

"How could I forget it, when you're constantly harping on it? Maybe if you left me alone for a single day, I might," George said, then instantly regretted his words. He cursed himself for a fool. "Mother, I'm sorry. That was unforgivable."

Standing before him in the throne room of the Hasek Ancestral Palace, his mother—now in her sixties—was still a beautiful woman. With her blond hair, which she'd worn in an austere bun as long as he could remember, and her lightning-blue eyes, her face was almost angelic. George often imagined how easy it must have been for his father to fall in love with her in their youth. Right now, he saw another look in her eye, however, one that cored him to the soul. He'd seen it only once before, when news had reached them of his father's murder. That he should be the cause of a similar pain was more than he could bear.

Turning away slightly, he said nothing for many moments. He could not, would not, hurt his mother in this fashion. He would feel disgraced in the eyes of his father, who he'd loved and admired more than anyone he'd ever known. But to have to give in on this? Now? It was infuriating. Softly, he spoke the only words he could. "All right, mother, I consent. I'll start seeing your prospects starting tomorrow."

He expected to see her nod sagely, letting him know that the decision was for the best. Instead, she was already moving off, her slippered feet a whisper on the mosaic floor of the Hall of Audience. Anyone else might have thought she was retreating, but he had seen her work the various marquees, counts, and barons who'd owed fealty to Duke Morgan Hasek-Davion once too often not to recognize the look of victory. Her regal bearing spoke volumes; she'd accomplished her task. Though still annoyed that she continued to manage him so easily, he nodded grudgingly in her direction.

Point to you, mother, he thought.

She had been attempting to marry him to one noble daughter or other ever since the start of the civil war. Whether it was a reception where young hopefuls were seated on either side of him at the banquet table, or during some review of the planetary defenses when he would have a "chance" encounter with this or that female warrior of noble birth, his mother's scheming only became more ingenious the more he resisted.

You must have an heir, she would say. You are the scion of Morgan Hasek-Davion, one of the greatest heroes of the Federated Suns. What if something should happen to you during this terrible war? History is filled with dynastic struggles because no clear successor was left.

The fact that he agreed with her on the importance of a successor made it all the more frustrating. No matter how often he argued that his two siblings were also in line for the Hasek throne, that would not satisfy her. *He* was the heir and it was *his* child who must take his place. Nothing less would do.

The pace of her suggestions, of her entrapments, had increased until not a day went by that she did not find some way to bring it up. His only respite in the last year and a half were the months he'd spent traveling to and from the Star League conference on Marik. But today was the final straw. With the unexpected arrival of one of his father's oldest friends, she had pounced on him in a moment of vulnerability.

Though he hated to admit it, he had done similar things in his drive to maintain the integrity of the Hasek holdings and the strength of the Capellan March. And all of it learned at his mother's knee. Though Morgan Hasek-Davion was a man most would have followed unquestioningly across the river Styx and beyond, it was George's mother who'd taught him how to move those who would not budge of their own volition.

A voice interrupted his thoughts. Snapping back to reality, he looked up to see a guard in the traditional livery of the Hasek Ancestral Palace standing before him.

"What did you say?" he asked, so distracted he hadn't even caught the man's words.

"My lord, your visitor comes," the guard repeated, while nodding down the twenty-meter length of the Hall of Audience. Through the open doors flanked by a pair of guards, Morgan saw a tall man making his way through the topiary-filled Garden of Roses, which occupied the central court of the Palace.

As a child, George had often wondered why the Hall of Audience, which was where Hasek dukes received nobility and honored guests, was positioned as it was. Why force people to travel through most of the palace and then through the garden until they arrived at the Hall? His mother had noted that the original architect had wished every visitor to be awed by the might and majesty of the Hasek dukes, as symbolized by their Ancestral Palace. Now, as an adult, it all made sense. Even in that, his mother had schooled him well.

"Thank you," he said to the guard, who took up position beside the throne raised on a three-step dais behind them. From the moment he'd learned of the visit, George had decided he would receive this particular guest in the Hall of Audience. The two hadn't seen each other in years, but the man was an old friend of his father's, and George had known him during his childhood. The man was also firmly in Victor's camp, another connection with George's father, who had been a Davion loyalist to the bone.

Much as he revered his father's memory, George was his own man. He had favored Victor at the start of the civil war, but he was no longer so sure that his childhood friend was the person most fit to rule. Victor had changed since returning from the Clan homeworlds campaign, and George feared that if Victor won the civil war, it would only set off another series of challenges to his power. George wanted peace and prosperity for the Capellan March, not more centuries of bloodshed and bitterness.

What better way to make it plain to his guest that George Hasek was not his father than to receive him in the Hall constructed to put every visitor in his place? George gazed around once more at its opulence. The entire floor was laid with slabs of black marble. Cut into shapes that fit together like the pieces of a puzzle, they portrayed the vastness of the Capellan March outlined in lines of malachite. Each solar system was represented, with large white marble circles for stars and small red ones for the planets. There were far fewer than George ruled today, as the palace had been constructed several centuries before; the March had less worlds back then, most of them taken from the Capellan Confederation.

Along the walls marched ten fluted columns rising to a height of twelve meters from floor to the ceiling. Carved from marble of the purest white, they were a stunning contrast to the gleaming black floor. Between each column was a small alcove set with a red velvet bench and a white-curtained backdrop.

The room's ceiling was a single, uniform piece of titanium, buffed to mirrorlike perfection. Its effect could be mesmerizing at times, as though a person traversing the Hall of Audience was actually striding through interstellar space, leaping light years with each step. For someone approaching the throne, it was a reminder that the supplicant was coming before the master of hundreds of worlds stretching across vast reaches of space. For the lord of the Hall, the effect was empowering, as though the duke were a god striding across the cosmos. George Hasek had not thought of such things since his youth, when his father had seemed so omnipotent to him. But now, he realized it was another piece of his father's legacy, a gift from one generation of ruling Haseks to the next.

Deciding that he would greet his visitor while seated on the throne, he ascended the three steps and turned to sit down. It would be better, he decided, to clarify his position from the beginning. Misunderstandings had already started too many wars.

His visitor finally reached the doors, and the two guards ceremoniously moved to block his path. George could not hear what they said, but he knew their traditional challenge by heart. Then, one of the guards turned, calling out in a voice that filled the Hall, "My lord, Marshal Ardan Sortek requests an audience."

Nice touch, George thought. Sortek was apparently

not above political intrigue himself. A life-long friend of Morgan Hasek-Davion as well as the late Hanse Davion, Ardan had also served Victor. Under him, he'd been assigned to the advisory council for the Commanding General of the Star League Defense Force, but it was rumored that he had resigned his post in the AFFC to join Victor's Armed Forces of the Federated Suns. Today, he came dressed in a non-descript jumpsuit that showed no insignia, yet he'd had himself announced as "Marshal," a rank that existed in both militaries. Apparently, he hoped to gain some advantage by trying to keep George guessing.

"Permission to enter," Ardan said, then began crossing the long hall toward the throne. Head held high, he gave not the slightest sign of being intimidated. Considering all that he had seen and done in his seven decades of life, that was no wonder. With his full head of snowy white hair and still youthful face and body, he looked much younger than his years. Like a ghost from the past, his presence evoked memories of a better time. A time when the FedCom was not tearing itself apart and George's father still lived and breathed.

If Ardan's presence affected him like this, George wondered how his mother would handle seeing Ardan again. Then he reminded himself that she was a rock that only death would dislodge. Though he didn't like thinking of his mother and death in the same thought, Ardan's visit was a harbinger of the coming storm. Of the attack that Katherine would soon launch at his beloved home world. Death would be no stranger when that happened.

"Duke Hasek, it is good to see you again," Ardan said as he halted a few steps from the dais and bowed smartly. The two men locked eyes, sizing each other up while not betraying their thoughts.

George realized that Ardan might be feeling a similar anxiety. He knew that his actions and words had left most people unclear about his true aims or intentions. Of course, that had been his purpose. He had specifically charted that course to keep Katherine from guessing what he would or would not do. It hit him that his friends and allies were probably just as confused.

He stood up suddenly and descended from the throne. "Ardan, you're a sight for sore eyes," he said. Though it might be dangerous to greet Ardan so warmly after making his point with the throne, perhaps it would not matter in the end. If their views were in conflict, then George's actions would only sow more confusion for Ardan, which was fine with him.

Reaching out, George embraced Sortek, clapping him firmly on the back. Then he stepped back and grasped him by both shoulders. "You've not called on New Syrtis since before the Clan invasion, if memory serves."

Ardan smiled, the lines around his eyes crinkling pleasantly. "Yes, it has been far too long. I was on my way for a visit in '57, but then some upstart decided to invade us and I had to return to New Avalon as quickly as possible."

George laughed without mirth. "Yeah, an upstart. And now look at what he's accomplished. He has practically reunified his whole realm, signed mutual-defense treaties with two Periphery powers for the first time in history, and he just sits there content, watching his most hated rival tear itself apart." There was no need to speak aloud the name of Sun-Tzu Liao.

"Yes, but his time will come," Sortek said. "His House does indeed look impressive, but not even his famous juggling act can last forever. Then it will be your turn to sit and watch with satisfaction."

Still unsure of Ardan, George steered away from a topic that might reveal too much of his own thoughts. "Yes, you may be right. We'll have to drink to that. Come, walk with me." Leading the way, he began to head down the Hall toward the Garden of Roses.

Ardan gave a slight bow. "Yes, your Grace."

"Please," George said with a dismissive wave of his hand, "not that. Though we haven't seen each other in over a decade, you've been a part of my family's life for much longer. Inside this palace, you've no need of such formality. George will do."

Ardan smiled and gave another slight bow with just his head. "Thank you, George."

They continued to stroll toward the far doors, their out-of-sync footfalls sending discordant echoes through the hall.

"So, to what do we owe the honor of this visit?" George asked. "I doubt you were just in the neighborhood."

Ardan chuckled at the absurdity of the idea of being "in the neighborhood" when dealing with astronomical distances. "No, I'm here for a purpose."

"Oh. It wouldn't have to do with a woman in white sitting on a throne somewhere, would it? Or with the 'incident' that's currently going on?"

"As a matter of fact, it does."

"Which one. The woman in white or the incident?"

"Both actually, since they're one and the same."

"Are they?"

"Yes. They couldn't possibly be any more intrinsic. George, I realize you're trying to feel me out, and I'm not here to dissemble. That would waste your time and tarnish a long-standing relationship I've had with your family."

George crossed his arms as he walked. "I'd also hate for you to waste my time, Ardan. Besides, I have only fond memories of you. It would be disappointing to discover that we no longer have things in common."

"I guess that all depends on what you consider common ground."

Passing through the large double-doors constructed of the finest hardwood and lead glass, they continued leisurely into the Garden of Roses. Before Kym Sorenson had married George Hasek, the place had been known simply as The Garden, and boasted dozens of flower varieties from across the Capellan March. His mother, however, had loved roses to the exclusion of almost any other bloom, and now more than half the garden was filled with their jewel-like colors and arresting perfume.

Moving off the gravel walkway, George paused and crouched to scoop up a handful of freshly tilled dirt. He took a deep whiff of it, then squeezed it between his fingers and let it sift back down to the ground.

"This is our common ground, Ardan. Though this dirt lies at the center of my palace, it is ground that could be found anywhere on New Syrtis, or on any world in the Capellan March. It is ground that has given sustenance to my people and to their fathers and their fathers' fathers. It is ground my father taught me is almost sacred." His voice caught slightly with emotion.

"Beyond all the fancy words and trappings. Beyond all the barons and counts and other functionaries. Beyond the JumpShips and DropShips that roam between planets. Beyond all the BattleMech armies that march at my command. This is what matters. This is what my stewardship is about. Protecting my worlds and, in turn, protecting the people who call them home. Is that common ground enough?"

Ardan stood looking at him intently, and then bowed much deeper than he had in the Hall. "Your Grace, your father taught you well. I can see why the men who followed him now follow you with equal devotion. Yes, that is a ground that I find common enough, indeed. And it is a ground that is being taken away from you. Taken away by one who has no right to it."

"Oh. And who does have that right?"

Ardan hesitated for just a moment before speaking. "Is that a question that must be answered right now? Isn't it enough to know that her claim is not valid?

That everything in our power should be done to remove her and stop the madness?"

"Perhaps. But will that really stop it? For many men—military, commoners, and nobles alike—*we* are the rebels defying the crown. If we remove her, who's to say that we will not put someone else on the throne who has just as little right?"

A long silence stretched between the two men, and Ardan slowly looked away. "There are those with the right to the throne," he said softly. "Those who have proved their worth time and again."

George clicked his tongue softly as though scolding an errant child. "Ardan, you promised to speak plainly, and here you are beating around the bush. I'd ask you who—"

Then he stopped and smiled. This conversation had gone approximately the way he'd thought it would. There was no denying that Ardan was firmly in Victor's camp and that he was here to swing George Hasek into that camp. Yet, he could see that Ardan was still the open-hearted man he had known from his childhood. They might not see eye to eye, but he almost looked forward to the mental and verbal sparring that would surely take place over the next few weeks. He was confident of his own stance but wondered what arguments Ardan would bring to the table.

He clapped Ardan on the back once more. "Don't worry. I won't make you answer that question now. Instead, we'll just agree that Katherine does not deserve the throne of the Federated Suns. Afterward, well, we'll deal with that soon enough, I imagine.

Come. Let's find that drink I mentioned earlier. Who knows, it might just signal Sun-Tzu's downfall.''

Both men chuckled, and turned to retrace their steps back into the palace.

7

REPORTER: "Mr. Secretary, can you confirm or deny the rumor that a move against New Syrtis is in the offing?"

MR. MAGERS: "And we've all heard the rumor that a plan to invade Luthien is also underway. I'm surprised you'd give credence to such hogwash, sir."

REPORTER: "Isn't it true that Duke Hasek confronted the Archon-Princess at the Star League conference on Marik and told her he would see her unseated by the end of the year."

MR. MAGERS: "It's true that Duke Hasek attended the meeting on Marik. The Archon-Princess met with him and even suggested he join her delegation, which he declined because of his need to return to his duties. However, what possible reason could the good duke—one of her own field marshals, I might add—have for making such a statement? And why in the world would the Archon-Princess move against her own duke?"

REPORTER: "I could site numerous reasons, but you still haven't answered my question, Mr. Secretary."

MR. MAGERS: "Yes, I have. You, from the Federated News Services, next question."

—Press Secretary William Magers, Daily Press Briefing, Davion Palace, New Avalon, Federated Suns, 20 September 3065

Avalon City, New Avalon
Crucis March
Federated Suns
20 September 3065

Dressed in the white she often favored, Katrina Steiner-Davion, Archon-Princess of the Federated Commonwealth and Archon of the Lyran Alliance, made a rare appearance in the Fox's Den. From this subterranean chamber in the palace on New Avalon, her generals directed the forces of the Crucis March as well as kept tabs on the militaries of the Capellan and Draconis Marches and the entire Lyran Alliance. The place had been named for her father, known in his time as the Fox, but she thought of it more as an ant colony filled with worker ants, busily going about their duties for their queen.

One worker ant was not serving his queen as he should, she thought with a frown that she erased as quickly as it came. Too much frowning would only wrinkle her. With numerous generals and scores of marshals to help her direct this war, she almost never set foot in the Den. They were schooled in their art and she in hers. She usually left them to scurry about carrying out her orders, going about her business in their small-minded ways.

Today, however, she'd tired of waiting for Marshal Simon Gallagher to come to her first, and she'd sent one of the ubiquitous comm techs who seemed to fill every niche of the military to find him. Those, she thought, are surely the male ants, desperately attempting to be useful and generally getting underfoot. Nevertheless, with the peak of her satisfaction at the current state of the war waning slightly and boredom setting in, she toyed with the idea of stripping Simon of his Prince's Champion title and naming someone else as Director of the Crucis March Regional Command. She quickly tossed the notion aside. It had taken her far too long to find a doormat to fill that position. Someone who would simply do her bidding without attempting to deflect her plans with his own irrelevant ideas. Infinitely easier to let him know of her displeasure than to waste the effort finding another drone to fill his shoes.

"Highness, if you will come with me, I'll show you to the marshal's office," she heard someone say. Looking around, she saw a young officer standing in front of her, bowing. It dawned on her that he'd been standing there for several minutes, and she hadn't even noticed him. Then again, why should she have? He was just another worker ant.

With a gracious nod, she gathered up her dress around her and waltzed after him, confident of her power. All of this belonged to her, and soon there would be no one left to thwart that ownership.

Heading away from the main command center, the young man led Katrina down a short hallway that led to a sizable door. He rapped sharply on the metal, then waited until a muffled voice bid them enter. Bowing smartly to Katrina, the officer then turned to open the door and stepped aside.

Having already forgotten him, she brushed past him into Gallagher's office. She'd been here before, and it struck her again what a strange place it was.

There were no holopics of Gallagher alone or with other officers or the usual vain and repulsive holopic of a soldier's first 'Mech. There were not even maps on the walls. The whole place was an empty expanse of white, broken only by an impressive mahogany desk and a small beechwood filing cabinet to the right of it.

Settling her gaze on Gallagher, she couldn't help thinking that the anonymity of the room was a reflection of the man himself. He was just another ant, devoid of any use except to follow her orders without question. He was a thin man, almost gaunt, with a balding head that he vainly attempted to hide by brushing several greasy strands of hair across the top.

He rose quickly and came around the desk to perform a bow worthy of the most skilled courtier. "Your Highness, I apologize for the delay, but it was unavoidable. I'm honored by your visit. What may your humble servant do for you?" His words were the finest silk, but as empty as the little eyes that looked at her almost hungrily.

Katrina studied him impassively, thinking he looked like a gangly puppet waiting for the pull of her strings. Under her steady gaze, a slight twitch began near his right eye, and a thin film of sweat broke out on his broad forehead. He knew better than to say anything more.

She let the silence drag on further, letting him twist in the wind, while she took his seat. Though they both knew that Simon had the much weaker position at all times, it provided a small amusement, a diversion from his stupidity, to inflict further discomfort on him.

Finally, she broke the silence. "Where is Marshal McCarthy?"

Gallagher tried surreptitiously to mop his brow while speaking in a voice more nervous than usual. "He'll be here shortly, though I'm not sure why you need him."

Katrina hardened the look in her eyes, and he almost took an involuntary step backward. The tick near his eye showed graphically that he was aware of overstepping himself again with such a question. Too many of those, and she would toss him aside. After all, even doormats wore out.

"This war is finally coming to a close, Marshal. With the midget pushed back and crushed, I believe the time has come to deal with thorny problems in our own pastures."

Gallagher suddenly looked as though he was about to swallow some particularly noxious concoction, but he spoke anyway. "Highness, Victor may have vanished from sight, but I would not count him out yet. As your Highness has pointed out numerous times, he may not have your political deftness, but he is a military man. Unless we see his warm, dead body at our feet, I do not think it wise to assume that we've seen the last of him."

Katrina raised one eyebrow, which brought an audible swallowing sound from Gallagher. She wondered where he'd gotten this sudden courage. He'd never spoken this way to her before.

"I did not say the war was done. I said it was coming to a close." She placed her hands on the smooth mahogany surface of his desk. "You're correct that my brother is an excellent soldier. Perhaps even one of the finest since the days of Alexandr Kerensky, but what has soldiering gotten him so far?"

She paused for effect, holding Gallagher's eyes. "He foolishly attempted to make his way into my world—the world of politics—and I've shown him the error of his ways. Shown him in a way I believe has crushed him completely. Yes, he is a fine soldier, but he gives himself too freely, and that is his weakness. He will not overcome this setback, General. I know my brother too well. As for his warm body, I'll be more than happy to drive a stake into it when he's here. He's come back from the dead once too often.

"But I didn't come here to speak of him," she said. "I believe it is time to show one of my nobles that I am the ruler of the Federated Suns, and that his obedience and loyalty are required, not suggested."

Gallagher nodded sagely. "Are you speaking of Tancred Sandoval?"

Katrina snorted derisively and softly slapped the desktop. "That upstart? Hardly. That battle is a fight between him and his father, and I've been assured it will stay that way. No, I'm talking about a much bigger thorn in my side."

A sick look slowly crossed Gallagher's face, and a few heartbeats of silence filled the room. He obviously had some objection to make, and Katrina wondered if he'd have the spine to voice it. To her surprise, he cleared his throat and spoke in a voice that sounded like someone trying to lift a BattleMech with his bare hands.

"Highness, is that really wise? Up to this point in the war, the fighting between troops loyal to you and those professing loyalty to Duke Hasek has been spontaneous. I agree that he is defiant and that he must be stopped. However, in the eyes of many soldiers, he has walked a fine line to keep from appearing an outright rebel. Moving directly against him might push some regiments who've supported you until now into his camp. Or worse, into your brother's camp."

Looking sharply at Gallagher, Katrina decided that his backbone had suddenly and unexpectedly become too firm. Somehow, in the last few months, he had outlived his usefulness. She had plenty of other generals, not the least of them Marshal of the Armies Jackson Davion, to admonish her on the military consequences of her plans. Simon's job was to rubber-stamp her orders and find ways to circumvent the standard chain of command through Jackson. He had no other job than that, and since he appeared to think he actually mattered, it was time to find a new doormat. Perhaps it was her preoccupation with other matters that had allowed this to occur. Shaking her head slightly, she spoke softly but with iron resolve.

"Marshal, if there are regiments that think they can take sides against my right to enforce the laws, then we should flush them out. They are not loyal enough to me. But you need not worry about George Hasek.

When the time comes, I'll have proof of his treachery against me. All I need from you is the orders to the appropriate regiments."

"Yes, Highness," Gallagher said. He sounded weary, resigned to her decision.

Without looking at either a noteputer or a file, he began to rattle off names and lists of regiments that were in range of New Syrtis and were not currently engaged. His photographic memory was another one of his uses that she would be hard pressed to replace. "Two front-line units are in a position to launch an assault on New Syrtis in less than a month. The Eleventh Avalon Hussars RCT is currently on Ridgebrook, along with the Ridgebrook CMM, who could also join the assault. The Fourth Donegal Guards RCT is on Taygeta. Hauptmann General Amelio is a staunch believer in the united Federated Commonwealth, and he thoroughly supports you. More important, his unit has not seen action in the war thus far. The Eleventh, on the other hand, sustained heavy casualties during the initial fighting when they retreated off Brockway after tangling with part of the Lexington Combat Group. If we strike now, the defenders would actually enjoy a slight advantage in numbers, never a good idea. In two months, I could have two additional regiments—"

"No," she interrupted. "We must hit New Syrtis as quickly as possible. The demoralizing effect of Victor's disappearance from view will help our cause. The cancer of George Hasek must be cut out immediately."

Gallagher looked for a moment as if he would

speak again, then curtly nodded his head in submission.

"I want detailed plans for the assault on my desk no later than tomorrow evening. Do I make myself clear, Marshal?" Katrina did not really care about such reports, trusting her generals to do their job. However, you always had to remind those beneath you of who actually held the reins of power.

"Yes, Highness."

"You may leave."

With a smart salute, he turned crisply and moved to depart the room. Though she was actually ordering him from his own office, it was a final reminder of his true station. Perhaps it would be enough to keep him in check until his replacement could be found.

Only a heartbeat passed from the time the door closed behind him and when it opened again to admit Marshal Christian Robert McCarthy. A completely unassuming man, he could have vanished into any crowd with no effort. Which, of course, made him perfect for his job.

Katrina might have reprimanded him for such lack of formality but felt no need. Through as many checks as her Lyran Intelligence Corps could unobtrusively carry out, McCarthy had passed with flying colors. Either he was a master at his game, which meant she was doomed, or the man was fanatically loyal to her. More likely, he was fanatically loyal to any person on the throne who allowed him free rein to carry out his job. He was commandeer of MI6, the special forces division of the AFFC's military intelligence, who dealt in everything from anti-terrorism to hostage rescues and foreign extractions and on occasion internal targets. Katrina had provided the man with more work than the Foxes had seen in the last decade, which perfectly suited one of the psychological profiles assembled on Christian McCarthy. He liked wielding his men, some of the finest such agents anywhere in the Inner Sphere, like surgical instruments. She had begun having him report directly to her, and his exemplary performance over the last two years had earned him the right of familiarity.

"Highness." He never used many words when few would do.

"Marshal. As usual, I've a job for you," she said. "There is a duke who has stepped out of line one too many times. Marshal Gallagher will launch an assault on the duke's world, but the need for a speedy resolution will not permit Gallagher to gather sufficient resources to do the job right. This duke is a problem that needs a solution, and that solution will help our marshal whether he wants it or not."

The way McCarthy's eyes glittered at her words only confirmed her thoughts about him. The challenge of his work provided all the loyalty she needed. And this was a challenge, indeed.

"A permanent solution?" McCarthy asked.

Katrina nodded once. As usual, the less said, the less possible collateral damage should things go disastrously wrong. She knew her power and flexed it continually. However, she was fully aware of the limitations on such power. At times, petty nobles and the rabble found ways to call her to account. As such, her hands must be as clean as the white-virgin disguise in which she sheathed herself.

As he too departed the office, Katrina leaned back and slowly closed her eyes. After so long, the end was near. Soon, the Federated Commonwealth and the Lyran Alliance would know without doubt that she was undisputed ruler by right. Then, it would be time to turn her eyes beyond the borders of the Federated Commonwealth. When the Star League convened again in 3067, it would be her year. There would be no one to stand in her way, and as First Lord, she would show the whole universe her greatness.

8

In other news, we have just received confirmation that the fighting on Freedom, capital of the Freedom Theater of the Skye Province in the Lyran Alliance, has ceased, following the surrender of remnants of the Eleventh Lyran Regulars. Pundits are already saying that this is the death knell of the Skye Rebellion.

Colonel Jeremy Donner, ex-commander of the Eleventh, has already been arraigned, and it appears that the LAAF High Command has every intention of making his court-martial quick and very public. General James Ellis, commander of the Freedom Theater Militia, said: "I knew Colonel Donner personally. Hell, Donner and I go all the way back to the Nagelring. But his actions on Freedom were unequivocally reckless and unbecoming an officer in the LAAF. I've no doubt the board will court-martial him in short order."

Inside sources have also mentioned the possibility of a trial for treason for his actions against the State in support of the Skye rebellion, but a statement of "no comment" is all we've received to date. Stay tuned for updates on this unfolding story.

—From *News at Noon*, Federated News Services, New Syrtis, Federated Suns, 9 October 3065

Morgan Hasek-Davion Memorial Park
Mawreddog Glacier, New Syrtis
Capellan March, Federated Suns
10 October 3065

For early October, it was a cold, cold day, fitting his mood perfectly.

Duke George Michael Hasek moved with alacrity across a final, small crevasse and onto the ferrocrete foundation of the three-acre Morgan Hasek-Davion Memorial Park. Though the foundation was a marvel of modern technology—sunk some nine hundred meters through the almost world-spanning ice sheets to the bedrock below—that did not, could not, keep the ice from its inexorable march of destruction. If not regularly maintained, the entire park would become a medial moraine in less than a century, scoured from its bedrock by the moving ice and dumped as crushed sediment hundreds of kilometers away. Or so said his top hydrological scientists at the University of Saso whenever they asked for more funding to study the interaction between the ice and his father's final resting place.

At the entryway to the park, George stopped to adjust his polarized sunglasses against the harsh, blinding light reflected off the unending desert of purest white. He pulled his fur cloak closer around him and caught his breath in the ten-kph easterly wind. At minus twenty degrees Celsius, he couldn't breathe through his nose without momentarily freezing his sinuses, and every inhalation sent spikes of cold jabbing down his throat. The thumping of the blades of the Cavalry Attack Helicopter, where he'd left his detail, had finally slowed enough to fall below the keening sound of the wind blowing across five hundred kilometers of uninterrupted ice. The walk had been just over a kilometer, no easy trek across this treacherous terrain, but George never allowed the VTOL to land too close. Chunks of ice whipped by the whirlwind of the craft's landing could cause unintentional damage to the park.

Glancing around, he could see the park's treasures, the reason someone would risk breaking an ankle or even death trying to get here. More than a thousand ice-sculptures dotted the three-acre park, some as small as the robin's egg frozen for eternity in a perfectly sculpted nest not a meter from his foot. The largest ice structure stood at the exact center of the park and could be seen clearly even from this distance. A full-scale replica of Morgan Hasek-Davion's BattleMech, the ice sculpture sat on back-canted legs, perfectly capturing the menace of the hundred-ton monster. One of the most powerful war machines ever built, it was the one known to the Clans as *Dire Wolf*.

An appropriate guardian for the man who *had* been a dire wolf to the various enemies of the Federated Commonwealth, George thought. From the Clans to the Capellan Confederation and even to fractious elements within the Commonwealth itself, Morgan Hasek-Davion had been universally feared.

As he began his slow descent down the winding path that led to his father's tomb, he admired the other ice sculptures that fell somewhere between the delicacy of the robin's egg and the enormity of the *Dire Wolf*. A mythological unicorn pranced with such precision that George could almost see its flanks heave with the simple thrill of existence. A rose blossomed, with several ice-petals caught in mid-fall. A magnificent lion roared its defiance to the universe, an appropriate symbol that Morgan had adopted for most of his adult life. A mother cradling a new-born to her breast cast her eyes toward Morgan's tomb, a look of complete trust on her finely sculpted features, trust in the man who had protected hundreds of millions for decades. In another miniature scene, a JumpShip extended its sail to capture energy from the solar winds while its DropShips burned toward a far-distant planet. A New Syrtis polar bear stalked an aquatic creature through bone-chilling waters, a reminder of why George wore its fur.

Unbidden tears leaked from his eyes and froze his lashes together, blocking his view of the rest of the thousand sculptures. Today, he would not clear his vision; he could not bear to see what this park represented. Not when the last few months would have broken his father's heart. Though Morgan had been feared and respected throughout the whole human sphere, these sculptures showed the true mettle of the deceased hero: love. The hands of the people who had adored him—the citizens of the Capellan March of the Federated Commonwealth, the seat of power where Haseks had ruled for centuries—had crafted each masterpiece. Beyond his military career, beyond even his family at times, Morgan was a man of the people, dedicated to their protection and welfare, and they loved him for it.

Almost without exception, every world of the Capellan March had sent craftsmen to New Syrtis during the final construction of the park, and they had used their skill to call forth images from the ice to show what Morgan had meant to them. Dozens of other worlds across the rest of the Federated Commonwealth—as well as many in the Lyran Alliance—had also sent craft-workers. It was this unconditional love that showed who his father had truly been. In a universe filled with giant walking tanks that could level a city-block in seconds with lasers, charged particle beams, and autocannons, almost any man could be hated and feared. But to be loved? More, to be loved by billions? That was an accomplishment most leaders of the vast interstellar states that ruled all of known humanity could not claim.

So, blinded by his own frozen tears, unwilling to be further burdened by the love his father had received from his subjects, George moved slowly down a path his feet knew by heart. Memories of his childhood burst into his mind like strokes of lightning, illuminating past experiences with his father before plunging him back into darkness.

It was always like this. George Hasek was a strong man, a determined man. A man raised by his father to rule hundreds of worlds and billions of people with justice, mercy, and courage—a charge laid at his feet many years ago by his father and taken up some five years back when an assassin's hand had struck

Morgan down. A charge that George felt in the depth of his soul that he was failing to keep. It did not matter that events beyond his control were conspiring to unravel his father's work, which was now his. What mattered in the end was that the people in his care were paying for his inability to stop the madness that had engulfed the Federated Commonwealth. Like a viral sickness, civil war had infected the body of the interstellar state and spread uncontrollably. From the first terrible act almost three years ago, George had tried his best to keep the people of his March out of the fighting, but it had simply not been possible. Too much hatred. Too much distrust. Too much . . .

He thought he had further betrayed his father by not coming here immediately upon returning from the Star League conference. For the first time in five years, he'd skipped his private ceremony on the anniversary of his father's death, unable to face Morgan's shade so soon after his play against Katherine. Knowing she would soon reply, he needed to bare his soul before his father if he was to have any peace with himself over the trial to come.

While his thoughts raced on, his feet remembered the path and gradually came to a stop. A silence broken only by the wind settled as the last crunching footfall fell away. Minutes passed. Far from this place, in the world of Duke Hasek, George could never show weakness. Here, before his father, surrounded by the majesty and colossal indifference of nature, the shields could fall and the doubt and uncertainty could surface—he could be George.

But only for a moment. His father had taught him too well. Slowly, he raised his gloved hands and pulled away his sunglasses to dash away the ice that clouded his eyes. Then, in a ceremony he had practiced at every visit, he lowered his hood and shrugged the bearskin cloak back onto his shoulders. He would be bare-headed and vulnerable before his father. Nothing between them—in death as it had been in life.

Standing 1.9 meters tall, George Hasek Davion lacked his father's height, but his leonine head of hair and piercing blue eyes accentuated his rugged good looks and underplayed his age. At only thirty-five years, he was equal in authority but half the age of the other three field marshals of the FedCom. Some considered him young and inexperienced, but George thought that an advantage against those who would underestimate him. An advantage he had most recently asserted in showing up uninvited at the Star League council meeting last year.

Under the fur coat, he wore his full-dress military uniform, a coat and pants of deep green, with gold cuffs and a red stripe running down the outside of each pants leg. He also wore black boots, but without the stirrups; the first time he'd worn them while trying to walk across the ice had been his last. Gold, white-edged epaulets with a silver sunburst rode each shoulder, pronouncing his rank of field marshal. In a civil war almost three years old, the uniform declared his allegiance, and it was not to the throne on New Avalon and the Archon-Princess who occupied it.

Ahead, frozen in the ice of his father's tomb, he saw the cylindrical metal coffin that had borne Morgan's body home from the Clan homeworlds. Giant, ice-clawed feet stood guard on either side, rising into the air to form the legs and body of the giant 'Mech that stood eternal vigilance over the resting place of one of the nation's greatest heroes.

"My father," George said. The words, like all sounds in these unrelenting elements, were quickly swallowed. Though Morgan had been a devout member of the New Avalon Catholic Church, a faith that had given him great inner strength, George did not share that belief in a supreme being. He had never witnessed any proof for the existence of an omnipotent, omniscient being. Rather, the universe seemed more like a vast, uncaring place where men and monsters lived in the same skin, and love, hatred, and violence were meted out in equal measure. Standing at the foot of his father's final resting place, he could not bring himself to believe that Morgan lived on in glory, next to angels and his god.

George believed that only the actions of this life mattered. If people came to your graveside because of what you'd done, if people honored and remembered you, if the very history of humanity mentioned you, whether it was to glorify or demonize, that was how one lived on. His father would live for a long, long time.

And yet, coming here made him feel close to what he sensed as his father's indomitable spirit. He never thought Morgan would suddenly appear, like a prophetic vision from the Bible or the Unfinished Book.

Yet, speaking to his father as though he was alive always seemed to help him find guidance in the midst of confusion or despair.

Today, as always, he spoke aloud, sending his voice against the wind. "Am I doing the right thing?" he called out. "Was I wrong to defy her so? I learned from you that the time for action is when doing nothing will be your undoing. I thought to take the initiative so that her reaction would come when and how I wanted it. Right?" As the words began to tumble from him, his voice gaining strength, he began to pace in a slow, tight pattern, which he was wont to do when working through his thoughts.

"Perhaps openly wearing this uniform was too much," he said. "Especially at the Star League council, where the leaders of the other Houses saw one of her own dukes defying her. But she left me with no options." He was silent then, his mind reeling with unanswered questions. How she prattled on about the horror of this civil war, about how it was all Victor's fault for wrongly accusing her of their brother Arthur's death. According to Katherine, only Victor was to blame for this bitter, bloody civil war.

"Can she be so blind?" he asked, the wind carrying his murmured words. Victor instantly became a hero upon his victorious return from the Clan homeworlds, a rallying point for people who were tired of Katherine's Lyran bias and who wanted to see a loyal son of Davion on the throne of New Avalon once more. Even if Victor had died the day after his return, he would have become a martyr to be used against her. A few more years might have passed, but the end result would have been the same.

As he paced, words intermittently erupting from him while he tried to puzzle out his dilemma, the shadows began to lengthen and the sun sank toward the horizon. Every New Syrtan knew the dangers of being exposed to this kind of cold in full darkness. Yet, he was oblivious, his need for an answer consuming him.

"And Victor! What of him?" he almost shouted against the wind. "Every time he can draw breath before a holocamera, he claims that his only intention is to remove his sister from the throne. Is it simply to place himself there instead? Will we merely replace one despot for another? Will this civil war drag on for a decade as we see one Davion after another on the throne, only to have them removed by a rival faction? Father, you know our history. It's happened before, and I fear it will happen again. Even if we can unseat her, will that be the end?"

The anguish he felt was palpable, pulling at his energy and soul, draining his very being. He was close to tears of frustration when a sound reached his ears. Slowly turning, he could just make out a shadow moving toward him along the same path he'd taken here. Only then did he realize that his face and chest felt like frozen slabs of meat. Looking around, he noticed for the first time that the sun had set, turning the park into a surreal landscape of crystal shadows. The wind had picked up, and the temperature was dropping precipitously.

"Sir," he heard someone say, then gradually made out the approaching form of Deborah Palu. She tossed back her hood so he could see her face.

"I apologize for interrupting, sir, but you've been gone for almost two hours, and the sun has set. It'll be hard enough to get back to the safety of the Cavalry if we leave right now, much less when full dark is upon us." Though her voice expressed only respect, Deborah was a good, dear friend who never failed to let him know when she thought he had taken a misstep.

He nodded once to show that he understood, and turned a final time to his father's tomb. Though he gave silent thanks for all his father had been, he had not found what he had come for. He drew his hood back into place and fell into step with Deborah as they returned to the waiting VTOL.

The silence stretched, filled only with the moaning wind and the echoes of their footfalls on the ice-covered ferrocrete. Nearing the edge of the park, Deborah produced a small but powerful halogen lamp, which she played over the ground as she led the way out onto the glacier. Another fifteen minutes of intense concentration passed.

"You know she'll come," Deborah said finally.

"Yes." George's voice was thick with emotion. Deborah was one of the few people who he permitted to see him with his guard down.

"The only question is when. You're too much a thorn in her side, especially after attending the Star League conference without her permission." There was no need to mention the uniform. Except for the honors and rank device, Deborah wore one identical to her duke's.

"You still disagree with me on that?"

"Yes. We both know she'll come, but why poke a stick into the bear's cave? Look what that got the Combine."

He nodded soberly. When the Draconis Combine's military had launched an unsanctioned attack into Clan Ghost Bear territory, the response had been swift and devastating, the Ghost Bears falling on House Kurita with savage intent.

"I don't think she can dedicate enough force to take New Syrtis," George said. "The war is too spread out, and her resources are too thin. Where would she get that many regiments?"

"Don't ever underestimate her. Everyone's been doing that for a decade, and look where that got us. She'll find the regiments, and they'll come. Not tomorrow, no. But soon."

Another few minutes passed as they concentrated on some particularly treacherous ground, picking their way carefully between desiccated mounds of ice. They both knew you had to be careful not to put your weight on a corrupted piece of ice, riddled with air pockets. If you did, a broken leg was the least of your worries.

"When?" he asked, after the worst of the danger was past and the landing lights of the Cavalry shown ahead in the darkness.

"Before the end of the year, maybe sooner. She can't wait much longer or you might find additional regiments to bring here. And she knows we've had almost three years to dig in. She's confident that the war is going her way, and this might seem like the perfect moment to her. You threw down the gauntlet, and she'll take up your challenge.''

As they came within the last dozen meters of the VTOL, Deborah raised her right arm and circled it several times—the signal to start the blades. Night had fallen, and the temperature was quickly approaching minus forty degrees Centigrade. Staying out much longer would be fatal. As it was, the ride back would be no picnic.

As the wail of the turbine engine kicked in and the heavy blades began to claw at the air, the answer George was seeking suddenly materialized where it had always been. His father had been a man of action, and so was he. What he'd done was right. The time for words was past. Though he did not necessarily want Victor back on the throne, he must do everything possible to remove Victor's sister. Once that was done, then the problem of Victor could be dealt with.

Turning toward Deborah, he raised his voice to speak a few more words before speech became impossible. "You're right, Deborah, but Katherine Steiner-Davion will find that *this* gauntlet is heavier than any BattleMech fist. Let her accept the challenge, but she'll live to regret it."

9

In recent fighting with the Combine, the Eighth Striker Regiment of the Fighting Urukhai was destroyed on Addicks, as was the Twelfth Deneb Light Cavalry, when the Combine retook their world of Al Na'ir.

Has the Archon-Princess become so obsessed by her rivalry with her brother that she has completely failed to see the enemy at the gates? While our blood spills our blood, the Dragon's banner still flies over Davion worlds, and Commonwealth citizens must bear the yoke of that dictatorship. When will the Archon-Princess right this grave injustice? When will she stop squabbling in the house and realize that the wolf is already blowing the house down?"

—*Word from the Underground*, pirate broadcast, Robinson, Federated Suns, 26 October 3065

Damien Hasek *Recharge Station*
Zenith Jump Point, New Syrtis System
Capellan March
Federated Suns
31 October 3065

"Sir, I've got multiple IR spikes," the young ensign said. "To be exact, I'm reading seven of them."

Captain Joshua Hetfield looked across the command center of the *Damien Hasek* recharge station. Total silence greeted the announcement, followed a moment later by some anonymous crewman's soft curse of, "Blake's blood."

They all knew that there was only one reason so many JumpShips would be arriving so close together at one of the New Syrtis jump points that their IR signatures could be detected at the same time.

"So, the invasion has finally begun," Hetfield said. Another silence stretched out as ensigns and comm officers exchanged quick glances telegraphing emotions ranging from fear to excitement. "Ensign Jones, send a Priority Alpha message to New Syrtis immediately, as follows: 'My Duke, the attack has begun. We are reading seven, I repeat, seven, incoming JumpShips. The invasion has begun. Out.'"

"Yes, sir," Ensign Jones responded, followed by an explosion of furious key-tapping.

Striding over to his command chair, Hetfield opened up a general frequency to the entire station. The enemy armada would be arriving within minutes. Better that the thousands of individuals, many of them civilians, on the space station got word of the invading ships from him than being taken totally by surprise.

"All hands, this is the captain speaking. We have detected an incoming invasion force consisting of seven vessels. Execute response plan immediately."

With those few words, the gears were set in motion. In a universe where the construction of massive space stations had only recently become possible once more, they were still treasure troves of what had previously been known as lostech. For that reason, *Olympus*-class stations like the *Damien Hasek* were rarely, if ever, targeted for destruction by military forces, especially since their massive energy banks could be used to quickly recharge an enemy JumpShip fleet just as easily as a friendly's.

It was common practice to simply surrender the station to the invading force, thus sparing irreplaceable technology and saving a few lives. Later, when the planet was retaken, the space station would be intact. Though the *Damien Hasek* had some minimal weaponry—generally used to keep pirates at bay—the most the ship could do at this point was send a warning to New Syrtis. They also had a few chores to accomplish before they were seized and boarded, and those measures were already underway.

First came the energy banks. Just like JumpShips and WarShips, the *Olympus* had a massive solar sail, which it used to collect solar energy from the system's K5IV star—energy it stored in eight energy-collection banks that could then serve to quick-charge a JumpShip's Kearny-Fuchida hyperdrive. With all eight banks currently full, all seven incoming vessels could quickly recharge their drives and depart the system, but not if Hetfield had anything to say about it. In a purge that would take exactly nine minutes, the same microwave transmissions normally used to charge a JumpShip began to vent the energy into space, at a rate exponentially greater than a JumpShip's delicate drive could ever handle.

Second, all cargo was ejected into space. Some of it would survive and could even be retrieved by the invading fleet, but that would take days, if not weeks, a waste of precious time and resources. With its massive, one-hundred-sixty-thousand-ton cargo capacity in twelve holds, an *Olympus*-class station would never have enough time to eject the contents of those holds in the hour or so between the arrival of the first ships and the detachment of a DropShip to secure the station. The *Damien Hasek*, however, had been operating under imminent-crisis mode for over two months, and it carried only sixty thousand tons of cargo at any given moment.

In the one move that could possibly damage parts of the station, those holds were opened rapidly for an explosive decompression that jettisoned everything from ammunition and spare parts to fuel and clothing. After all of the simulations and preparation, it was still a miracle that nine of the twelve bays managed to eject their cargo without serious mishap. As it was, multi-ton cargo containers smashed into Bay Doors Three and Seven as they ejected, warping the metal, which would prevent the doors closing. The damage would take ten days to repair.

Bay Ten was almost a catastrophe, as the crewman responsible for aligning its cargo had inadvertently placed volatile inferno fuel for 'Mech flamers in the same container as spare ammunition for the *Olympus*'s weapons. When decompression of the bay occurred, the container was skewed off its track and slammed into the outer bay wall, several meters from the door, rupturing the tank. This, in turn, caused the fuel to cook off under the heat, resulting in an explosion that rocked the station and punched a three-meter hole through the bulkhead. Though the structural integrity of the *Damien Hasek* was not compromised, the detonation caused several minor injuries around the station, and it would be six months before the bay was usable again.

Finally, came the most important action, that of systematically purging the station's computer banks of their data. This practice occurred only in the direst situations, when it was not known whether the enemy would strictly follow the Ares Conventions in its prosecution of their invasion. Hetfield knew there had already been too many cases of infractions on both sides to allow the invading commander any benefit of the doubt. The purge would not affect the station's performance, as no key data systems were destroyed, but all non-critical information was wiped from the system.

Exactly ninety seconds after the first IR spike was detected, the space twenty thousand klicks directly in front of the *Damien Hasek*'s prow was split open by an expanding ball of energy as the emergence wave of a JumpShip flashed outward and the incoming ship solidified into reality. Though almost anticlimatic after the captain's announcement, warning klaxons began to toll all across the station.

"Turn those damn things off," Hetfield growled. "We all know what's happening, and they're just giving me a headache." Laughter erupted around the command deck, relieving the tension slightly as a comm officer typed in the order to cut off the sound.

"Ensign Franks, identify that ship immediately," Hetfield said.

"Yes, sir." A few keystrokes zoomed the view toward the incoming vessel. It showed an *Invader*-class JumpShip, with a DropShip capacity of three. "Sir, it's an *Invader*, and her IFF identifies her as the *Red Sickle*."

"I don't recognize that ship. Run it through the system and see if we can identify it."

"Uh, sir."

Hetfield looked at his comm officer for a moment, then was angry with himself. He should have waited longer before purging the computer system.

"Sir," someone else said.

Turning, Hetfield saw Ensign Jacks and remembered that she'd served on several stations in the Lyran half of the Federated Commonwealth. "Yes, Ensign."

"I can't be certain, but I believe I've seen that ship before. I think it's attached to the Fourth Donegal Guards. Sir, from my calculations of the jump, the vessel originated from Taygeta, which I believe is where our latest intel placed the Fourth."

Hetfield stood staring at the vessel, which had already begun aggressive maneuvers to move away from its incoming jump zone. The ship was too distant to see any insignia, but he'd read the same intel. The Fourth had always been a prime contender for an assault on New Syrtis, as the unit was loyal to the Archon and had been sitting for many months on Taygeta, a single jump away.

"Well, ladies and gentleman," he said, "it would appear that our enemy has a face." As he spoke, another JumpShip materialized. Several members of the bridge crew gasped involuntarily.

"Holy cow," Ensign Jacks said. "I can't believe how close they emerged!" Any vessel entering a system distorted the very fabric of space and could damage any craft within two thousand kilometers of its entry point. For that reason, it was SOP for all vessels to clear ten thousand kilometers before another one entered the system. Yet, the computer indicated that less than twenty-five hundred kilometers separated the two enemy ships.

"They seem to be in a hurry to get insystem, and I'm not sure why. Perhaps they think New Syrtis will simply surrender if they get to the planet quickly enough." Another round of laughter swept the control room. Not only were the defending troops completely loyal to the duke, but the duke himself had proven time and again that he could stand up to the best.

"Sir, the IFF on the second ship identifies her as the *Galloping Void.*"

Hetfield grunted as though sucker-punched. He knew that ship, as it had made several ports of call to his station in the last fifteen years.

"Captain, should I query the crew?"

"Unnecessary, Ensign. I know her. She's attached to the Eleventh Avalon Hussars."

The announcement stripped away all levity like a PPC eating through 'Mech armor. Everyone present knew that a civil war was ripping their nation apart, but they were used to thinking of the battle lines being drawn along Davion-Steiner loyalties. They had heard of a few exceptions, where traditional Lyran or Davion units fought on the other side, but on a world spared the ravages of civil war till now, it was easy to dismiss those as aberrations. The Avalon Hussars had been a part of the Federated Suns since its inception, and for one of their own to be attacking New Syrtis was more sobering to the crew of the space station than the invasion itself. The term civil war was quickly gaining new meaning.

Another ship hove into view, and the despair in the room became almost palpable. Dead silence reigned for several long moments as the sight of a WarShip robbed everyone of speech. Massing seven hundred-seventy thousand tons and some eight hundred meters long, the Federated Suns' newest War-Ship was an awesome sight, and the devastating firepower at its command was almost mind-numbing.

"Blake's blood!" Ensign Jacks said, her unusual use of such harsh vulgarity overlooked by everyone.

Hetfield tried to relieve the tension. "Well, the Archon must be pretty scared of us. With only two *Avalon*-class WarShips left in service, we should feel honored that she sent one of them against us." Several officers tried to laugh, but it was obviously forced.

"Yes, Captain, and we'll send it down in a fireball just like they did to the *Robert Davion* on Kathil," Ensign Jones said loudly, then he and the officer next to him slapped palms in a gesture of confidence. Their bravado, whether feigned or real, spread through the command center as growls of defiance and determination filled the air. *If we survive this, you just earned yourself a promotion,* Hetfield thought.

"Ensign Jones, send another Priority Alpha message to the planet. 'My Duke, at this time, we have confirmed the arrival of the Eleventh Avalon Hussars and the Fourth Donegal Guards in system, with what appears to be hostile intent. An *Avalon*-class WarShip has also jumped insystem as well. We will surrender in less than an hour, as per your orders.'"

He paused for a moment, confident of the duke and the men under his command but wary of the strong show of force currently arriving in system.

"'Good luck, my Duke,'" he added.

10

To the people of the Federated Suns, this is to tell you that it has begun. As I broadcast this, a naval battle raging in the New Syrtis System. The Ice Queen on New Avalon has finally showed her hand and struck at the peaceful inhabitants of New Syrtis. Has the duke raised a hand against her? NO! He has remained neutral in a terrible civil war tearing our once Great House apart. Any who hear this broadcast, know that the Archon has finally shown her true colors, her lily-white façade stripped away to reveal her blood-drenched garments underneath. It is time for the common man to rise up against her tyranny. It is time to unseat the tyrant from her throne and give it back into the hands of the savior of the Inner Sphere. It is time to lay down our pitch forks, hoes, and hammers and take up the banner of a righteous cause, following Prince Victor to peace once more!

—Pirate broadcast, source unknown, New Syrtis, Federated Suns, 31 October 3065

Hasek Ancestral Palace
Saso, New Syrtis
Capellan March
Federated Suns
31 October 3065

It was a cliché, but no matter how often he'd been in these situations, storm drains and sewer systems were still the easiest way into any building. Foremost was the ubiquitousness. Unless a building belonged to some cult that didn't believe in technology like those insane Omniss of the Outworlds Alliance—now that had been an assignment!—every edifice large or small was equipped with such systems and, therefore, vulnerable. Good security chiefs recognized this fact and went out of their way to neutralize the possibility.

The problem was that installing security measures in such dirty, liquid environments was difficult at best, not to mention that the longevity of the equipment was severely limited. Only the finest and most patient security details did a good enough job of sealing a path. That was why a good operative could always gain access to the vast majority of the nobles in the Inner Sphere—and even among the Rabid Foxes, Larry was very, very good. Then again, getting your hands on a set of blueprints for the entire sewer system of the palace never hurt, and he'd spent the weeks journeying to New Syrtis memorizing it.

On his belly, inching his way through wretched-smelling human waste that covered him almost completely, he crawled in utter darkness. Hovering before him in his mind's eye were the architectural drawings he'd committed to memory, informing him that he was approaching the right access hole. Less than a meter above that hole was the covered opening into the basement. Motion, light, infrared, and perhaps even electronic detectors would surely be in place around the aperture, but he was prepared with the latest espionage technology available.

He wore a combination camo/IR/ECM sneak suit that covered him head to foot and even had a built-in oxygen rebreather that would let him completely submerge himself for twenty minutes at a time. Built of heat-absorbent material, woven through with lightweight ceramic mesh, and containing thousands of sensors, the suit cost more than most white-collar civis made in a year.

Strategically placed throughout the suit were three types of sensors. There were infrared sensors to detect the ambient temperature and to adjust to conceal his own body's heat signature. There were thousands of electronic detection/suppression devices, which picked up incoming electronic-detection signals and fed them to an integral microcomputer that identified the type of signal and determined an effective electronic countermeasure, which it then broadcast. Finally, sensors in the suit detected the color and amount of light in the immediate area, and another built-in computer analyzed the data and changed the suit's color to mimic the surrounding environment.

Though the suit was a marvel of current technology, none of it could work without the skilled hand of the surgeon who would use the tools to cut away the cancer infecting the Federated Commonwealth.

Yes, he thought, it was time to put his skills to use. Easing his arm out of the filthy water, he took some malleable polymer composite from a small container, and spread it painstakingly until, fifteen minutes later, it covered the entire hole. Then, even more slowly—if he moved too fast it would rupture the membrane—he worked his arm through the substance until it was up to his shoulder. Now, he would see if the pain was worth it.

With the underside of his forearm against the bolted cover, he flexed his arm, attempting to keep the rest of his body as still as possible. His entire arm quivered, and the continuous headache he'd had for the past four months suddenly surged. His hand jerked spasmodically, the knuckles cracking, and he thought his deltoid muscle would tear right out of his pectoral. For a long half-second, the world turned a painful white as he lost his vision to the flashing white splotches of a full-blown migraine. He fought back the nausea, and a moment later, the cover gave, the bolts on one side shearing off with a rasping metal-on-metal sound that worked its way through the membrane and painfully into his cranium. He did not move for several minutes, afraid the sound might have set off one of the sensors. He also needed to give the auto-injector in his carotid artery the chance to minimize the headache pain.

Damn doctors! he thought. They'd promised that the pain would go away after a month or so. Pain or not, there was no denying he was a walking piece of science fiction, something only dreamed about or remembered vaguely from the vaunted Star League, before all those centuries of warfare had ground technology to dust.

Elective Myomer Implants, originally re-pioneered by the Capellan Confederation in the early sixties, were part of an ultra-secret testing program by the FedCom's Ministry of Intelligence, Investigations, and Operations. Myomers, used as muscles to power BattleMechs for centuries, had first been implanted into humans during the Star League, but the art had only recently been rediscovered. Synthetic myomer effectively replaced a body part's entire musculature—in Larry's case, his right arm—conveying a significant, almost miraculous increase in strength. Though he'd just proven its worth, there were serious drawbacks. For one, the damn migraines. They came and went with no discernible pattern, never truly departing, and always flaring to maximum pain when he put the arm to excessive use.

He'd also become addicted to several substances, though he'd never previously used drugs in his life. Out of the blue, he'd developed an uncontrollable craving for alcohol and amphetamines. The doctors simply tsked-tsked and consulted under their breaths while scribbling gibberish on their clipboards. That had given him the almost equal urge to use his new-found strength to throttle the lot of them. Of course, he had it easy compared with some other cases he'd seen. He still got the shakes just thinking about them.

But everything for god and country, right? That's what he kept telling himself.

Despite what the implant had done to his body, the operation was declared a success, and he was given this assignment. One of the reasons he found himself submerged in filthy waste, attempting to overcome the headache while remaining absolutely still, had to do with that arm. As far as the rest of the Inner Sphere was concerned, only the Capellans were experimenting in human myomer implants. In the unlikely event that he was captured or killed, his implant would point a most accusatory finger at House Liao. After all, it was well known that George Hasek, on his own authority, had launched discretionary raids against the Confederation back in '60-61 in an effort to save the beleaguered St. Ives Compact. Nothing could save that old ally, and in '63, the Compact was absorbed back into the House it had left thirty years earlier. No one would be surprised if the Capellans retaliated against the duke.

After another pause of some five minutes, he began to carefully push his way through the membrane, the pain subsiding into the constant, dull background throb he had learned to ignore. Any breach would let light and sound through, not to mention creating a drastic change in the air pressure and temperature, setting off alarms from here to the Cave.

Another twenty minutes passed before he was through the membrane. He emerged into a small closet, where he levered the hole cover back into place. Through his night-vision goggles, he inspected the washed out, green-tinged space that appeared to be a large maintenance closet, complete with tool locker, mop, and bucket. Moving to one corner, he sprayed his body with the contents of an aerosol canister he took from another pouch. The foam quickly dissolved the filth on his suit, sloughing it onto the floor, while eliminating the smell. It wouldn't do to have the distinctive odor of a sewer give him away. Another three minutes saw the job finished, and another two dried his suit completely.

Moving confidently, he crouched down next to the door. He took a micronoteputer with an attached fiber-optic cable from another watertight pocket and slowly slid the end under the door. Rotating the end back and forth, he was able to see a very grainy picture of the darkened, empty hallway beyond. When done, he slid the hand-held device back into its pouch.

He checked the Mauser & Gray flechette pistol that he carried at the small of his back and that he used with his left hand. A vicious weapon, the needler shaved off flechettes, or needles, from a polymer-composite block and fired them with a blast of compressed gas. Though the pistol had an extremely short range and almost any armor would block it, it had no recoil to speak of. Best yet, it was almost completely silent while able to devastate human flesh better than any personal slug-thrower or energy weapon on the market. Though this particular model was favored by the Lyran Alliance, almost every special-forces agency in the Inner Sphere used the weapon. If something was good, you adopted it, even if you had to purchase it from your enemy.

Also at the small of his back was a sonic stunner that he wielded with his right hand—how people could function without being ambidextrous he could never understand. A sweet little device, it emitted an ultra-high frequency that could render even armored targets unconscious, sometimes even scrambling their brains if the target was close enough.

Opening the door, he slipped into semi-darkness and began to travel down the hall. Under any rational circumstances, this operation would have been suicidal. You simply did not sneak into a duke's palace and assassinate him on such short notice, especially this ancestral dwelling that had seen so many similar intrigues over the centuries. Too much could go wrong. Most of the time, getting in was easy. It was getting out after doing the job that could prove your undoing if you didn't get the chance to study your case, maximize all potential opportunities, and minimize the threats.

On some wet-work missions, he'd cased the subject for over four months before striking. But time was a luxury he did not have on this mission. The Archon had called on MI6, the elite special forces team also known as the Rabid Foxes, and he'd been given the assignment. Any other time it might have gone to Charlotte, probably the best agent in the unit. He still couldn't believe the bitch was siding with Victor in an ever-growing fracture that was threatening the integrity of the Foxes.

Shaking his head to clear it of distracting thoughts, he moved down a hall perpendicular to the one he'd first entered. After another dozen meters, he slipped into a stairwell and began his ascent to the upper levels. There was a camera at each landing, which forced him to move particularly slowly, trusting his suit to spoof the security.

As he passed the door to the second floor, an older woman wearing what looked like the smock of a household servant opened the door and headed toward the steps leading back down. He'd been moving slowly enough that his camo suit was painting him the off-white of the wall, but some sixth sense made her turn and look directly at him. Not wanting to have to dispose of a body right now, he would have preferred to wait her out. Her pause, however, was her death sentence.

His right hand flashed out in a superhuman blur to fire the sonic stunner. The barrel was practically touching her nose and set on its highest frequency; her brains were scrambled instantly. Already dead, her body jerked as though having a spasm and fell noisily down the stairs. The little gun, almost completely encased in his gloved hand, would not stand out on the security camera. He stayed motionless for a moment to give any security guard viewing the camera-feed a chance to glance past his form and focus on the fallen body. Then, he began to make his slow way upward again, the corpse already forgotten.

On the fifth floor, he again slid the fiber-optic cable under the door to view the hallway, which was empty. This one, however, was better lit and showed the opulence of a duke's palace. Easing the door open, he slipped through and slowly stalked closer to his target. From his own internal clock, he knew it was about two a.m., and that news of an invading fleet would soon reach the palace. The duke would surely go to his palace office before heading for the Regional Military Headquarters. This was the moment to strike.

Having traversed the entire length of the corridor, he took a branch that led him further into the palace. He was right on schedule and should enter George's office shortly before he did. It was always best to strike in a place where the target was most comfortable; the target was more vulnerable that way. The hallway he'd entered was approximately twenty meters long, and was obviously undergoing renovation. The floor, walls, and ceiling were concrete slabs, with no exit paths.

Trying to move more quickly without compromising his suit's camo ability, he suddenly heard voices from the end of the junction. Glancing back, he saw that he'd traversed most of the hall. With no side exits should any security guards come around the corner, his mind worked at a feverish pace. Once again, it seemed he would test the limit of his new implant.

Launching from a crouch position, he used his superb physique to propel himself toward the ceiling. As his hand came in contact with it, he braced for the pain and dug his fingers into the concrete. To his ears, accustomed to near total silence over the past four hours, it sounded like the roar of an avalanche. His fingers tore through the sneak suit, as well as most of his skin. That pain was nothing compared to the white-hot knife thrust in the right side of his head as the migraine almost sent him into oblivion.

Fighting the reflexive nausea that threatened to spill his stomach's contents all over the floor, he heaved himself into the air and pulled his body as flat against the ceiling as he could. Drawing the sonic stunner with his left hand, he prepared for the worst-case scenario. Though he could no longer see much, his ears still worked fine.

Seconds later, a pair of guards entered the hallway, walking leisurely as they chatted about inane things that only mattered to the insignificant. Larry slowed his breathing with a quick yoga exercise, and began to count his heartbeats as he imagined himself an actual part of the concrete ceiling: solid, stable, insensate, invisible. The two guards kept walking, not knowing how close they came to death.

After counting his heartbeats up to exactly five hundred, which allowed the drugs for both his migraine and his hand to kick in, he slowly lowered himself to the floor. Looking up, he could see his hand imprint on the ceiling, slightly stained in places by his own blood. It was a good thing his genome was not on file in any database. Unless you looked closely, all you really saw were a few holes screwed rather sloppily into the concrete. Workmen these days were so shoddy, he thought sarcastically.

He gave his hand not a second thought, except to

curl it in toward his body to protect his suit's chameleon ability. He didn't have to worry about losing too much blood. His body was seeded with exceptionally strong coagulants; he wouldn't bleed to death from such a minor wound.

Continuing unerringly toward the office, he passed without incident through several other corridors before reaching the one leading to the duke's office. Surprised to see the door open and light flooding into the hallway, he paused to consider his options. Was the duke suffering from insomnia, or had he already received news of the invasion?

He calculated swiftly, knowing he was out of time. Either the duke was already aware of the invasion—a distinct possibility, considering the time Larry had just wasted—or he was awake for some other reason and would know soon enough. Confident of his speed and skill, Larry decided quickly. He stripped off his night-vision goggles and darted forward. With guns splayed wide, he dropped to the polished flagstone floor and slid through the doorway into the office. He felt a momentary tug against his knees as alarms began to blare throughout the palace and the hallway suddenly exploded with bright light.

His mind, already in a heightened state, moved into hyper mode that almost made the room seem to move in slow motion. Even as he brought his weapons to bear on the two individuals he could see, he could not believe what was happening. He'd just spent the better part of four hours defeating the finest security technology the Inner Sphere could produce, only to be fooled by one of the oldest protective measures known to man—a trip wire. Though his chances for escape had just gone from fifty percent to less than one, he had every intention of accomplishing his mission and getting away.

With his right hand, he fired at a guard standing against the wall to the right of the duke's desk. Pawing for a handgun, the man convulsed and smacked his head against the wall as the slight hum of the stunner dropped him.

Larry's left hand simultaneously drew a bead on the duke with the M&G, but the alarm had given the target a second's notice. The duke was already catapulting himself backward from the desk, pushing his chair over to gain cover. The pop of expended air was followed by a hail of black flechettes that clawed into the duke's left hand and arm. Blood exploded against the wall as the needles shredded the hand to the bone, then walked partially up the arm. Not a lethal wound, but the scream ripped from the duke's throat was ample proof that he'd been wounded.

Movement in Larry's peripheral vision had him tracking the M&G back to his left as he twisted his head to follow. He pulled the trigger in the same instant he felt a stab of pain in his lower abdomen and down his right leg. He cursed his luck as his own weapon tore out the throat of another guard. The man was killed instantly, but Larry knew from experience that he was just as dead; he'd just take longer doing it. The energy beam had cauterized his wound, he thought. He wouldn't bleed to death before he could finish off the duke.

He attempted to get up into a sitting position, but fire lanced through his entire body as his severely wounded stomach muscles tore even more. Gritting his teeth against a scream he refused to emit, he rolled onto his stomach, which put his head in the wrong direction. He could now make out the thudding of boots coming down the corridor over the bleat of alarms, and it dawned on him that he just might fail for the first time in his life.

He clawed himself around on the floor. His right leg was useless, and he scrabbled at the floor, trying to get around the desk. An avalanche of sound exploded into the room as several guards rushed in before he'd gone a meter. As laser beams sliced his body in half, his last thought was that at least it was death that had beat him and not another man.

After all, no one could win that one forever.

11

ANNOUNCER: The Archon-Princess has called an emergency press conference. As she has not directly addressed the press concerning any aspect of the war for several months, this session will likely have every news agency in the Inner Sphere in attendance. We go now to the press conference, where our own Timothy Browne informs us that the Archon-Princess has just taken the podium.

ARCHON-PRINCESS: Good people of the Federated Commonwealth, it is with a heavy heart that I stand before you today and impart this grave news. This tragic war, which my misguided brother has foisted upon us for these three long years, has reached a new, tragic level. As the rightful ruler of the Federated Commonwealth, it is my duty, yes, even my right, to expect the loyalty of the men and women who serve in our military. Like my brother, many of those troops—your own sons, daughters, wives, and husbands—have become misguided. I cannot fault them, however, or even hate them for their actions. In fact, I must admire them, as they are obeying what they perceive as their duty to protect this great nation, regardless of how imprudent their actions might be. Furthermore, as in any military, most of those men are simply obeying their superiors.

It is those superiors that I speak of now. Through the rigorous work of both the Department of Military Intelligence and the Ministry of Intelligence, Inves-

tigations, and Operations, it has been proven
beyond any doubt that Field Marshal George Hasek
has been conspiring for years against the throne of
New Avalon. Not just to support Victor in an errone-
ous bid to take the throne of New Avalon. No,
Duke Hasek's crimes are much more insidious, as his
eventual plans call for the secession of the entire
Capellan March from the Federated Commonwealth
and the establishment of a new Great House under
his dictatorial control. It grieves me that in our most
desperate hour, men of such great authority and
command would allow their greed and avarice to ob-
scure their vision and responsibility in safeguarding
the lives of every citizen of the Commonwealth.

As such, a task force today entered the New Syrtis
system with the hope of changing Duke Hasek's
mind by a peaceful show of force. Sadly, he only
proved our worst fears when naval forces under
his command launched an unprovoked attack, forcing our task force to defend itself.

That is all I have to say at this time. My press
secretary will attempt to answer any further questions you have, as well as providing additional information on the actions of Field Marshal George
Hasek.

—Archon-Princess Katrina Steiner-Davion in an emergency
   press conference, Davion Palace, New Avalon, Federated
   Suns, 31 October 3065

DropShip **Proletariat**
Near-Planetary Orbit, New Syrtis
Capellan March
Federated Suns
2 November 3065

Clenching his fists in frustration, Hauptmann General Victor Amelio, commander of the Fourth Done-

gal Guards and overall commander of the forces sent to subdue New Syrtis, gazed out the main viewscreen of his command DropShip as it decelerated in preparation for atmospheric insertion in fifteen minutes. Several thousand kilometers beyond, almost blocked by the curvature of New Syrtis, a giant fireball plowed through the upper atmosphere. It left a blazing trail that must surely stretch across the entire visible sky from the planet's surface, accompanied by a host of smaller fragments, a veritable school of firefish swimming in the wake of a glowing whale. There went the FCS *Hanse Davion*, one of the FedCom's few remaining *Avalon*-class cruisers, destroyed and burning up in the atmosphere. It was locked in an embrace with the *Covenant*, whose suicidal ramming had fused the two behemoths in a kamikaze blaze.

The Archon would not be pleased, he thought. As the fused form continued to plunge into the atmosphere and fall beyond his visible horizon, another thought occurred to him. Take New Syrtis, bring her the Duke's head on a platter, and she won't care about anything else. That was the task she'd given him, and he would carry it out.

For a moment, his thoughts sidetracked as he wondered what would happen when the fused WarShips impacted a glacier on the planet's surface. Maybe the thing would land on the duke and spare Amelio a lot of trouble.

A voice he recognized instantly came over the speaker. "Well, General, it appears you owe me a hundred kroner," said Hauptmann General Justin Leabo, commander of the Eleventh Avalon Hussars.

Amelio glanced at the speaker as though it were actually Leabo's smirking face, and shook his head in disgust. "I don't believe this is the time for levity, General. Or do you laugh at the loss of almost three hundred men and women, not to mention the cost. Gads, man, the cost!" He clenched his fists.

"You misunderstand me, General," Leabo said, his voice carrying a note of pique through its digital reprod· .ction.

Let him be piqued, Amelio thought. How the man had earned so much political influence with such a caustic manner was beyond him. At least he wasn't in charge of the invasion.

"First, I'm simply pointing out what I stated weeks ago. Second, I'm not laughin;; at their deaths, which I find very unfortunate. I'm simply pointing out the irony of the situation, though most will probably not see it. Need I remind you that the origins of the *Covenant*-class WarShip that rammed the *Hanse Davion* are very likely a *Kirishima*-class cruiser the Combine handed over to Victor Davion in return for his help in Operation Bull Dog? To see the *Hanse Davion* struck down by a WarShip of Combine origins—never mind that it took the *Covenant* with her . . . Come, General, you must see the irony, no matter how unpalatable it may be."

Amelio walked over to the comm officer and placed his hand on the back of the young man's chair. He got his voice under control. "General, I appreciate what you're trying to say, but frankly, I don't give a damn about irony. If it would help me to land an additional battalion on planet, or better, if it could bring back the *Hanse Davion*, then just maybe I might. Until then, I suggest we prepare for planetfall. If you'll excuse me, I've a mercenary unit to purchase."

Tapping the officer on the shoulder, he signaled for him to break the connection, then turned to the comm officer to his left. "Have you been able to patch through to the Legion?"

"I'm still working on it, sir. There's a lot of jamming going on, not to mention trying to pinpoint his location."

"I understand the difficulties, but we're about out of time. You've got to patch me through now."

"Yes, sir."

With nothing to do but wait, Amelio strode over to a bank of monitors manned by a set of MechCommanders. The position was a relatively new development in the AFFC, and the general was not sure exactly how he felt about it. Though he'd served in the Lyran Commonwealth Armed Forces before its full integration into the Armed Forces of the Federated Commonwealth in 3042, he'd never been a lover of 'Mechs to the exclusion of all other forces the way most of his contemporaries had been.

For some reason, the Lyrans had esteemed assault 'Mechs as the be-all-end-all of warfare, but the years spent wedded to the Federated Suns military had not only turned most of the old Lyran 'Mech-only commands into combined-arms units but had also softened that view. Or, at least, so he'd believed. Now, just a little over six years since the Lyran half of the FedCom had seceded to form the Lyran Alliance, many in the military upper echelons were already falling back to old ways. It made him glad that his own Fourth Donegal Guards had stayed in the FedCom. Never mind that he and his unit now firmly supported the Archon-Princess. But these Mech-Commanders . . . he wasn't so sure.

As the most technologically advanced of the Great Houses, the Federated Commonwealth always attempted, and usually succeeded, in providing its military officers with the best training and equipment. This led to the finest officer corps in known space and had made the FedCom juggernaut a fearsome opponent. Their latest attempt to push the envelope had resulted in a new generation of field commanders like these sitting at their console banks before him.

By combining intensive new training techniques that included the latest, top-of-the-line Command/Control/Communications and logistical software from the prestigious New Avalon Institute of Science, the AFFC had created an integrated, "whole-picture" suite of software that removed the logistical burdens of command. This allowed the MechCommanders, who directly controlled anywhere from a lance up to a company, depending upon the mission profile, to do what they did best: win battles.

But this new type of officer was removed from what he'd known most of his life that he didn't know what to make of them. However, their first deployment in Operation Bird Dog against the Smoke Jaguars had been a spectacular success. Now, with the resources at his disposal barely adequate for taking the planet, the Archon had once more shown her trust in his command abilities—not to mention emphasizing the importance of this mission—by giving him a cadre of these officers. He would soon be utilizing them in the orbital insertion of his 'Mechs before the DropShips themselves made planetfall. He only hoped they would not flame out like the *Hanse Davion*.

A glance at the first MechCommander's console showed him several monitors, a keyboard, and a light stylus that the officer was busy using. The main monitor currently displayed a topographical map of what Amelio assumed was that company's designated landing site. To the left of that were small monitor feeds from all twelve MechWarriors under the officer's direct control. They were giving him information on everything from their own visual feeds to their 'Mechs' general status and their current physical condition. Finally, several other monitors above and to the right conveyed additional battlefield conditions: a weather-satellite feed, a tie-in to the feeds from the two MechCommanders whose units would drop closest to this one's, and, surprisingly enough, what appeared to be a standard, local news broadcast.

Why that would be important, Amelio could not fathom. Then again, it was not his job to understand it. These officers had been trained for this technology; let them do the work. It was his task to tell them what he wanted done and then trust them to carry it out, no matter how strange he found their type of warfare. Of course, nothing much was occurring right now. The MechCommander's men were still sealed in their metal cocoons, awaiting the order to drop onto the planet. Only then would the battle unfold.

"General, I've got a feed," the comm officer said, interrupting his thoughts.

Returning to his side, Amelio prepared for his first battle of the day. He'd had no direct command over the *Hanse Davion*, beyond ordering it to deal with the *Covenant*. Looking at the screen, he could see a poorly pixilated image of a MechWarrior in his neurohelmet and cooling vest. He knew immediately that his techs had managed to patch a feed into Colonel Chad Dean's battle frequencies while the Legion was out in the field. A most impressive feat, he thought.

He squeezed the officer's shoulder silently in approval. It would have been preferable to see Dean's eyes. You could always bargain better with a person when you could see into his soul, but he'd make do.

"Good morning, Colonel Dean," he began, keeping his voice friendly yet respectful, one military man to another. "This is Hauptmann General Victor Amelio, commander of the Fourth Donegal Guards and overall commander of the invasion force that you are preparing at this very moment to repulse. Such a rapid response speaks volumes about you and your unit's acumen—a testament to the Vanguard Legion's history." A little buttering-up never hurt.

"Additionally, I bring you compliments from her

Highness, the Archon-Princess Katherine Steiner-Davion. It has come to her attention that your three-year contract with the Federated Commonwealth will expire next month. As your service to our House has been sterling, she would like to employ the Legion for another three-year contract. Though it is unusual, she hopes that, by sending me, she shows her respect for you and your Legion. Of course, I'm aware of how strange it might seem to negotiate a new contract on the eve of battle, but there are abundant precedents."

Amelio paused to give Dean time to digest his words and to speak if he had a mind to. When no answer was forthcoming, he decided it was time to tackle the touchy part.

"We are well aware of the difficulties that your unit faced under Lyran command, but you'll not encounter the same problems here in the Federated Commonwealth. Though the Archon-Princess may sit on both thrones, she understands how important it is to treat each realm with the respect it is due, and that includes the military and mercenaries of each realm. I can personally attest to this fact."

Again he paused, but Colonel Dean only sat like a statue, as uncommunicative as the 'Mech he piloted.

Somewhat vexed, Amelio didn't know what to do except keep talking. "As for the specifics of your contract, I've been authorized to increase your original fee by an overall twelve percent, while increasing your percentage of battlefield salvage to eighty percent."

"Eighty percent," Dean said dryly, as though tasting the number with his tongue. It was a huge increase from the fifty in the Legion's current contract, and one of the highest that Amelio was aware of. "That's something. And a twelve percent overall increase to boot. My unit sure could use it. However, General Amelio, is it? Um, I'm a little confused as to why you make this offer now. Our contract with the FedCom isn't up until the end of November. I don't wish to be disrespectful, but there's plenty of time to send a mediator to Outreach to negotiate a new contract. What's the hurry?"

Through the entire delivery, Dean had not changed posture or batted an eye—at least as far as Amelio could tell through the small faceplate of the man's neurohelmet and with the picture still pixilating at odd moments. Irritated, Amelio couldn't imagine a colonel that dense.

"Colonel, the reason for the rush is the invasion about to occur. It's no secret that we've come to take control of this planet for the Archon-Princess. Its duke has blatantly defied her Highness, and it's time to put a stop to it. The forces under the duke's command are another matter. As in all such situations, they are simply following his commands. If they lay down their arms, they'll not be harmed in any way."

"But you'll take their 'Mechs."

Amelio pursed his lips, noticing that Dean had not included his unit in the statement. Every MechWarrior feared becoming dispossessed. Though Amelio operated at a level where he commanded a desk more often than a 'Mech, he knew what it was to stalk the battlefield from ten meters up. His ninety-five-ton *Banshee* would shake the ground like an earthquake, and he felt like a god incarnate, ready to subjugate the poor mortals who could not partake of such glory. Though dispossession was not so common now that 'Mech production had increased, it could still occur.

"Yes."

"So, to keep my 'Mech, my unit—not to mention a nice, shiny new contract—all I've got to do is, what? Switch sides?" Again, Dean paused, as though carefully weighing his words. "Let's say I do that. Don't you think the other units on planet will object? I've been training extensively with them, and I wouldn't relish going up against the Light Guards or the Fusiliers for real. What then?"

"I'm confident that if you show your resolve to stay neutral, or perhaps let it be known that your unit will march to the drumbeat of the Archon-Princess, this world would fall without a shot being fired." Of course, Amelio was confident of no such thing, nor had he ever been. The suicidal run of the *Covenant* against the *Hanse Davion* was proof enough that George Hasek had the complete loyalty of his men.

Apparently, Chad Dean agreed. He gave one barking laugh. "Ha! So that sun-bright fireball we saw streaking across the sky doesn't count as a 'shot being fired.' "

Amelio ignored both the comment and the sarcasm. "If it comes to a fight, which I don't believe it will, then we'll just have to take this world."

"Ha!" Dean barked again, his body actually convulsing with mirth. "Um, general, I really do appreciate your taking time away from your busy schedule to contact me. However, you can tell your Archon to shove her compliments up her dainty little white ass."

Amelio's face drew back at such a vulgar and familiar curse thrown at his rightful ruler. Was the man simply trying to provoke him? Perhaps he could further sweeten the deal. Dean was a mercenary, after all.

"Colonel, I would appreciate it if you left her Highness out of this. Second, I've been authorized to offer you up to—"

"General, I don't think you're getting it," Dean cut in, his voice filled with a cold fury. "I don't want your money. I don't want your contract. I've got a new contract. One that will let me sleep at night. As for taking this planet, I'm not sure you could do it even if I switched sides. I told you. I've been training with the Guards and Fusiliers, not to mention the Militia, for months. On their home terrain, you'd spend the next year just trying to dig them out. But with me on their side, they can't lose. So, please, General, welcome to our winter wonderland and prepare for frostbite when I knock you right out of your 'Mech, you arrogant Lyran bastard!" Then the line went dead.

Staring at the screen, Amelio couldn't help but wonder how the Lyran Intelligence Corps had been so wrong. They'd done several profiles on the new colonel of the Legion and were confident he did not share the unit's old grudge against the Lyran Alliance.

He shook his head slowly. This was not a good start, not a good start at all.

═══ 12 ═══

Good evening and welcome to Nightline. Our top story involves the cessation of hostilities on the world of Inarcs. Though it cost them the Ninth Lyran Regulars, the Third Alliance Guards RCT has destroyed the Seventh Crucis Lancers, and they remain in control of the planet. This gives the LAAF High Command and the Archon-Princess a critical 'Mech production facility in the Melissia Theater of the Alliance, an important development since the loss of Coventry to Victor. Not only will this victory boost the morale of the loyalists, it will also provide them with desperately needed supplies to help push back Victor's forces.

—From Nightline, Donegal Broadcasting Company, Donegal, Lyran Alliance, 2 November 3065

Saso, New Syrtis
Capellan March
Federated Suns
2 November 3065

Just past three in the morning, the coffee simply was not doing anything for her anymore. She'd been up for almost forty-five straight hours, and Major General Deborah Palu told herself she wasn't a spring chicken anymore. You just couldn't do this to a body her age and not expect repercussions. Then again, she'd had no choice. After the duke's . . . no! She shied away from that thought. More coffee.

Getting up from her computer console in the Cave, she headed for the coffee table, an item known to every military complex since the first use of such buildings—and even beyond that several millennia to when warriors in ancient Ethiopia on Terra had chewed the beans for energy. She wished she could chew some beans herself right about now.

Screw this brewed crap and give me the pure essence! she thought. Anything to keep going. She grabbed the full pot of coffee off the heater, tossed out the used filter and grounds, and started a new pot going—double-black! She couldn't chew it, but it'd be close.

"General Palu, we've just received confirmation from Alpha station," said a comm tech from a station a few steps away. "They're under attack as well." She did not respond, concentrating instead on the slow trickle of black liquid into the coffee pot.

"Ah, General?"

Deborah held up her hand for silence as she waited for enough coffee to trickle through the filter and fill a portion of her cup. A few seconds more would make absolutely no difference, and if she didn't have something to hold her demons at bay, she'd be useless anyway.

Drip, drip, drip. Strange how you could sink all of your concentration, all of your consciousness, into a single act that really was no act at all. Piloting a 'Mech, flying her ultra-light, making love: these she could expect to sink her soul into. But watching fluid splash onto itself? Was it simply the lack of sleep, combined with the mind-numbing knowledge of an invasion plunging down on her beloved New Syrtis, while her darling—no!

She tried to blank her mind again until only dripping black coffee consumed her consciousness, swallowing her whole. With a slight start, she suddenly realized that some ten minutes or more must have passed. The pot was completely full. Shaken by her lapse, she reached unsteadily for a large cup, poured, and then took a long, long draught, scorching her mouth. Slamming the cup down on the table, she burned her hand, too, when some hot coffee sloshed out. Fine, she thought. Your penance, Deborah, for such an inexcusable lapse of concentration. At least it should keep you awake.

She turned toward the comm tech who'd spoken before. "Why didn't we receive a report yesterday? Is this a new assault?"

"No, General. Alpha station was apparently caught in an extremely violent blizzard that has only now diminished enough to allow communications." On a world where blizzards were a daily occurrence in one place or another, for a native to call it "extremely violent" was the understatement of the year, equivalent to saying that the men loved their duke.

No! No!

She stood there, paralyzed by her own thoughts, one side yelling "no!" while the other shouted the same thing. The commtechs looked at each other silently as if wondering whether Deborah was about to crack under the pressure. It was known to happen, and even she wasn't sure whether she'd survive the ordeal.

She wasn't completely out of it, though. She had enough presence of mind to realize that if she didn't stop denying the truth, she risked betraying not only her men, but her duke. There—she'd done it—the bastard Capellans had struck down her duke! Her life. Her whole reason for existence. Even in the confines of her own mind, she could barely utter the truth—the man she loved.

She had listened silently, in disbelief, as the doctor had given her the report, his greens covered with the duke's blood. The injury to the hand was bad enough. It now appeared that the duke had also suffered an atrial fibrillation, which had gone undetected until now. The trauma of his wound had sent him into deep shock, but the heart defect had brought on cardiac arrest. A heart attack! She laughed hollowly at the thought. He was only thirty-five, for heaven's sake, always as strong as a bull, handsome as a prince. Now his life hung in the balance and her sanity as well.

His hand! She was in anguish at the thought of its loss, but could not bring herself to even contemplate the possibility of his death from the fibrillation. Oh, she had wanted, just once, to feel those strong hands caress her, but now it was to never be. They'd maimed him and, in doing so, had robbed him of his soul. Would he ever pilot a 'Mech again? But losing a hand wouldn't kill him, while the fibrillation might. She'd seen the look in the doctor's eyes.

A hand on her shoulder brought her back with a violent start. "General, perhaps you should rest for a while," her aide said. "Right now, we can't affect any of the battles. Our plans have been set for weeks, and now we have to trust our men to carry them out."

Looking at Major Ericcson, Deborah despised him immediately for the pity she saw in his eyes. She was also momentarily horrified to think that he might know of her secret desire—that they might all guess at her shame. No, that couldn't be. She'd been too careful; no one knew. Ericcson probably just thought she was nervous about the invasion. Better that than the truth.

"I'm not going anywhere," she said loudly, causing all heads to turn in her direction. She lowered her voice. "Not until we've word of the duke."

"But, General, we'll wake you as soon as we hear anything."

"No, I said," she snapped, her lips tight. She knew she must look a fright—her uniform wrinkled, bags under her eyes, and her hair hanging out in clumps from the bun she usually wore.

"Yes, sir," he said.

Her lapse would be talked about, sending ripples out from this central pond to affect the men in the field. She must try to mitigate the damage. "Ensign, any word of additional units?"

"No, General, as far as we can ascertain, the invading force consists only of the Fourth Donegal Guards, the Ridgebrook CMM, and the Eleventh Avalon Hussars."

Though she'd known for more than a day who was invading New Syrtis, Deborah ground her teeth at the words. The Ridgebrook CMM were militia troops, play soldiers who didn't know the end of a 'Mech from a hole in the ground. But the Eleventh? It galled her to think that they were attacking a Davion world. How could they?

"So, they've landed almost all of their DropShips by now, with most of their forces actively engaged and yet they've come nowhere near us. Why?" It wasn't that she needed someone else to analyze the situation for her. She could do that herself. The talk was meant to distract her anguished heart.

"We thought they might try a direct orbital assault against us, but what they're doing also makes sense," Ericcson said. "I'm still surprised more troops aren't involved, but perhaps reinforcements are already on the way. In any case, they couldn't come against us head to head, not when we're intimately familiar with the terrain and they're not. We diverted a significant portion of our assets to protect Saso and the Cave, which gave the invaders superior numbers against us in the field. It will take us days to redeploy some of the forces we have stationed around Saso to relieve those beleaguered units."

Deborah nodded at the assessment. "You're right, but we can't leave the Cave completely undefended either, and that will continue to tie up assets that could otherwise deploy to stop the invaders at other key points. The enemy would simply load up a few DropShips and drop on our heads."

Ericcson looked worried. "So, this allows them to maintain numeric superiority in the field, where they eliminate our troops while they gradually encircle the Cave. There's no doubt in my mind that this place will be their final target. They're going to need more than just numbers to defeat us, but it's a reasonable plan."

"Yes, especially if they've got reinforcements on the way. Reinforcements that they could throw at us after we've reassigned some of Saso's defenders."

"I've been thinking about that, General, and, though I'd never underestimate Katherine, I'm not so sure she's got reinforcements to send. I've been poring over our intel, and all units in a sixty-light-year diameter from New Syrtis are embroiled in fighting. Of course, she could've sent a unit from some distance, but again, from where? Most units all across the FedCom are either tied down in the fighting or are licking their wounds after getting pounded. It's almost a miracle she was able to dredge up a force even this large to send against us."

Deborah crossed her arms in thought. If Ericcson was right, perhaps they had already seen the extent of the invasion. Yes, the Fourth and the Eleventh were formidable units, but she commanded superior numbers and knew the terrain. It was a classic win-win situation. Of course, if the duke died, it would be a devastating blow to the troop morale, but how could anyone have known that the Capellan bastards would strike at the start of Katherine's invasion? An idea was beginning to coalesce in her mind, but a familiar voice interrupted her thoughts.

"General, may I speak with you privately?" the doctor said, crossing the bowl of the Cave to reach her.

Deborah turned slowly toward him, as though her eyes were a tracking device that could give her some warning of what he might know. Though everyone in the place became suddenly intent on working at their stations, she knew they were as anxious as she was to learn whether George Hasek was alive or dead. "Doctor, whatever you have to say to me can be said in front of my men. Death comes to us all, and soldiers are no stranger to it. If the duke has died, I'll not hide it from my troops." She was amazed that her voice remained calm and controlled. Inwardly, she was shaking like a leaf in a high wind.

Though he looked exhausted, the doctor smiled. "I've come with good news, General. We've just downgraded the duke from critical to good, and we're confident the worst is past. He'll live. In fact, he's already demanding to know what's going on."

A round of cheers and whoops erupted all around the Cave. What the doctor said sounded just like their duke, and they all knew it. Though Deborah, too, could've cried with relief, she read the look in the doctor's eyes. They'd been unable to save the hand. George Hasek would never pilot a 'Mech again.

Tears welled in her eyes, and she turned away. Some of the men saw and pretended they hadn't, though they probably thought they were tears of joy.

Some of the eyes around her also sparkled with unshed tears. Like her, they loved their duke.

She turned from the doctor to a nearby officer. "Ensign, inform the men in the field. The duke lives!"

REPORTER: What do you consider the current hot spots in the civil war, Mr. Lewis?

LEWIS: Well, Tom, without a doubt, I'd say they are Cavanaugh II, Dalkeith, Giausar, and Marlette, where the fighting currently involves at least three regiments each. Success for either side will permit the reassignment of units to other hot spots, creating a domino effect for whichever side can exploit it. Cumbres would have been on the list, except that the Twentieth and Twenty-third Arcturan Guards recently subdued the Third Donegal Guards. Unfortunately, they lost their sister regiment, the Twenty-fifth Arcturan Guards, in the process.

REPORTER: I notice that your list does not include New Syrtis.

LEWIS: That's because the fighting on New Syrtis is in a class unto itself—a nova-hot spot, if you will. Not only is it by far the largest conflict currently underway anywhere in the Alliance or the Federated Suns, it is the single most important world being contested. A win in either direction will be devastating to the other side, not to mention the boost and loss of morale. Like it or not, New Syrtis has become the current proxy world for New Avalon. Of course, the fact that Duke Hasek seems to have some additional, personal agenda only makes the outcome more critical. I think we're looking at a long and bitter fight for the capital of the Capellan March.

   —Interview with military analyst Geoffrey Lewis, *Conflict*,
   Federated News Services, Robinson, Federated Suns,
   2 November 3065

Deep Space Observatory Bell 1
Hangover Hell, New Syrtis
Capellan March
Federated Suns
2 November 3065

"**L**eftenant Peterson," said Subaltern Dora Peltran from the cockpit of her *Fireball*, "looks like we've got incoming bogeys."

"What!" Samuel Peterson stared out the viewscreen of his *Men Shen*, unable to believe what he was hearing. How the hell could the Lyrans know about this facility out in the middle of the New Syrtis tropics?

"Looks like a demi-lance, coming in two-six-niner, just over a klick away from my position. They're moving fast, too, Leftenant. Must be mostly lights or some awful fast mediums."

"Damn," Peterson said. His thoughts raced, trying to decide on the best course of action. His was only a recon lance, after all. Nobody had expected the invaders to know about this secondary HPG station.

A demi-lance put the enemy at eight units—likely all 'Mechs. That was double the strength of his force. Though his lance had the defender's advantage, plus familiarity with the terrain, being outnumbered two to one was not a recipe for success. Especially since, at fifty-five tons, his *Men Shen* was by far the heaviest machine in his unit.

"Leftenant?" Peltran prodded.

"I'm thinking, dammit. Give me a minute." Peterson told himself this shouldn't be happening, but he probably should have called for help yesterday when word came that the main HPG in Saso had been sabotaged and was off-line. An invasion was no time for a communications blackout—the whole reason to guard this HPG relic, once a part of the Star League's Prometheus Inc. Though the station had not been used in over a century, it was kept in good enough repair to serve in an emergency. Though outnumbered, he didn't dare retreat. He'd be cashiered so fast the door would smack him in the back on the way out. Not to mention the way his fellow Mech-Warriors would treat him. Then again, he'd be alive.

"Leftenant, I don't mean no disrespect, but they're coming really fast. We've got only minutes until they're on us."

"Subaltern Petran, I heard and understood your first report," Peterson snapped. "I want you back here now. We're already outnumbered. The least we can do is face them as a lance." With a top speed of over one hundred-eighty kilometers per hour, he knew of almost no other 'Mech that could catch Peltran's *Fireball*.

Looking out the main viewscreen, he sighed heavily. The HPG station was at his back, and before him stretched an idyllic beach, fronting a sea whose white-capped waves he'd surfed on many a sunny afternoon. Palm trees swayed in the breeze, and he could see his hammock strung between two of them from here. Just the other day, he'd gone out on a catamaran and caught the biggest fish he'd ever seen. Under ordinary conditions, this was the cushiest assignment on New Syrtis—if you didn't mind basking in the tropical sun after so much snow and ice. It was often hotly contested by units up for reassignment.

Now, it really would be contested, and Peterson was terrified, not only for himself, but for this little piece of paradise on the frozen ball of New Syrtis. He turned and began to walk his *Men Shen* away from the beach, up past the old deep-space observatory and its HPG. He might not be the greatest warrior or commander, but he was a competent soldier who'd survived his fair share of battles. He'd give as good as he could, and no one could ask for more.

He clenched his jaw to open a general frequency to his lance. "Okay, Recon, we've got problems. There's eight bogeys coming at us fast, and we've got to stop them. We can't just sit here and let them come for us, so I want to go to them. We've got the speed to meet them halfway, and in the sink-hole terrain they're coming through, we can take 'em." At least he hoped that would the case. "Let's move out."

A chorus of voices acknowledged the order with varying degrees of enthusiasm.

Dora Peltran, whose twenty-ton *Fireball* was as fast as lightning but had papier mache for armor, sounded excited. Either she was foolish, or very confident—likely both.

Subaltern Lee Suh also came in loud and clear,

adding some invective about where the invaders would find their 'Mechs after he finished with them. Though his thirty-ton *Battle Hawk* was on the light side, it was a superb light in-fighter. It also had the speed to get in and out quickly and a trio of medium pulse lasers that could rip up even medium 'Mechs.

Gary Russo, the final member of the lance, piloted an ENF-5D *Enforcer*, renowned as one of the most solid medium 'Mechs ever produced. Nothing fancy like the *Men Shen* Peterson had acquired in a raid against House Liao, but good enough. Russo barely made any sound at all, his voice almost a whisper on the line. It was paradoxical that the two Mech-Warriors in the heaviest machines were the most worried, but maybe that was because their greater field experience told them what to expect. Dora and Lee had less time in the Fusiliers than their two lancemates.

Peterson pushed such thoughts from his mind and forced himself to concentrate on the task ahead. Working his foot pedals, he began to move the *Men Shen* forward, letting his body roll with the up and down movement. It had taken him a while to get used to the way the *Men Shen*, with its back-canted legs and forward-jutting cockpit, moved. But now it felt as fluid as water, a deadly elemental whose emerald energy beams would rip the life from enemy machines.

After several minutes of working his way through ever-increasing sink holes that provided excellent cover for a 'Mech, he heard the klaxon warning him of an enemy target lock. Jinking left and right, Peterson attempted to throw the lock as ten long-range missiles raced toward him. As happened so often with standard LRMs, they lost their lock and fell far behind him. Not even the dirt kicked up by their detonations hit his *Men Shen*.

"Contact! I repeat, I have contact, but have yet to engage the enemy," he said into his mic. "These sinks are preventing me from identifying any enemy units."

"I read you, Leftenant," Russo answered. "I can't make out a thing with all of this blocking terrain."

"Yeah, but it means they can't see us, either," Suh put in.

Dead silence on the line told Peterson that her comment had hit home. His lance didn't want to be found, and the longer it took the enemy to concentrate their superior numbers, the longer his unit would last. And the longer they lasted, the more chance they had to actually pull this off.

Reaching a particular sink that was covered on three sides and fell away to an open area on the fourth, Peterson maneuvered to back in. He hoped that would give him a free shot at any passing enemy 'Mech before it ever noticed him. Hunkering down, he shut down as many heat sinks as he dared, and reduced the power on his fusion reactor to hide his IR signature. It was a dangerous gamble that might keep him from being able to bring the *Men Shen* back to full power quickly enough.

On the commline, his lancemates were also reporting contact with the enemy.

"I've got a *Wolfhound* bearing down on me. Looks like a standard WLF-2," Suh said.

Peterson didn't like the sound of that. In open terrain, the *Wolfhound* would tear her *Hawk* apart. He just had to hope Suh's jump jets would keep him safe.

"I've got a *Talon* trying to keep up with me, too, but I'm running him ragged," Dora Peltran reported. She sounded elated.

Listening, Peterson felt like his heavy neurohelmet suddenly weighed a ton. Sure, she could outrun the *Talon* all day long; its top speed was only slightly greater than Peltran's cruising speed. But one connecting shot from the *Talon*'s PPC would penetrate the armor in any location on the *Fireball*. In some places, like the arm, the armor would tear clean off. How long could she keep playing Russian roulette?

"I'm taking heavy fire. I need reinforcements now," Russo called. "I repeat, I'm holding off a *Nightsky* and a *Clint* and request immediate assistance. Leftenant— Samuel!" That shout almost brought Peterson out of his hole, where fear had his entire body slicked in sweat despite the fact that his cockpit was almost cool.

Terror had set in. Not just for himself, but for his whole lance. How could he have thought they might prevail? The enemy *Nightsky* alone weighed as much as Russo's *Enforcer* and could out-maneuver him. Not to mention that the *Nightsky*'s depleted-uranium-tipped ax was enough to give any MechWarrior nightmares. Toss in the forty-ton *Clint*, and it was over. And there were still four other 'Mechs out there!

Yet that shouldn't have been enough to paralyze him like this. This might be the worst situation he'd ever faced, but it wasn't his first time in combat. He wasn't sure what was different, except that today he was fighting his own countrymen.

His proximity alarms shocked him out of his reverie, making his heart race and his vision spin as though he'd stood up too quickly. Streaming into his forward field of vision was a pair of deadly Fulcrum heavy hovertanks, a scant one hundred meters away. Ruby fire from their turrets was already slicing armor off his 'Mech.

The shock of being attacked by hovertanks instead of 'Mechs stopped him cold. Kilajoules of energy shredding his *Men Shen*'s armor broke through his surprise. Grabbing his right-hand joystick, he triggered a flurry of jade darts from his four medium pulse lasers. But he'd waited too long, and both hovertanks had already passed out of his line of sight. Worse, he'd shut down all but one of his heat sinks while trying to hide, a fact he'd forgotten in his momentary haste to sting his tormentors. Now, heat swam through the cockpit, and another warning klaxon threatened imminent shut-down. He slammed his fist down on the override, angry that he'd been suckered by his own stupidity.

Leaning forward, he threw the reactor switch, reassured by the rumble of his fusion engine powering up to full capacity. He pushed the throttle full-forward, but the *Men Shen* was sluggish as it rose to its full height, slowed by such a massive dose of heat. Its three-toed, clawed feet dug furrows into the ground in their haste to gain speed. Throwing additional switches, he brought his heat sinks back on line as quickly as possible.

Abruptly, he was thrown forward against the straps of his restraining harness, which bit into his shoulders. The whine of his gyro attempting to keep the *Men Shen* upright almost drowned out the sounds of multiple explosions and armor blowing off his back. Checking the rear-facing portion of his display, he swore savagely to see that the fleeing targets were a pair of Drillson hover tanks.

"A lance of fifty-ton hover tanks!" he yelled, beside himself. He'd already lost a ton-and-a-half of armor to the Fulcrums, and now another ton littered the ground, thanks to the Drillsons' long-range missile packs. He was outnumbered four to one, each hover-craft weighting in at fifty tons—only five less than his 'Mech—and each with superior maneuverability. Though he packed more firepower, their combined armor and armaments outdid him. He was cut off, outnumbered, and outgunned.

As laser and missile fire continued to systematically reduce his 'Mech to slag, Peterson couldn't help wondering if his comrades fighting these invaders elsewhere on New Syrtis were encountering the same kind of odds.

He didn't know it was his last thought as ruby fire lanced through his weakened head armor and flash-exploded him into red mist, but Samuel Peterson couldn't bring himself to hate an enemy who was his own countryman.

══ 14 ══

It has come to our attention that a most heinous act has been laid at the doorstep of our Great House. That our shared pasts have not been amicable does not excuse such a gross breach of the Star League concords, when not a shred of evidence has been presented before the council members. If the House of Davion is willing to strike down their own blood and launch its nations into a bloody civil war, then how can one doubt that some fanatic from within their own state might attempt a strike against one of its March lords? It is our wish that the Council Lords censure the Steiner-Davion seat for their unwarranted accusations. Furthermore, we demand a public apology for this slight against our honor.

We thank the Council Lords for their time and forthright effort in this matter.

> —Message from Chancellor Sun-Tzu Liao to the Star League Council, Sian, Capellan March, 9 November 3065

New Syrtis Metals Ltd., New Syrtis
Capellan March
Federated Suns
9 November 3065

With twenty-four people packed into the ready room of Hauptmann General Victor Amelio's command DropShip *Proletariat*, it was bursting at the seams. Having stationed the ship near the ruins of New Syrtis Metals, he had called together his commanders for a planning session.

Amelio couldn't shake the feeling that something was wrong. It was nothing he could put his finger on, but it had dogged him from the moment they'd entered the system. He'd carefully reviewed their plans, poured over the latest intel on the planet's defenders and their last known location, checked his stockpile of consumables, ammunition, and spare parts, had even gone so far as to review the latest personnel transfers to the units currently under his command, but he could detect not a single item out of place.

And yet, he felt the itch between his shoulder blades that decades of military service had made into a sign that something important was off. Shrugging his shoulders as though to physically dislodge the sensation, he pushed the thoughts from his mind. After all, he and his force had taken almost all of their primary targets. What was the problem in that?

Standing at the head of the table where his officers were seated, he rapped his knuckles on the pressed-board top, calling the meeting to order. Around him sat the invasion's RCT and brigade commanders and their aides. Though this meeting had pulled them away from direct command of their units, Amelio believed in one-on-one planning sessions. The synergy created by such gatherings—not to mention information to be gained from the nuances of his officers' gestures or body language—was enough for him to ignore any complaints that this would take too much time away from the actual mission.

To his left sat Leftenant General Lynton Tucker, Leftenant General Raie Samuels, and Leftenant General Ivan Bersch, the brigade commanders of his own Fourth. He had entrusted them with his own life any number of times.

Beyond them and stretching around the far end of the table sat Generals Seth Miller, Emeline Jones, Emma Lazenby, and Frank Jenkins, commanders of the Ridgebrook Capellan March Militia. Although Amelio had been skeptical of their inclusion in his task force, so far the militia and its commanders had accomplished the objectives he'd assigned them. More important, they were solidly behind the Archon-Princess.

To his right were the officers of the Eleventh Avalon Hussars, whose commander, Hauptmann General Justin Leabo, wore the perpetual look of smugness that Amelio always tried unsuccessfully to ignore. Down from Leabo were Generals Robin Kim, Saffron Gale, and Ayse Crosby, the Eleventh's brigade commanders. The various aides to the generals occupied chairs along the walls, while Amelio's own aide sat ready at a stenograph machine in the corner. Amelio was a big believer in getting down every word spoken at such meetings. You never knew when something might come in handy.

"Gentleman, what've you got for me?" he asked.

Seth Miller leaned forward and punched a button in the tabletop, activating a small holoprojector mounted in the center. A white-blue ball with a thin band of green around its equator sprang into view, slowly rotating above the table—the image of New Syrtis. He manipulated several more buttons, which brought three Lyran-blue squares burning into existence on the planet's surface.

"General, as you can see, my militia has successfully captured our three primary targets." Miller pointed to the northernmost corner of the northern continent of New Syrtis, which contained all three squares. "However, the supply depot on Purgatory Glacier had been cleaned out top to bottom when we got there. Either the New Syrtans needed those supplies, or they somehow managed to discover it was one of our targets and cleaned house."

"Impossible," Leabo said. Despite Amelio's several talks with him about his "meeting manner," the man still came across as though he was reprimanding Miller for his ignorance. "How could they possibly know about our primary targets? A month ago, this plan wasn't even finalized."

Another officer might have bristled at the rebuke, but Miller stayed calm. "I've no idea, General. According to our intel, that depot has been in use for fifty years. That they would abandon it just before the invasion seems too convenient for coincidence."

"Bah. More likely our intel was wrong."

Miller shrugged as though to say that, of course, that was a possibility. Moving on, he pointed to the other two blue squares. "The second, but much smaller supply depot, has been secured. Finally, we've taken the main head for Purgatory's oil pipe-line." With that, he sat down.

It was Leabo's turn. Moving almost laconically, he leaned forward and hit several keys on the tabletop, adding four more squares to the rotating globe. "We've established our main base of operations on Julius Crater in the Coppolin Isles," he began. "Our other targets, the main northern continental oil pipe-line junction, the Bearing geothermal plant, and the Syrtis II landing field, are also firmly in hand."

Amelio couldn't let that pass. "Firmly in hand, General? It was my impression that a counterattack occurred at the plant only yesterday."

Leabo waved away the remark with a casual flick of his wrist. "A mere muscle spasm of an already dead corpse."

"That *mere* spasm cost you seven 'Mechs, General." Amelio did not want to criticize Leabo in front of the other officers, but he'd have the full truth disclosed. "I'm not sure I would call that a mere anything." For the briefest instant, something like anger flashed in Leabo's eyes, but it vanished so quickly it was hard to tell whether Amelio had only imagined it. In the short months he'd spent in Leabo's company, this was the first time he'd seen the man express even a hint of anger. Then again, he was being called out.

"My master technician has assured me that three of those 'Mechs will be operational within a week's time," Leabo said coolly. "Considering how easily we secured the pipeline junction and the landing field, I did not think it relevant. I'm not concerned about such losses. They will not affect the next stage of the invasion in any way."

Meeting Leabo's gaze straight on, Amelio again wondered how such a man had risen to command of an entire regimental combat team. Was he truly so careless, or did he simply hide behind a façade of nonchalance? After a long pause, he realized it was like staring at a wall, so he looked away to punch several buttons of his own, adding four more blue squares to the holographic New Syrtis.

"The Fourth has also secured its four primary targets: the Jasper oil refinery, the New Haven landing field, the secondary HPG site, and the site we currently occupy, New Syrtis Metals Limited."

"Ah, General," Leabo interrupted, "if I recall correctly, your Fourth was supposed to take the plant intact, correct? What happened? On landing here, I noticed that the factory has been virtually leveled. This was to be one of our major repair staging areas. Now what?"

Amelio glared at Leabo. He'd been about to explain the situation, but Leabo's comment made it seem as though Amelio, too, was attempting to conceal a partial failure from his men. Are we really on the same side? he wondered.

"I was about to explain, Justin," he said, hoping the omission of rank and the use of Leabo's first name would reinforce who was in charge. He turned to the others. "We dropped directly into the center of the plant, and things went well until we'd almost secured the entire facility. Then, an entire lance of defending 'Mechs turned their fire on the building. Such wanton destruction of their own assets took us by surprise, and we reacted by returning fire with everything we had. Not once did they attempt to defend themselves. They simply moved forward like wheat-cutters, methodically lancing holes into the crucibles, cutting swaths through presses and the troves, chopping through conveyer belts, and generally destroying everything in their path. It took us over five minutes to destroy the last 'Mech. Not one of them ever fired back at us."

An eerie silence settled over the table, and even Leabo looked stunned by the report. Right then, Amelio realized how much this incident was part of his unease. The feeling had begun with the *Covenant*'s suicidal ramming of the *Hanse Davion*, proof of how far the defenders would go. And now, they were showing the same ferocity on the ground as well. He would never forget the twisted, hammered shapes of those 'Mechs as they struggled forward through withering fire to deliver one more salvo, to fire one more beam, to inflict one more blast that would prevent the invaders from making use of the facility. That was bad enough. The worst part had been the reaction of some of his own men, who had fired again and again and again into the already dead corpses. Amelio couldn't really believe it until he'd watched it again on the battle ROMs. Was his entire force going to descend into that kind of savagery? He prayed it would not, but knew that he was the only one who could prevent it.

Trying to keep his troubled thoughts from his face,

he spoke again. "Needless to say, I believe the 'easy' part of our invasion is over. The rest will be both difficult and painful. This is not simply a war. This is about who has the right to lead us, to whom we owe our allegiance. Those are the bloodiest battles of all. Keep that in mind as we launch the second wave."

15

I believe it is time for new leadership. Not just the removal of the Archon-Princess, but the end of the Davion ruling line completely. Though the Davions have led our peoples for centuries, the Great Satan compromised their blood forever by joining with the filthy blue. Some say that there are other Davion blood lines, that cousins or half-breeds exist whose pedigree runs pure. However, when one of the greatest Davions to ever live can fall from grace to become the Great Satan and sully himself with filthy merchants, then I say the Davion blood has thinned too much. Only calamity upon disaster awaits us if we continue to cleave unto their brood. Instead, it is time to raise up new blood, to return once more to our own path, to again become the most powerful Great House the Inner Sphere has ever seen. It is time to purge the Davion ranks and accept a new destiny.

—Pirate broadcast by the radical sect People for Davion Purity, Robinson, Federated Suns, 28 November 3065

Heaven's Top
Purgatory Glacier, New Syrtis
Capellan March
Federated Suns
29 November 3065

Leftenant Bette Severenson fired at the Ridgebrook *Enforcer* just as it dodged behind a rocky spire high on Heaven's Top. Water cascaded in a long arc from the jagged outcrop, plunging some one hundred meters before hitting the unyielding surface of the glacier. In the subzero weather, most of the liquid froze into irregular chunks of ice as it fell, and the pieces jumped, bounded, and shattered as they slammed into the ice. Additional kilojoules of energy instantly sublimated ice into vapor, generating giant white clouds that increased the almost total lack of visibility from the raging snowstorm. Residual heat from the shots, as well as ambient heat bleeding off the 'Mechs themselves, melted ice to water, creating the first waterfall on Heaven's Top in close to seven thousand years.

Almost directly north of Saso, Heaven's Top was one of the few mountain peaks to breach Purgatory Glacier, and it housed a supply bunker. It was defended by elements of the Davion Light Guards.

"Where'd he go, John?" Bette asked. Scanning her various targeting-acquisition apparatuses, she saw nothing. She'd lost the enemy *Enforcer* behind the rocky outcropping and was unable to relocate it. Not good, not good at all.

"Sorry, Leftenant, but I've lost him, too. Simply can't make out anything in this crap."

Bette was about to respond when a particularly violent gust of wind knocked her *Argus* slightly off balance. She took a step back and braced her legs wide. The last time she'd assumed her gyro was up to the wind and ice, she'd ended up flat on her back.

The *Argus*'s wide, three-toed foot dug easily into the ice, shattering the top layer and clawing into the snow that lay beneath. Lucky for all of them that the snow had been packed into almost ferrocrete hardness over the centuries. If not, they'd have found themselves hip-dip at every step, and that was no way to fight a battle. Her enemies were in the same boat, but that was no consolation because they had jump jets and she did not. Though Clifton's *Helios* and Geoff's *Blackjack* also mounted jump jets, the 'Mechs were relatively slow for their size, limiting their maneuverability. Comparing them with the enemy *Enforcer*, *Hatchetman*, and *Quickdraw* she'd seen had her a little worried. Bette didn't even want to know the identity of the final 'Mech of the Ridgebrook lance.

A harsh gust of wind heralded the arrival of hail. It hammered at her *Argus*, knocking almost a half-ton of armor off her left leg, her right arm, and all across her chest. What the hell, she thought, checking her monitors to the wail of shrill alarms. She'd been in some devastating storms before, but never one with hail that could penetrate aligned-crystal steel.

She was about to report this new development to

the rest of her lance when a proximity alarm sounded. Jerking backward, she began to pivot her upper torso even as a cascade of brilliant ruby energy cored into her 'Mech's right side. The large laser easily sublimated her armor, leaving a metal cloud that created even more confusion as a vortex of wind trapped it briefly near her *Argus*. As she lined up her own weapons, she cursed herself for a fool. The *Enforcer* had practically announced himself with a cluster shot, and she'd stood out in the open begging for more like a cheap whore.

Grabbing her joystick, she continued to backpedal and bob in an effort to throw off the enemy's aim while waiting for her targeting reticle to burn gold. Lock achieved, she fired a steady stream of depleted-uranium slugs from her rotary autocannon. Totally baffled at why the invaders were attacking such a paltry weapons depot as the one her lance was protecting, she recklessly toggled her autocannon onto its highest muzzle-velocity mode, looking to make her first score. The banshee wail of the cannon cut through the wind until she had to grit her teeth against the pain of the sound.

Attempting to cycle six autocannon loads in the same time it took for a standard shot, the multi-barrel weapon spun at its highest velocity, creating a vibration that only her advanced targeting computer could compensate for. Through the thinning metal cloud of her armor, which the wind was finally streaming away from her, she could see the slugs slamming into the *Enforcer* and sending up a shower of white-hot sparks and shards of broken 'Mech armor.

Grinning savagely, she was frantically attempting to keep the shots on target when a sound like a 'Mech's arm being torn off rang hollowly through her *Argus*. The steady stream of shells was cut off like a capped water spigot. Warning alarms sounded, and glaring red lights lit up half her screen. Quickly scanning her damage schematic and internal monitoring systems, she cursed vehemently, pounding one leg with her fist.

"Damn, damn, damn, damn, damn!" she shouted above the noise.

If she thought her rant would change the situation, it didn't. The barrel casing of her rotary autocannon, unused for long hours, must have gotten packed with too much ice and dirt. On top of that, her negligent use of its highest muzzle velocity without warming up or clearing the weapon had caused a catastrophic jamming, rendering her *Argus*'s primary weapon useless. Had there been time to spare, she might have been able to un-jam it, but another scintillating beam of energy cored into her right torso, stripping off the last of the armor and lancing inward to destroy delicate internal machinery. Another alarm and a blinking light informed her that her Beagle Active Probe had also been rendered useless. That was almost anticlimactic after the loss of her main weapon.

"John," she said. "I need some help over here." She hated to admit she'd jammed her main weapon—her lance would never let her forget it—but that was preferable to the alternative. "I've jammed my rotary, and I've lost almost half of my armor. What's your situation?"

She continued to dodge and weave as best she could, using the storm and the constant presence of stony outcrops to hide her *Argus*, while returning intermittent fire. She had lost her primary weapon, but her 'Mech could still sting with a pair of extended-range medium lasers and a ten-brace of long-range missiles.

"I'm coming, Leftenant. I haven't spotted any enemy 'Mechs since I lost the *Enforcer*. I think I know where you are. Be there in two minutes." Though slow, John's JM7-D *JagerMech* was the largest 'Mech on this snow-tipped rock, and its duel rotaries and advanced targeting computer would, she thought, make short work of that *Enforcer*.

More alarms bleated their warnings as a dark shadow abruptly fell across her *Argus*. Again, she attempted her trademark bob-and-dodge, but this time the enemy was too quick. Like the hand of some metal god, a *Hatchetman* fell from the sky. It was a 'Mech she'd spotted about thirty minutes earlier, but it had apparently moved above her position on the mountain. She screamed, bracing for the impact.

The *Hatchetman* slammed into her 'Mech, and her teeth jammed together so hard she bit her tongue. Stars exploded in front of her eyes as her neurohel-meted head whipped back against her command seat. She was further disoriented as her machine canted backward, and a sudden draft of bone-cold wind sliced across her bare legs. With sudden clarity, she saw that it was over for her. The *Hatchetman* must have breached her cockpit. With most of her armor lying at her feet, her main weapon neutralized, and her bare skin exposed to the elements, she wouldn't last another minute against the two enemy machines. At least they'd pick her up, she thought, hitting the eject button with one fist.

Explosive bolts blew off the top of her *Argus*'s head, slamming her down into her command couch as it rocketed into the air and toward safety. She recognized her mistake only after she lifted into the sky. Merciless winds instantly overpowered her ejection seat's primitive auto-stabilizer, sending it into a frenzied spin like a drop of water sizzling on a hot plate.

Blinded by the snow, she vomited the contents of her stomach into the wind. Shaking uncontrollably from the cold, blood from her nose blowing across her face, she careened off the ground on her first bounce, her collarbone snapping like a twig. The second bounce severed her left foot when it caught between the edge of her couch and a rock outcropping. That sent her into shock, and the blackness of unconsciousness almost seized her. Through sheer force of will, Bette held onto the light. The final landing, which slammed her into a tall tower of rock, broke a rib, puncturing her lung. Again, the void loomed, and again, she held it at bay.

Looking up through a pain-fused daze, the cold already leaching what little body heat she had left, the knowledge that it was not a rock tower that she'd butted up against finally penetrated her tortured consciousness. With every inch of her aching and her life's blood already staining the snow red, Bette understood that her ejection seat was leaning against the leg of the enemy *Enforcer* who'd been trading shots with her.

Relief flooded her. She would be saved! She might never again pilot a 'Mech, but surely the enemy warrior would pick her up. The rock tower turned leg suddenly lifted into the air, and for a breathtaking moment, terror gripped Bette. The *Enforcer* pilot had not seen her! He was leaving! She attempted to raise her hand, while drawing in a breath to yell. Before she could utter a sound, the triple stab of pain from her broken collarbone, rib, and punctured lung finally capsized her into the dark waters of unconsciousness.

Bette Severenson never did see the *Enforcer* casually plant its foot down on top of her, squashing her like an ant.

16

LANSING: Now that the fighting on New Syrtis is moving into its second month, what do you expect will happen?

DRANNIGAN: I have no doubt that Hauptmann General Victor Amelio will attempt to encircle Saso and the Regional Military Headquarters. In fact, I'm surprised he didn't try a direct orbital-insertion on the capital in the first place. The losses would have been tremendous, but I believe his Fourth Donegal Guards could have pulled it off. The battle for New Syrtis would already be over, and Duke George would probably be on his way to New Avalon, provided he survived the assault.

Amelio seems to be taking a slower, safer route to victory, which I believe George Hasek will exploit through his troops' more intimate knowledge of the terrain and counter-attacks against the enemy's command and supply bases. I also believe he will order a scorched-earth policy, though on a world as inhospitable as New Syrtis, that isn't saying much.

—Chief correspondent Dwight Lansing interviewing military strategist Reinhold Drannigan, on the holovid newsmagazine *The Real Deal*, Marik, Free Worlds League, 11 December 3065

The Cave
Saso, New Syrtis
Capellan March
Federated Suns
11 December 3065

"General, he's coming." The words hit the Cave like a splash of ice-cold water, immediately creating utter silence around Deborah Palu. Gradually, the others noticed and also fell quiet. Deborah stopped where she was, turning slowly toward the door.

The last six weeks had not been easy. After the first few days, which almost destroyed her, she'd dug deep and found an inner reserve she hadn't known was there. The invading force struck like a hammer, smashing through their preliminary targets, then moving on to take secondary targets, demolishing her troops again and again. Her men fought with passion, valiantly opposing those who would take New Syrtis from them. But, with George Hasek lying in a coma, they were losing their edge.

She had tried to impart courage to her troops by never showing the least sign of doubt or weakness, but it wasn't enough. She was their general, but they needed their duke. Had he died, his martyrdom would have spurred them to drive the invaders from their shores. But this gray middle ground had left them in a kind of limbo not suffered by the invaders. Damn them!

Then, the miracle they were waiting for had happened. The duke had emerged from his coma late last week. Deborah's being hummed with pent-up

emotions that threatened to spill into the open. She
knew her first sight of him coming through the door
would be her greatest trial. Greater than the last six
weeks of watching her assets dwindle. Of watching
her men and women die in the field. Of seeing each
new city and town fall under the control of the invaders. She feared her first sight of the duke might
finally break her in front of her officers.

With an iron will, she pushed her feelings back
into the same hard knot where she'd kept them hidden for years. She was a commoner, regardless of
her exalted military rank. The duke would as soon
bed a cow as her. It would be a young cow, too.
How many gray hairs do you have, Deborah? she
mocked inwardly, knowing it always worked.

Now, finally, he was back. He was here.

With an outward calm that belied the wild fluttering in her stomach, she looked around at her men
and saw them restored. It was obvious in the way
they walked, the way they held their heads, the
strength of their voices. Even the tapping at their
computer consoles sounded brisker than usual.
Seeing their duke alive and well had inspired his
troops once more.

Never in her life had Deborah doubted the Duke
of New Syrtis. From the towering father to the courageous son, she had always known they would keep
her and her homeland safe. Their noble words and
actions had created a synergy between them and the
people, a bond that had let New Syrtans survive everything fate had thrown their way. When George
Hasek was struck down, it had almost paralyzed

them. Where his death would have ignited a sacrificial fire, his coma had them vacillating between anger and fear in a sine wave that seemed to suck away at their strength.

A sudden commotion at the back of the Cave pulled her back to the present, and she braced herself. Those not already standing leapt to their feet, snapping to full attention. The soldiers nearest the entrance to the Cave stood like statues, their backs blocking the rest of the room's view. For a moment, their silence almost frightened her. Did he not come? Did he look so bad? Then, almost as one, they snapped a salute and held it for a few long beats before exploding into cheers. The wild edge to their cries of joy was contagious and soon spread throughout the underground cavern. Everyone joined in, even though many could still not see the duke.

Only Deborah held herself aloof, as was only fitting for a general. Besides, she had no idea what her emotions might do if she let them slip even a notch.

Then, he came into view, working his way through the crush of soldiers at the entrance. Her heart pounded, drowning out the sounds around her. Drinking in his features, she felt like she'd been wandering in the desert and now suddenly tasted the manna of the Promised Land. He looked a little older, a little more fragile, but his ready smile and strong step—the pinched look around his eyes the only admission of pain—radiated strength. He came wearing his full field marshal regalia.

Deborah's eyes were drawn involuntarily to his left hand, which was sheathed in a glove. She knew he'd lost the hand, but the temporary prosthetic looked almost completely normal. Only if you knew what to look for was it obvious. Pain washed over her. He would never pilot a 'Mech again, and she ached for him.

Struggling for composure, she watched as the duke saluted and shook the hand of every soldier he passed. He also spoke a few words to each one, including the techs. The cheering and clapping only intensified at this show of affection from her duke. An itching in the back of her eyes threatened to explode into a river of tears. This was the duke she loved. This was the duke they all loved. The duke who would help them take back their world.

It was almost thirty minutes before George Hasek finally made his way down to the main floor of the Cave. During that time, Deborah had the image of him as a moth, fluttering in circles but inexorably drawn toward her flame. Perhaps it was the weeks of tension. Perhaps it was her knowledge that he would never again pilot a 'Mech. Whatever the cause, as he finally stood before her and she returned his salute, something must have slipped past her carefully constructed façade.

A strange look glittered in his eyes, then was gone. Had she imagined it? She wondered in horror if she had failed to hide her true feelings. For more than a decade, she had worked alongside him, and never once had anyone suspected. Now, in front of her entire command, she couldn't be sure. She felt her face get hot, and she wanted to flee, but was forced to stand at attention and pretend that nothing was wrong.

"It's good to have you back, Marshal," she said, her voice a little shaky.

As he continued to stare at her, her agitation increased so much that she began to sweat. She had to get away from here. Then, he slowly shook his head as though to dislodge an unwanted thought and said, "I can't tell you how good it is to be back, Deborah. I've read your reports, and I want to commend you on the work you've done."

He turned in a slow circle to take in the whole room. "I want to commend all of you for your hard work and dedication during my absence. Even as I lay in a coma, you safeguarded our home and our world until I could find my way back. Thank you."

Several long moments passed. Then, the room exploded into another round of wild cheering.

After almost a full minute, the duke raised his right hand. The whole room instantly fell silent. "Men, the time has come. The plans we laid have been implemented almost flawlessly, and other plans have been set in motion to stave off this invasion. But now we must make one last push to drive off the enemy. I want all foreign troops off our soil by the new year. Let the snow of New Syrtis be pure once more!"

As the room erupted for the third time, it was like a physical force uniting them in a common cause. From here, the energy would spread outward, infusing every soldier with a determination to make their beloved duke's words a reality. Deborah had never loved him more than she did at that moment, and she was terrified that it showed.

17

On most worlds of the Federated Commonwealth and the Lyran Alliance, people are celebrating, or attempting to celebrate, the yule season. Here on New Syrtis, however, it has been a grim season.

Behind me is what was once the town of Gatlin, a small but thriving community serving the oil fields approximately fifteen kilometers east of here. Now, it's a ghost town, its empty houses and broken windows like white skulls stripped of flesh, their empty eyes mocking the living. And though scenes like this have occurred on numerous worlds, the town of Gatlin is a particularly evil example. The media has reported that a battle for the oil fields spilled over into Gatlin. However, our sources report that when the invaders could not dislodge the defenders after days of pitched battle, the enraged enemy commander ordered the destruction of this peaceful town.

The hatred and fear that is the life's blood of this civil war have once more fueled an act of savagery beyond anything we can conceive of as human.

—Pirate broadcast from the People for Unity, New Syrtis, Federated Suns, 27 December 3065

Julius Crater
Coppolin Isles, New Syrtis
Capellan March
Federated Suns
28 December 3065

"Do you think you can pull it off?'' asked Leftenant
General Justin Leabo of the officer standing before
him.

"Yes, General. I believe I can," the man said.

Leabo contemplated Kommandant Jason Niles and
never doubted that he spoke the truth. In the ten
years that he'd known the man, Jason had never
failed in a mission. That was why he'd pulled the
necessary strings to get his Forty-second Battle
Armor Company reassigned to the Hussars several
years ago. The unit represented the largest concentration of battle armor in the invasion force, and though
Amelio had been holding them in reserve until the
right moment, Leabo thought the moment had come.

"Good. It's time this battle was won, don't you
think?"

Jason nodded firmly, still at full attention. "Yes,
General. I thought we'd broken their spirit in the
first attacks, but something seems to have galvanized
them in the last few weeks. I heard that the
Ridgebrook CMM actually lost one of their primary
targets to a counter-assault. That isn't good."

By this point in his career, Jason Niles could have
been commanding an RCT had he wanted it. He was
obviously competent enough, and his service record
was sterling. Yet, he'd turned down promotions

twice, saying he believed his skills were better used in the field. More the loss for him, Leabo thought, but a gain for me. Looking around his ad-hoc office on Julius Crater, he couldn't help thinking for the hundredth time how much he wanted off this ice ball and to get back to civilization. The only good thing was that his base camp was in the semi-tropical Coppolin Isles. He shuddered to think what it would have been like if he'd been forced to set up on some accursed glacier.

He broke the brief silence. "It's never good to have your enemy counter-attacking, and even worse if the attack is a success. Then again, what can you expect from a militia, right?" He laughed derisively, ignoring the fact that Jason did not join in.

"I think I know what restored our enemy's backbone," he went on. "I've just received a report from our beloved MIIO stating that an assassination attempt by the Capellans put the duke in a coma for awhile." He paused, expecting some reaction, but Jason didn't even blink. "From what they say, it occurred on the very eve of our invasion, and he only recently regained consciousness and is back in command."

"Too bad we didn't find out about this two months ago," Jason said. "Maybe we could have turned it to our advantage. Still, the timing was quite a coincidence. Makes you wonder if ol' Sun-Tzu is suddenly on our side, eh?"

Leabo decided to ignore the implications of the assassination attempt. He had his doubts about the "truth" of the MIIO report, but he didn't plan to voice them. More military men suddenly found themselves reassigned to command of a militia unit protecting the realm against the great nothingness of the Periphery because of their loud mouths than for any mistake in the field.

He stood up and began to pace behind his desk. "Well, that's behind us now. An opportunity we weren't aware of is not one lost. I have to admit that I'm sick and tired of this place. And now that their duke is back, who knows what these bloody traitors will do next? I'm not forgetting what they did with the *Covenant.*"

"No, sir," Jason said.

"The report made me wonder what would happen if they lost their precious duke for good . . . along with most of their top brass?" The sudden look of understanding in Jason's eyes was gratifying. Leabo loved a mind that could keep up with his own.

"A surgical strike," Jason said.

"Yes. Cutting off the proverbial head of the snake. If successful, the confusion and loss of morale would put the world in our hands by the end of the year."

Jason didn't answer right away, giving Leabo's words some thought. "Won't they be expecting such a strike?"

"I don't think so. For one, they did a superb job of blacking out the news of the attack on Hasek. We didn't hear the faintest whisper of it until now, either from our own sources or even rumors circulating through the general populace. Something like that would have reached our ears had it been generally known. Another strike—one that succeeded and that we would make sure became known—could demoralize the entire planet's population, not just its soldiers."

"Wouldn't you risk creating a martyr?" Jason asked.

Leabo nodded. "Possibly. That's why I believe we need to eliminate their entire Command and Communications, taking as many comm techs and brass as we can."

"The Cave."

"Exactly."

"Best protection on the planet."

"I'm well aware of that, Major," Leabo said, slightly annoyed. He hated obvious statements. "That's why you're here. An orbital insertion by your Forty-second could accomplish what an entire battalion of 'Mechs would fail to do."

"We would need some diversion."

"The entire Third Battalion of the Hussars will be driving toward Saso. Of course, we won't even get close this time, but it will put us in a better position to take advantage of the fall-out from your operation."

For a moment, Jason stood still as a statue. Leabo could almost see the images of the strike moving in front of his mind's eye as he went over every possible contingency. He'd submit a full written report by tomorrow morning covering the plan and several possible contingency plans, but he probably had figured it all out in just these few moments. Wonderful, Leabo thought.

"And if it fails, I'll take the fall," Jason said.

Leabo stiffened, then reminded himself not to

praise the man for his mind, only to get upset when he caught up. He laughed silently to himself. "Well, Kommandant, once more you prove why you're my most able field commander. You are correct. General Amelio does not know about any of this. As long as I succeed in accomplishing the mission parameters handed down by our esteemed general, I have complete authority over my own troops."

"A successful strike will hand you the world, and you'll be seen as the conqueror of New Syrtis."

Leabo couldn't help himself. He almost puffed up for a moment, Jason's words sending a tingle down his spine. If he won New Syrtis, it would bring him to the personal attention of the Archon-Princess, vaulting him into the elite of elite. He'd be promoted to the rank of marshal for sure. Perhaps even to field marshal. After all, with the duke dead, who better to take control of the Capellan March than its conqueror? He was almost light-headed at the idea.

One look at Jason, who had a knowing look as if he guessed exactly what Leabo was thinking, brought him quickly down to earth. One step at time, he told himself, trying to clear his mind of such lofty fantasies. It was all about one step at a time.

He'd been working toward an opportunity like this for years, and he mustn't let anything spoil it. He told himself to calm down. "Yes, that's right," he said aloud. "And I wouldn't forget anyone who helped me."

A small smile creased Jason's face. "My report will be on your desk by oh-six-hundred." With that, he saluted sharply and departed the room.

For a moment, Leabo was taken aback, and then he began to laugh softly. He should have known. After so many years of turning down advancements so he could stay in the field, Jason probably looked at this as the greatest challenge of his military career. And that would be enough for him. He had simply been trying to let Leabo know that he knew the score.

Turning toward his desk, he pulled open the top drawer and withdrew a cigar. He bit off the end and smelled the length of it, then pulled out his lighter and lit up. Ah, he thought, I love such minds. Especially when they're on my side.

18

I have intercepted a courier packet between Demi-Precentor X Peter Fedt, commander of the 299th Com Guard Division, stationed on New Avalon, and Archon-Princess Katherine Steiner-Davion.
Among other things, it is a complete readiness report. It also suggests that he is confident that all but one of the other six Level III commanders would follow his lead if he supported Katherine in the event of a battle for New Avalon. He believes that only Adept IX, Thomas Atkins, commander of Bad Omens III iota, might be questionable. Though the 299th is only rated at regular, I believe this veiled suggestion represents a significant boost in Katherine's on-planet defense.

—Intelligence communiqué from Agent Curaitis to Prince Victor Steiner-Davion, 31 December 3065

Above Saso, New Syrtis
Capellan March
Federated Suns
31 December 3065

Sixty-four metal-clad figures fell at terminal velocity through the ice-cold skies above Saso. Among them, Kommandant Jason Niles glanced toward the upper corner of his faceplate, where a digital altimeter ticked off thirty-two thousand meters. With dawn hours away, he could see nothing. The mathematical part of his brain knew that if the sun was out and no clouds obscured his view—a rare occurrence on New Syrtis—he would have had an unobstructed, circular view of the planet some twelve hundred klicks wide. Though most of his previous HALO insertions had been at night, he knew the heady feeling evoked by such a sight—all of that vastness stretched out below as you fell at over forty meters a second. He'd known troopers so hypnotized by the awe-inspiring sight that they forgot to open their parafoil until too late. There usually wasn't enough of them left to scrape into a can by the time they hit the ground.

"Kommandant, I've got—

"Silence," he snapped. Those were the first words spoken since the team had ejected from their DropShip in ceramic cocoons at one hundred klicks above Saso. Whichever soldier had broken radio silence would be on latrine duty for a month. A year, if the slip caused any problems.

Silence descended once more. As with all such jumps, not even the sound of the wind existed to break the eerie silence. Air pressure was simply too light at this altitude to create the phenomenon. As the altimeter ticked down to twenty-seven thousand meters, his speed began to bleed off. The sound of rushing air started as a low moan and built toward a keening howl as the thickening atmosphere began to slow his falling battle armor. More long minutes passed before his company fell into the clouds, their current ceiling at ten thousand meters. At just over six thousand meters, the cloud cover let go to reveal sparkling jewels nestled in a snowy landscape: the city of Saso and their target, the Regional Military Headquarters.

At exactly one thousand meters, parafoils at the backs of sixty-four battle armor deployed in unison. The sudden air resistance yanked Jason's Infiltrator Mk II into an upright position, making his stomach drop like a rock and causing him to swallow reflexively several times to keep the nausea at bay. After so long in freefall, the full effects of gravity were always dramatic. Plummeting toward the ground, he marveled at the technology that allowed such a small parafoil to arrest his fall in such a short space and time.

His company swooped toward the entrance of the Cave like dark, avenging metal angels, bent on fire and vengeance. Looking at the weapon-control icon displayed on the inside of his faceplate, Jason brought his gauss rifle on line. Then he looked at the targeting icon, and a targeting reticle appeared, moving across his field of vision as he brought his right arm up. The reticle burned gold, and a targeting lock sounded in his ear; he squeezed his right index finger.

An oblong, ferro-nickel slug shot forth at supersonic speed toward the hapless guard standing at the entrance. At the same moment, twenty other such rounds fell from the sky, targeted on ten individuals. Designed to easily penetrate light armor and even to damage 'Mech-strength armor, the Federated-Barrett

"Magshot" gauss rifle was guaranteed to kill a soft target every time if the slug hit in the torso. Several shots missed. One took off only a leg, but a second landed squarely below the sternum: the size of the shells and the transferred kinetic energy was enough to kill ten guards messily and instantly. The sound of the impacting slugs, not to mention the clatter as guard weapons fell to the ferrocrete, would quickly alert the interior that something was drastically wrong. Even worse would be if there were video feeds patching this exterior entrance in to the command center. If the defenders managed to seal the Cave before Jason's men secured the blast door, the chances of penetrating inside were almost nil. His troops began to hit the ground seconds later.

With surprise gone, the need for radio silence was over. "Hauptmann, secure that door now," Jason said.

Keeping noise to a minimum, two squads of Infiltrators moved forward to secure the door, which had already begun to close. Jason knew it would happen, but he swore nonetheless. Either the planned diversion had not been enough of a distraction, or the defenders had anticipated an attack like this. Either case was academic at this point. He smiled when he realized this was going to be more difficult than he'd thought. So much the better.

Just then, several explosions rocked the night, lighting the sky with flashing strobes. Looking toward the Cave entrance, he saw that his men had used several packs of pentaglycerine on the inside hinges of the door. Once closed, those blast-doors could withstand numerous direct hits from even 'Mech-class weaponry, but apply enough force to the delicate hinges and they became so much scrap metal.

"Kommandant, the door is secure. Alpha Squad has already inserted. Proceeding with Plan Jugular," Hauptmann Jefferson said.

"Confirm," Jason replied. "I repeat, Plan Jugular is go." With those words, fifty-two metal-clad warriors made their way through the entrance, while three squads of Infiltrators dug in, prepared to keep this escape exit open. Jason could see several troopers strategically placing command-detonated anti-personnel and anti-armor mines in an overlapping semi-circle in front of the entrance. As the enemy could not allow such a bolthole for his troops to remain open, he fully expected to resurface into a bloody killing zone.

Two Infiltrators had just finished pushing a truck onto its side, and they dragged it into position as makeshift cover. "Leftenant Johnson," Jason said, addressing the closer of the two.

"Yes, Kommandant."

"I know you'll keep it open for us."

"Yes, sir!" Johnson said and even managed a fair salute in the bulky battle armor.

With that, Jason followed the others into the depths. Lights placed every fifteen meters along the walls cast pools of radiance on the rough-hewn floor. Ahead of him, the sleek metal figures moved in smooth, overlapping fields of fire. Minutes passed as his men proceeded downward, without a single contact.

Something was wrong, he thought. The Cave's defenders should have responded by now. At the very least, his team should have stumbled into an errant guard or a comm tech trying to get some from a secretary. His unease continued to grow.

Abruptly, he and his team were plunged into utter blackness. "Silence," Jason ordered, cutting through the babble that exploded on the radio. "Alpha Lead, what happened?"

"I haven't tripped any wires or come across any pressure plates that I'm aware of. Looks like they cut power to this entire section. I'm not getting any ambient light at all."

Jason knew that his point man's comments would surely have set off another uproar if he hadn't cut off the first one so sharply. That was good. He needed to think. He couldn't believe the Cave defenders had cut the power.

The Infiltrators were packed with the finest IR-imaging equipment available, but without ambient light, the only images that could be picked up were ones created by heat from their suits. The visual effect was eerie—the ghostly green shells appearing almost insectoid against total blackness. The background wasn't the usual washed-out scene, but a void, with each warrior suspended above an infinite drop into nothingness in every direction. For a moment, Jason thought he heard someone retching, and even he experienced a moment of vertigo.

While mastering his stomach, he continued to think furiously. Why would they cut the power? All of his warriors had IR, but did the defending troops have it as well? A battle armor's package was better than anything a warrior could carry. His feeling of dread was mounting at an exponential rate. Something was going to happen, and he still couldn't figure out what it was.

Then, explosions echoed up and down the long corridor, accompanied by shouts, lights, and death. Desperately trying to understand what was happening, Jason hunched against the wall, hoping to avoid any collateral damage and to rally his troops. More explosions rent the darkness up and down his line of march, while stabs of coherent light, increasing in frequency, slashed in sickening reds and greens through the thick dust. Had they planted bombs that his point squad had missed? Was it possible that his entire command was about to be wiped out because of the incompetence of four individuals? He tried to head the anger off, knowing it would be a death sentence.

Suddenly, another explosion tore at the darkness just to his right, sending large blocks of stone slamming into his suit that knocked him over and sent him rolling across the uneven floor. Bruised and confused, Jason slowly realized that the explosion had not come from the floor, but had torn through the ceiling. Looking up through the dust and sputtering flames, he was just in time to see an armored individual drop through the ceiling to land lightly on the ground. Its right-arm-mounted small laser had already begun to cut into an Infiltrator to Jason's left.

When another suit dropped through the same hole,

it all made sense. The Cave's defenders had Cavaliers. Though not as good as his Infiltrators in some ways, they carried more armor, and these troops had probably been training for weeks, if not months, to fight in just these conditions. He'd been told that only a company of Cavaliers was on planet. From the boiling infestation of them coming down through the ceiling, he didn't doubt that every explosion in the tunnel had been a breach from a higher tunnel into this one. This was an entire battalion of Cavaliers, perhaps even more. Damn intel!

Raising his right arm, he sighted quickly, not even waiting for a target lock before letting fly with a gauss slug. The shot caught the nearby Cavalier directly in the chest, blasting away armor and knocking the warrior back.

Angry at a mission he knew was already lost, Jason let himself slip over the edge. Striding forward, teeth bared in a snarl of fury, he pumped three more slugs in quick succession into the trooper's chest until a blood-spattered hole was all that remained of the chest plate. He turned to find other prey, the back of his mind still cataloguing the losses to his command. He could see four Infiltrators lying near his position, broken and unmoving. Though several Cavaliers also littered the ground, the odds were changing fast.

Encountering another Cavalier, he sighted and fired, catching his target right over the faceplate. Finding some structural design flaw, the slug shattered the faceplate, instantly pulping the warrior's head inside. Jason felt no satisfaction.

This should have been the finest mission of his life,

and he had failed. It did not matter that he would lose his own life doing so. Dying was preferable to living with the shame of defeat. He went to find death while dishing it out.

19

In other news, the merchant JumpShip *Standing Deep* has been officially reported as lost in combat. However, inside sources report that the vessel simply failed its jump between two worlds, never emerging from hyperspace. With so many older merchant vessels drafted into the civil war, such accidents have increased considerably in the last half-year, as the military's heavy use of them pushes these antique vessels beyond their capabilities. Our sources report that this is the second vessel to meet such a tragic fate since the new year alone.

One merchant-ship captain, who refused to be identified, has stated that if the Archon-Princess refuses to acknowledge the limitations of the older JumpShips she has commandeered, one of two things will happen. She will either soon have a mutiny on her hands or the Commonwealth's interstellar travel capability will be crippled for a decade or more, as happened after the Marik-Liao invasion of '57.

Oddly enough, we've learned of no instances of merchant ships under the command of forces loyal to Prince Victor being lost through such mishaps.

—*News from the Front*, Federated News Services, Robinson, Federated Suns, 20 January 3066

Julius Crater
Coppolin Isles, New Syrtis
Capellan March
Federated Suns
21 January 3066

As Grayson carefully manipulated his 'Mech's controls to firmly plant his feet without destroying centuries of coral reef, he noticed a three-meter-long, silver-backed fish swimming past his cockpit viewscreen. Bemused by the sight, he couldn't place the fish, but it almost made his mouth water with hunger. After a solid week of military rations, a good boot stew would have tasted like manna.

"I have a depth reading of forty meters," a disembodied voice said in his earpiece.

"Confirmed, Leftenant. Forty meters," Grayson said, speaking loud enough for his throat mic to pick up. "All right, people. Looks like our week of hell is just about over. If our oceanography maps are correct, another hundred meters will bring us up out of this ocean and straight into their teeth."

In reprisal for the attack on Saso, the Vanguard Legion had already begun the strike on the Avalon Hussars' base at Julius Crater in the Coppolin Isles. While the 'Mechs of Grayson's force had spent the last week working their slow way along the coastline, the Legion had dropped straight into the teeth of the Hussars. The plan was for Grayson's team to burst from the ocean to finish the job the Legion had begun.

"From the frying pan into the fire," someone else said over the commline.

"More like from the kettle into the fire," someone else commented.

A round of good-natured laughter rippled over the line. Grayson smiled, too, not because the joke was so amusing, but pleased that his people had ridden out an exhausting schedule of underwater maneuvering in such high spirits. Not many units could have done the same.

"Call it what you will, people," he said, "but I'm not sure I'll ever be able to look at a fish in the same way. Let's not forget that this is going to be one hell of a fight, though. Julius Crater is their main base, and they won't give it up easily."

Silence greeted his words, which probably weren't really necessary. His men understood the importance of the mission. During the whole seven-day odyssey, not a single one had complained. The plan was to hit the Hussars' command post, with the intention of capturing or killing their entire RCT command. Though angry at the attack on the Cave by the company of Infiltrators, Grayson still was torn about where he should stand in this war. With this mission, he felt that he was being forced beyond a point of no return.

Most of his comrades, including members of his own lance, had no such qualms. Their hatred of the Lyrans colored their perception of this war, a fact that didn't bother them in the least. But these were *not* Lyrans they were about to attack. These were Davion troops, no matter how misguided. Grayson stretched his neck as though he could dislodge the unwanted thoughts. In the long underwater trudge through kelp and coral beds, these ruminations had chased each other around his cerebellum like a rabid cat and dog, each thinking it was chasing the other, not the other way around.

"I've got twenty meters on the depth gauge," came the leftenant's voice again.

"Okay, people, this is it," Grayson said. "I want three prongs formed up now. Per the plan, Assault Lance behind Command, Recon left, Force right. Move it, people. The Legion needs our help."

He began to move his *Templar* to the front of the line. He did not intend to lead this assault from the rear. Besides, his 'Mech carried more firepower than almost any other one in his reinforced company. It just made sense.

Another ten minutes passed as the depth gauge continued to rise, and the ambient light increased as the surface moved toward them like a giant mirror. Suddenly, his external mikes began to pick up the distinct sound of explosions and autocannon fire, muted through the water. Another ten steps, and the *Templar* broke through the crashing surf, a metal Poseidon ready with trident and lightning bolts to meet his enemies.

A quad blast of cerulean energy came toward him even as he emerged. Miraculously, two of the beams missed, sending up giant plumes of water vapor as they struck the surrounding waves. Grayson vowed not to make the same mistake as he fired back at the *Awesome*, which was standing less than thirty meters away. Four ruby beams sliced into the 'Mech's torso armor. Twin streams of autocannon shells followed, and eight short-range missiles brought up the rear, exploding armor in all directions and sending droplets of molten metal showering down on the beach. The *Awesome* dropped as though it had been cold-cocked.

Breathing heavily from the surge of adrenaline, Grayson was stunned for a moment. The eighty-ton *Awesome* carried more armor than some hundred-ton 'Mechs, and yet he'd taken it out it with one salvo. Then, he realized that the fallen 'Mech's armor was already pockmarked and scoured—it had been on its final leg. In fact, the *Awesome* looked like a strong breeze would have finished if off if Grayson hadn't come along. Breathing through his nose to calm his racing pulse, he gazed further up the beach.

The Hussars had landed two DropShips, an *Overlord* and a *Triumph*, approximately three hundred meters from the water's edge, but still within clear view of the beach. Forming a triangle with the two ships was the main command building, constructed of prefab slabs that were easily assembled in the field. Inside that triangle a brutal melee ensued, a whirling dervish of enemy and friendly 'Mechs engaged in a free-for-all.

Even he found it hard to distinguish friend from foe. That was probably why only occasional stabs of firepower shot out from the *Triumph*, which was apparently still operational. The enemy was probably having the same difficulty figuring out who was who. He sighed with relief at the condition of the

Overlord. Like an expired volcano, the entire top third of the ship had exploded outward, creating a wide circle of devastation around it. Coming out of the surf to confont an operational *Overlord* would have not been pretty.

"Time to earn our pay, people. Let's see if the Legion needs a little saving." A few appreciative snorts, especially from Jonathan, answered his slight sarcasm. Time for a fight.

Pulling free of the surf as seaweed and water cascaded off his 'Mech, Grayson struggled to keep his balance as each footstep sank almost a meter into the wet sand. It was all he could do to keep his 'Mech standing. Gaining more stability as he went, he brought up his targeting reticle and began target acquisition. "Recon and Force, I want that *Triumph* out of commission now. They may not be able to tell Legion from Hussar, but I'm betting they won't have the same problem picking out us Fusiliers."

A chorus of "yes sirs" came back.

"Okay, Command and Assault, hit them now." A moment later, Grayson brought up both his gunarms and registered a lock against an enemy *Owens* that was dueling with a Legion *Jenner*. Pulling both triggers, he hoped the Legion MechWarrior wouldn't mind the intrusion.

Four-meter flames leapt from both autocannon barrels, and dual streams of metal death bit into the *Owens'* torso. As the 'Mech was relatively damaged, the shot should not have been so devastating. Except that another new ammunition type had just lived up to the NAIS hype. Though he'd become almost addicted to the precision ammunition, today he was using a new type of armor-piercing ammo. A novel combination of advanced materials and high explosives, the new autocannon shells increased the likelihood of a penetrating shot by almost twenty percent.

Seeing the *Owens* drop like a puppet whose strings were cut, Grayson figured he'd taken out the gyro for sure. The downed machine was instantly out of the fight. In his peripheral vision, he could see a half-dozen Hussar machines taking a beating from his dual lance. Opening up a general frequency, he decided it was time to announce himself to friend and enemy alike.

"Colonel Chad Dean, the cavalry has arrived. Want some help?"

A few seconds passed with no answer, though many of the Hussar 'Mechs began to turn and engage his machines. "Well, if you've got nothing better to do," Chad finally replied, cool as ever.

"I was just passing this way, so I thought I'd see if we could join the fun," Grayson said with a short laugh. It was a tactic he'd used in the past. Offhand banter in the midst of danger would put his own troops, not to mention the Legion troops, who'd already been fighting for over an hour, at ease, while unsettling the enemy. The other guys would be wondering how a commander could utter such inanities on an open channel unless he was completely confident of winning. He laughed silently. Of such trickery were victories made.

And he could see that the battle was already being won. The Legion demi-company had done a masterful job with their orbital insertion, dropping directly onto the Hussars' base camp. Whether through sheer luck, bravado, or stupidity, only a demi-company of 'Mechs had been on hand to defend the base. Many of the MechWarriors had died even before they could mount up their 'Mechs. He could see four untouched Hussar BattleMechs standing silent sentinel over the death of their unit.

Of course, the Legion had taken a pounding, too, but with his own demi-company added to the mix, the Hussars were done for. And they knew it. Not even the *Triumph* could help balance the numbers, especially with Force and Recon Lances already engaging the DropShip. Grayson had yet to target another 'Mech before a broadcast from the Hussars came over the open channel.

"This is Hauptmann Bull Graves of the Eleventh Avalon Hussars. On behalf of my men, I surrender with the understanding that the Ares Conventions are in full force." Even through the electronic reproduction, his voice sounded like he'd just had the worst day of his life. Which he probably had.

"The Vanguard Legion, on behalf of Duke George Hasek, accepts your surrender," Chad responded. "Power down your machines, Hauptmann, and egress."

Grayson didn't mind that his unit had been left out of the exchange. The Legion deserved the credit for this victory. But as he began to shut his *Templar* down, he couldn't help thinking how anti-climactic the whole thing had turned out to be. He'd been arguing with himself for almost a week over the politics of this attack, and now he was disappointed that his part in the fighting had been so brief. Amazing how quickly the allure of battle could overpower his conscience.

Annoyed with himself, he continued his shutdown sequence while opening up a channel to his own men. "Assault and Command, you will stay combat-ready in case something goes wrong with the surrender. Force and Recon, I want two of your number with me, and the rest to also remain at combat-ready."

As his machine froze in place and the cockpit was plunged into darkness except for one small red light, Grayson leaned back and sighed heavily. He was almost frightened by his feelings now that the battle was over. He'd been so sure he wasn't slipping into blind hatred of the enemy like so many other Fusiliers, and yet now he didn't know what to think. Closing his eyes, he let himself drift for a moment, hoping to find again that safe middle ground he'd walked for so long.

20

A grand parade was held yesterday in Avalon City, celebrating the arrival of the Nineteenth Arcturan Guards and the Fifth Donegal Guards RCT. With pennants flapping in the wind and the units arrayed in their parade colors of white and blue-gray, the spectacle turned into a two-day holiday that drew tens of thousands to clap and cheer for the shiny 'Mechs and brave men.

Or so the traditional media would have you believe, thanks to whatever candy-coated bribes the Archon has used to seal their mouths. The bare truth is that two traditional Lyran units have landed on New Avalon, apparently to stay. That so many Avalonians filled the streets to cheer their arrival is a galling testament to the Archon's continued hold over them. Don't they see that this signals the first time since the beginning of the war that Katherine has felt it necessary to reinforce her position on New Avalon through military might? Have doubts finally begun to erode her arrogant self-confidence? Has Victor's slow but steady progress into the Federated Suns frightened the Archon enough to force her into a visible display of military strength, which she has been loathe to do until now?

Then again, if I had the destroyer of an entire Clan coming for my head, I'd probably also want to

pack as many Regimental Combat Teams around me
as I could!
   —Pirate broadcast by Death to the Archon, New Avalon,
      Federated Suns, 25 January 3066

DropShip **Proletariat**
New Syrtis Metals Ltd., New Syrtis
Capellan March
Federated Suns
25 January 3066

"You can't be serious, General," said Leftenant General Estelle McCartney, aide to Victor Amelio. Out-
rage was written all over her face.

"You think I want to do this? I've got no choice,"
Amelio said, unable to contain his frustration and
anger. "That idiot Leabo got himself killed, and the
Hussars are in complete disarray—they've been
routed twice already! If General Leabo wasn't already dead, I'd kill him myself. As it is, I wish I had
his skull here to piss into."

The shocked look on McCartney's face brought
him down some, but not much. Anyway, he meant
what he said. If he'd had the corpse, he'd already be
at work. Dismissing the whole thing with a wave of
his hand, he began to stalk around the table, though
the *Proletariat*'s ready room didn't give him much
room to do it. What he wouldn't give to have a real
conference room to stomp around in.

"General—

"Enough," he cut in. "I've heard your arguments
for half an hour, and none of them change my mind.

In case you haven't been paying attention to what's been going on in this war, the Archon-Princess has not been kind to those who fail her." Truth to tell, he tried not to dwell on it too much himself. He'd heard some ugly rumors, and he wasn't sure which disturbed him more: that he might soon find himself the subject of similar rumors or that his sworn liege might actually inflict such punishments on loyal officers, regardless of their failings.

"But, General, you're talking about sacrificing troops to take an objective. Not just some troops, but a lot of troops."

"And I'll take a lot of the defenders down as well. That's what a general does, right? Chooses how many of his men he'll sacrifice in order to defeat enemy troops. Depending on the objective, the ratio changes. Two of my men for two of his men if I can take the field, right? Two of my men for only one of his if it wins me the war—right?"

The troubled look on McCartney's face warned that Amelio's bitterness was starting to show. He couldn't seem to stop himself. Like a dam bursting inside him—the final straw being the ludicrous death of Justin Leabo in his own base camp—the pent-up emotions of the last few months of grueling combat had become a flood he no longer controlled.

He watched McCartney shake her head while trying to hide her shock. "That's all true, General. That's your job," she said. "That's what you've been trained for. But this plan . . . you're not talking about two for one. You're talking about sacrificing an entire command."

"But I'll take an entire command down with them," he said.

"Then, what have you gained? If you allow what's left of the Hussars to be destroyed in exchange for the destruction of the New Syrtis CMM, we're still at the stalemate of forces we started with. I just don't see what we've gained."

Amelio was surprised. McCartney had been with him for five years, but it was the first time she'd shown so much spine.

Apparently, there was more. "General, I know we have an objective to accomplish, and I've also heard the horror stories about how the Archon-Princess shows her displeasure with unsuccessful generals. But it was well known that you disliked General Leabo. Might you be taking out your feelings on his unit now that he is beyond your reprisals?"

In a fit of rage, Amelio took a step toward his aide, wanting to slap the offensive words off her face. Then he stopped almost in mid-stride as what she said sank in. He'd always considered himself above political maneuvering. It was one of the reasons he'd despised Leabo almost from the moment he'd met him. Was it possible that he was making a military decision because he feared the political consequences of failure? Would he really decide whether some people lived and some people died because of that? It was an ugly thought, and one he did not want to face. No man could hold a position like his for very long if he lied to himself, however. For almost five straight minutes, he remained frozen in place, searching his heart for the truth while mentally going over his plan.

He rubbed his hands together as if to wash them clean of doubt. Having thought it through once more, he still believed that his plan was the best means to turn the tide of battle back in his favor. "You make an excellent point," he said, "but I assure you that my personal feelings have not affected my judgment. The Hussars are almost finished. They lost their entire command staff and have taken almost thirty percent losses. I could spend precious time to extract and lift them off planet, or even to try and rally them, though I'm not sure that's even possible at this point. Either way, I lose ground I don't think we could ever make up."

"Shouldn't you call a command meeting of the remaining generals, sir?" McCarthy asked.

Amelio looked at her calmly for several long seconds. "No. We don't have time. If I extract the Hussars and send them off planet, I won't have enough troops to force an entry into Saso and take the Cave. And how long would it take to try and rally the Hussars while the enemy continues to harass our flanks and dig in even further?"

McCarthy gave a slight shake of her head. "They've dug themselves into the core of the planet by now, sir. A little bit more time won't make much difference at this point."

"What about reinforcements? We're certainly not going to get any, but do we know for sure that George Hasek hasn't scrounged some up and they may already on their way?" The look on McCarthy's face told Amelio he'd scored points. "We've got a time table that we can't break. If I leave the bulk of the Hussars disorganized and in place, they will be a target too tempting for Tia Caruthers and the New Syrtis CMM to resist. With her fanatical loyalty to the duke, she'll see it as the perfect opportunity to strike the final blow to end our invasion and save her precious duke. We then sweep in with our pincers, and the Syrtis CMM is effectively destroyed as a unit."

Amelio pressed the tips of his fingers against his temples. His brain felt like it was winding down just when he needed to be at his sharpest. He couldn't even remember how long it had been since he'd slept. "This is not a case of trading a command for a command," he said finally. "The Hussars are already destroyed. They and the Syrtis CMM just don't know it yet. I can use the Hussars as bait to eliminate a defending unit, and that's worth the sacrifice."

He could see the struggle on McCarthy's face even as she accepted his logic. "I don't have to like it, General."

His anger suddenly flared again. "Like! What does that have to do with anything we've done here? My god, McCarthy, we've been on a Davion March capital, killing its soldiers and its civilians, attempting to bring a March Lord to heel. How could you possibly think I'd like this, or that anyone would? This is not about liking. This is about keeping a rebel duke in line. This is about orders from our rightful liege. This is about orders I intend to obey!"

21

Our top story signals the end of Davion occupation of Combine worlds. We have just received confirmation from military sources that both the Eighth Striker of the Fighting Urukhai and the Eighth Crucis Lancers RCT were destroyed scant weeks ago.

Most military analysts believe that the Striker's stand for so long on Addicks was almost miraculous, considering the odds stacked against them. Much more tragic and closer to home, the loss of the Eighth Crucis Lancers has shocked many. Though information is sparse, inside sources state that at least three additional Combine regiments reinforced those already fighting the Lancers on Proserpina, dooming the Eighth. At this time, it is unknown whether remnants from either unit made it off planet or whether a prisoner-exchange might occur in the future.

—*Headline News*, Federated News Services, Robinson, Federated Suns, 11 February 3065

Bowerton Glacier, New Syrtis
Capellan March
Federated Suns
12 February 3066

Almost a half an hour passed as Major Tia Caruthers' column of 'Mechs and hovercraft moved up a lateral moraine in preparation for assaulting Bowerton Glacier, the last known position of the Eleventh Avalon Hussars.

"What do you mean they're gone!" she exploded at the report from one of her captains. "That's not possible."

"Um, General, sir, I don't mean to contradict you, but I'm looking at a deserted base. There's nothing here," Captain Roe Johnson said.

Thinking furiously, Tia tried to understand how that could be. None of her outriders had seen anything. She'd even set up remote sensors—heat, motion, seismic, and radar—two days prior in a rough semi-circle on the far side of her current location, in case the Hussars attempted to retreat away from her line of march. They couldn't have just vanished. Halting her *Victor* for a moment, she wiped her suddenly sweaty palms against her shorts. "How long since it was occupied?"

"Hard to say, General. The wind's pretty constant up here. They've definitely been gone for more than a few hours, but it could be as much as a day or two. Just no way of knowing without a closer look. Could be a trap, General."

"Of course, it could be a trap," she snapped, her

nerves strung taut. It was obviously a trap, but what kind? She seriously doubted this was simply a case of the enemy hiding. "Captain Johnson, I want a closer reconnoiter of that bivouac. I need to know how long they've been gone."

"Yes, sir."

"Major Charles," she said, opening up another frequency.

The screech of static gave her a moment to consider her current situation, but it only made her palms sweatier. As commander of the New Syrtis March Militia, she'd spent a lot more of her twenty-eight years in the AFFC teaching at the university than in actual combat. Militia units rarely saw the kind of action they were getting in this civil war, where they could do more fighting in a few months than they normally did in a few decades.

"General?" Major Charles finally answered.

"I want our flanks strengthened. It looks like the Hussars have bolted the hole. I can't take a chance of them hitting our flank."

"Aye, General. Should I inform the Cave?"

She hesitated for the briefest instant. "No, that's not necessary." Tia knew she could lose her command or even be cashiered for such a blatant disregard of the chain of command, but she didn't care. The duke would forgive all when she handed him complete victory by wiping out the last of the traitor-dog Hussars!

Almost a half an hour passed as her column of 'Mechs and hovercraft moved up in preparation for assaulting the enemy position. It was a good thing these glaciers were almost as hard as concrete, with only a thin top crust that gave under the multi-ton weight of walking 'Mechs. Things would get very messy otherwise, she thought.

"General, Captain Johnson here. Now that I've got a closer look, I'd say the base has been deserted for no more than a few hours."

Tia mulled that over before responding. "Any indication of their line of march? They have 'Mechs, for god's sake! Where are the tracks?"

"General, as I said—" Static cut him off.

"Captain! Captain!" Tia could feel the beads of sweat on her face turn into a thin stream that ran down her neck and runneled between her breasts. She had yet to fire even a single weapon, and she was already sweating like she'd taken two engine hits. Besides, firing a weapon wouldn't make her perspire in her heat-efficient 7K. Her mind was slow in telling her what her body already sensed. Something was up, and it did not bode well for her or her men.

Johnson's voice came back in her earpiece. "Sorry, General. Just noticed something. This simply doesn't look right. Almost as though this bivouac is fa—" Static once more broke him up as bright reflections flared over the horizon in a line parallel to her position. Moments later, she heard the dull thumps of explosions.

"Damn!" she yelled. "Captain! Captain!" She switched channels. "Captain Smithers, what's going on? Why have we lost contact with Johnson?" More static filled the line.

"General," Smithers finally answered. "We've got

aerospace fighters all over the place. A whole wing showed up out of nowhere and dropped infernos onto Johnson's company. There's nothing left, General. Nothing!"

"Get a hold of yourself, man!" she yelled back. She understood his fear, but they couldn't give in to it. Every MechWarrior had a dread of inferno missiles. The rounds were designed to set fire to a 'Mech and roast its pilot alive, though they weren't quite the same threat in the icy conditions of a glacier. From what she knew of the enemy's aerospace assets, she also thought it highly improbable that the invaders had an entire wing of twenty fighters. Of course, even a squadron of six could wreak havoc, which they were doing. A new thought suddenly hit her. Inferno rounds would burn on anything, including snow. If too much of the flaming mixture was dropped, it might turn the rock-solid glacier into a mushy coffin for many of her 'Mechs and vehicles.

Just then, her radar began to blare, warning of an incoming non-friendly unit. Before she could reach for her joysticks, a pair of what looked like *Stuka* aerospace fighters flashed overhead, spitting metal cylinders from their bellies like a grotesque parody of some egg-laying creature. These eggs were filled with death, however, not life. At fifteen meters above the ground, they burst, vomiting fiery jell that sprayed in every direction. Tia instinctively raised her hands as jell coated the front of her 'Mech, cutting off her forward view. Shaking even as she tried desperately to remain calm, she forced herself not to panic at the barrage of inferno missiles.

Then, her whole 'Mech was pushed backward like a toy soldier swatted aside by a giant hand. As it slammed against the ground, the breath exploded from her lungs, and she saw lights bursting before her eyes. Clinging to consciousness, she slowly rolled her *Victor* over and pushed it back onto its feet. Checking her damage schematic, she saw that she'd lost almost ten percent of her front armor.

Looking up, she saw that a Saladin hovercraft only twenty meters in front of her had exploded from the infernos. Her entire line of march was falling to pieces as 'Mechs scattered in every direction, trying to put distance between themselves and the burning vehicles.

As she watched an *Enforcer* flee the scene of a burning Pegasus, another explosion geysered snow into the air at a location almost five hundred meters from their line. Even before she could wonder how an explosion could be so far off target, a shadowy outline formed in the snow and rose to its feet, quickly resolving itself into a *JagerMech*. Additional geysers sprouted up and down the line as fire spewed from the *JagerMech*'s twin-barreled arms. Tia was about to call out a warning when she heard Major Benetine's voice on the line.

"General, we're under attack. At least a company of 'Mechs is moving toward our position . . . Make that two companies, General." Tia was confused at first. Benetine was on the side opposite her position. "Sir, I've just made a positive identification on one of the machines. These are Donegal 'Mechs."

Suddenly everything began to make sense. Peering

intently at the *JagerMech*, she toggled a zoom and found the shield-and-sword insignia of the Eleventh Avalon Hussars painted high on its right torso. A trap. The whole thing had been a trap. The Hussars were not disorganized. They'd only seemed to be in order to draw her in. And like a wet-behind-the-ears officer straight out of the Battle Academy, she'd fallen for it.

Clenching her teeth in anger, she lined up her right-arm gauss rifle on the *JagerMech*. Her satisfaction at seeing the nickel-ferrous slug tear into a machine so lightly armored as to be ridiculous was short-lived. With the Hussars on one side and the Guards on the other, not to mention aerospace fighters she could not contest, she had no choice about what to do next.

Hating the words she was about to speak, she opened up a general frequency to her troops. "This is General Tia Caruthers. Pull back. I repeat, pull back." She only hoped she could get most of her people out. Breathing heavily, firing off additional gauss rounds as quickly as the rifle could recycle, she knew that whether or not she survived this fight, her military career was over.

22

WarShips are incredibly expensive. The cheapest one currently in production by the AFFC is the *Fox*-class corvette, which comes in at over twenty-one billion D-bills. The pride of the Davion fleet, the *Avalon*-class cruiser carries a price tag of almost twenty-six billion D-bills. Factor in the amount of time each vessel takes to complete, and it's clear why both the LAAF and AFFC High Commands believe they don't get enough value for the money poured into their respective WarShip programs.

Though only a WarShip can hope to beat another WarShip in space combat, they simply cannot take or hold a planet. You need 'Mechs for that, and how many 'Mechs will twenty-six billion D-bills build you? Sure, a WarShip has the capacity for orbital bombardment, but in four years of fighting the civil war, that has never occurred. It would be too easy for either side to brand the act a violation of the Ares Conventions, and then who knows what horrors might be unleashed?

With almost half the WarShips of both the LAAF and AFFC fleets lost in combat at this point and all current construction on hold, very few WarShips will survive to the end of the war. After that, government funding will have to target the civilian sector: infrastructure on major worlds, reestablishing food production for resource-poor worlds, shoring up the loss of so much commercial interstellar travel capability, and so on. Without a doubt, Alliance and Commonwealth WarShip programs can be considered effectively defunct for some time to come.

 —Military analyst Dr. Judith Jamel, on *Conflict*, Federated News Services, Robinson, Federated Suns, 20 February 3066

Mawrydogg Glacier, New Syrtis
Capellan March
Federated Suns
22 February 3066

Grayson wondered if the snow would ever stop. If the war would ever stop. If the hating would ever stop. If the wind would ever stop up here on Mawrydogg Glacier, where the Fusiliers had set up their base of operations.

Getting up from his desk, he told himself that he distinctly remembered two whole days on New Syrtis without a breath of wind a few years back, and that, like all wars, this one had to end sometime. Even the hundreds of years of Succession Wars occasionally took a break.

The hating, though, would never stop. Two things had accompanied humanity through all time: war and hatred. He gave himself a slight shake, wondering if his thoughts could possibly get any darker. He wasn't sure how much longer he could live with this melancholy.

"Um, sir, you looked troubled," Adela said. She and Jonathan had arrived for an impromptu meeting of Third Battalion's commanders.

"You mean beyond my normal troubled look," he

answered, trying to make light of it. The attempt fell flat.

"Troubled look? I don't see a troubled look anywhere," Jonathan quipped.

Adela rolled her eyes, and for just a moment Grayson did feel more light-hearted. Then his spirit plummeted again into the bottomless abyss he'd inhabited for weeks as a third voice failed to chime in. Dennis Jenks would never again come to Adela's rescue, as he'd always tried to do even though she never needed it.

"It's Dennis, isn't it?" she asked.

The pain washed over him, red and raw as the day it first began. He ran both hands back over his bald pate as though to expunge the hurt. His skull felt ragged, unkempt, and prickly, no matter how often he shaved it. Just like he had for all of this accursed war.

"Not this again," Jonathan groaned.

"You shut up!" Adela snapped. Both men jumped and turned to look at her. Though she never failed to hold her own in any verbal sparring, Grayson had never seen her lose her temper. That was Jonathan's purview.

"Dennis was our lancemate. Our friend!" she said. "I've cried. I bet Grayson's cried." The vehemence in her voice kept Jonathan from interrupting, and his jaw hung open at the deluge directed his way. "But not you, Jonathan. Just because you've got the heart of a Capellan, doesn't mean the rest of us don't have feelings or don't have a hard time dealing with them."

"Hey," Jonathan almost yelled back, finally finding his voice as he jumped to his feet. "That remark was completely out of line. Dennis was my friend, too, in case you've suddenly decided to forget. And as a matter of fact, I did shed a tear. At his funeral! It's been three stinking weeks. I wasn't married to him, and I sure don't think Grayson was, either. Besides, Dennis took a lot of traitors with him. In my book, that helps even the score some." The angry words died away in the silence, leaving a tense tableau of Adela and Jonathan facing each other with clenched fists.

Grayson stared at them, knowing he should take control of the situation. But one of the reasons he'd felt so beaten down over the last weeks was that he felt like he no longer had control over anything. This terrible war had engulfed his House, and the fighting had come to his homeworld. Now, his friends, some of them soldiers under his command, were dying. And through it all, he felt as though his hands were tied behind his back. As though lady fate had decreed that he should be trussed up while New Syrtis burned before his eyes. Standing in the room with two of the people who meant the most to him, he felt helpless to stop their senseless quarrel.

Surprisingly, it was Jonathan who backed down first, making a great show of unclenching his fists, pasting a sloppy smile on his face, and going to sit down. "Adela," he said, "I'm sorry for what I said. You know I'm not the most diplomatic person." Though he never really sounded sorry when he apologized, Adela was more than willing to end the nasty fight.

"I shouldn't have yelled at you like that, Jon." Her voice was low and almost frail. "It's not just Dennis's death. Grayson thinks it's his fault, though we all know he couldn't have done anything to prevent it. Dennis made his own decision, and maybe he'd still be here if he hadn't disregarded a direct order."

"Yeah," Jonathan said, "but that's Grayson for you. Just needs to snap out of it somehow."

In all the years Grayson had known Jonathan, this was one of the few times when his friend actually sounded like he cared enough about something to be serious. From the way he and Adela were discussing him like he wasn't even there, he realized it was because he was so often somewhere else in his mind these days.

"Uh, I don't mean to interrupt, but please stop talking about me like I'm a piece of furniture," he grumbled.

Adela blushed slightly, but Jonathan merely shrugged.

"What did you find out from the general's secretary?" Grayson asked, deciding to get back to the reason he'd called them to his office.

"She confirmed that the New Syrtis CMM was destroyed up on Bowerton Glacier two weeks ago. The survivors have been straggling into our defense zones all along the glacier. I imagine the militia will be deactivated and the few fit survivors used to fill empty billets in other units."

Grayson looked at Adela, and he saw that she was

probably thinking the same thing he was. The loss of the CMM was devastating. Not only was the unit a significant part of the New Syrtis defense plan, but they'd been a piece of New Syrtis for . . . well, forever. Losing them was like losing a favorite uncle or aunt. Someone you imagined would always be there.

Though the CMM appeared to have left their position without authorization, the news of their destruction had galvanized the rest of the New Syrtis defenders into even more loud-mouthed vilification of the invaders. Just yesterday, Grayson had watched in horror as men from Second Company, First Battalion had gathered to burn the Lyran Alliance flag. Though he thought it a ludicrous and hollow gesture, it was one more sign of the hatred that had begun to take over. If something wasn't done, he feared they would all slide into ethnic cleansing or some other equally loathsome atrocity. Even worse was that the duke didn't seem to be trying to stem the tide. All he had to do was speak a few words about moderation, about remembering who these enemy soldiers were and what this war was really about. After all, the Capellans were still out there!

"Sir," Adela said softly.

"Yeah?"

"What do you think is going to happen next?"

"Beyond more fighting?" Grayson looked at his two comrades, trying to memorize their faces, to soak in their friendship that he cherished so much. A sudden lump formed in his throat, and the abrupt scratchiness behind his eyes warned him of tears. He had a terrible feeling that this war, which had already taken Dennis, would grind these two people into the grave as well.

He blinked to clear his vision. "I don't know, Adela. I just don't know."

23

With several ComStar divisions taking sides in the ongoing FedCom civil war, putting ComStar's avowed neutrality into question in the minds of many, Word of Blake has begun to rise in esteem among those same people. In the eight years since they split off from ComStar, the organization has managed to change their image from crackpot zealots to earnest believers.

In February 3066, the worlds of Caph, Keid, New Home, Bryant, and, most surprisingly, Epsilon Eridani publicly announced, in quick succession, that they were requesting military aid from Word of Blake. They cited the continuing instability of the Chaos March after a decade of attempts at peaceful co-existence, as well as the predations of nearby worlds and the inability of ComStar troops to stop such attacks.

On Caph and Bryant, the Eleventh and Eighty-third ComStar Divisions, respectively, were asked to depart as Word of Blake Divisions arrived to take their place. The ComStar troops quietly lifted off-world rather than further blacken ComStar's name by remaining to fight on a world where they were no longer welcome. The specific unit assignments are: Lasting Thoughts III from Second Division assigned to Caph; Fortunes of War III from Third Division assigned to Keid; Angel Wings III from Fifth Division assigned to New Home; Bells of Faith

III from Seventh Division assigned to Bryant; and Quality of Mercy from First Division assigned to Epsilon Eridani.

Precentor William Blane, a member of Word of Blake's Ruling Conclave and nominal spokesman for the organization, announced that this was the first step in demonstrating to every citizen and noble of the Inner Sphere that, unlike ComStar, the Word of Blake does indeed stand apart as a neutral party to whom all could come for succor.

Others, both in the Chaos March and the rest of the Inner Sphere, have cried foul and are alarmed by this so-called "peaceful" act. They accuse Word of Blake of strong-arming these weak Chaos March worlds into accepting occupation forces. These critics believe this is simply a gambit in a much larger game.

—From *Banner Headlines*, Atreus Free Press, Atreus, Free Worlds League, 15 March 3066

The Cave
Saso, New Syrtis
Capellan March
Federated Suns
16 March 3066

"I'm sorry, my Duke, but there simply are no reinforcements to be had," Major Lorena Felton said, her eyes almost pleading forgiveness for being the bearer of bad news.

George Hasek couldn't help feeling sorry for her. Her uniform looked rumpled, and her eyes were sunk deep in her face from days without sleep.

Before either of them could say more, a commotion

at the entrance to the Cave made him look up to see two people walking into the room. For a moment, he felt a mix of annoyance and anxiety, each feeling connected to one of the new arrivals. He closed his eyes to calm himself and remember that he was Duke Hasek, master of one hundred forty-one star systems. He needn't feel like a schoolboy with these two.

As he opened his eyes, Leftenant General Deborah Palu detached herself from the side of Ardan Sortek. Distaste for the man was written all over her face as she came to join George at the holotank. Their eyes met, and he felt an almost electric jolt that made his spine tingle. He gave her a small smile filled with that warmth. She smiled back, trying to look as though their friendship was unchanged. Only he would notice a slight shyness and a certain sparkle in her eye that had begun in the last few weeks.

"General," he said, inclining his head toward her.

"My Duke," she responded, nodding in return. When she spoke, he suddenly longed to be alone with her, hearing his name on her lips. He knew the thought was crazy when he was in the midst of a desperate fight to save his world, but it wasn't the first time it had happened. Though one part of his mind told him to forget the foolishness, another part savored the slow knowledge of these unfamiliar emotions. Perhaps it was because he knew he could die any time at the hands of the invaders. Perhaps it was his close brush with death at the hand of an assassin.

Whatever the reason, he was suddenly drawn to this woman who'd been a comrade and friend at his side for years. Even more surprising, his feelings were reciprocated. Drawing a deep breath, he told himself this was simply not the right time, especially with Ardan standing over him.

"Ardan," he said. "What brings you here?"

"Duke Hasek, as always, I offer my humble services. I recalled you saying that today you'd be running simulations to see how long it would take to bring reinforcements to New Syrtis, providing you could find any. I hoped I might be of some assistance."

"I appreciate that, Ardan, but things don't look good." George gestured to his aide. "Major Felton has been buried down here in the dark for weeks, contacting every unit in the March and beyond who might be able to reinforce us. There is simply nothing there. Every unit has been either wiped out or is so entrenched in its own battles that it's impossible for them to disengage. The good news is that it also means Katherine probably hasn't had any luck finding troops, either."

"What about local militias?" Deborah asked.

George nodded to say they'd already thought of that. "After two solid days of simulations, we finally discarded the idea. First, most of the militias on worlds near us have no 'Mech forces. And even when they do, the units are woefully under-trained, under-armored, and under-gunned. I'd be ordering them into battle as human shields for my own troops, and I'll not do that. Finally, to pull in enough such troops to make any difference would require a fleet of DropShips and JumpShips I simply don't have."

"ComStar," Ardan said.

George looked sharply at him. "I'm not Victor, Ardan. I refuse to ask ComStar to break their neutrality and fight at my beck and call."

Ardan shook his head slightly. "Duke Hasek, I've told you many times that Prince Victor never asked a single ComStar member to fight for him. After all, he did voluntarily step aside as both the Commanding General of the Star League Defense Force and Precentor Martial of the Com Guards. If he'd retained those offices, many more might have followed him, and yet he chose otherwise. Those units who followed him did so for their own reasons. As for asking ComStar to fight for you, that was not what I was suggesting. Call on them for arbitration. If I remember correctly, the 321st Division is on Warlock, which is only three jumps away. Perhaps they would intervene, not to fight on your side but to stop the fighting altogether. If nothing else, having a fresh BattleMech force on planet would give General Amelio pause for thought."

George thought for a moment and could not help a wry smile. "You seem to know an awful lot about Com Guard Divisions, Ardan. You probably even know the commanding Precentor's name, don't you?"

"Precentor Tamatha Sparks and I met while I was the Federated Commonwealth's assigned aide to the Commanding General of the SLDF," Ardan said simply.

That was what George continued to love about Ardan. He always had an answer. A good thing he knew his father's old friend so well.

"Ardan, you'd just love to get a Com Guard Division on New Syrtis soil. I'm sure Victor would, too."

"Duke Hasek, Victor is no longer Precentor Martial."

"Yes, just like I'm no longer field marshal. Ardan, if what you constantly tell me is true, Victor has no wish to sit on the throne of New Avalon. So, what does he intend to do with this mess when it's finally over? He's a military man through and through and one of the better generals of our generation. You think he'll simply take up station on Warren and become a gentleman farmer? No, if he doesn't take the throne, he'll march right back to ComStar, and they'll receive him like a prodigal son—with or without the backing of Anastasius Focht."

"Focht is retired, so—"

George cut in with a laugh. "No one is that naïve. Focht may not have his hands in the day-to-day business anymore, but when he speaks, it might as well be Jerome Blake talking from the grave, where most of ComStar is concerned. Victor will be Precentor Martial again, and I'd owe him for helping to rescue my world. I don't want to owe ComStar a single D-bill, much less the survival of my capital. And if Victor doesn't go back to ComStar but takes back the throne, he could still say his 321st only came to my aid because of their loyalty to him as former Precentor Martial. No, Ardan, I'll not have that hanging over my head, nor will you have me owing Victor that easily."

Ardan's face gave no hint that George's suspicions had any effect on him. His voice did convey a certain hurt when he spoke again, which George thought nicely done. "Duke Hasek, I'm sorry you think my suggestion was a subterfuge. If I believed you would accept Victor's aid directly, I would not resort to indirection and I would simply tell you, as I've done for months, that you should publicly declare for Victor. If you did so, another unit loyal to Victor might find a way to come to your aid."

"What are you saying, Ardan?" George was suddenly angry. He'd enjoyed sparring with his father's old friend before, but all that was gone now. "That some unit who has told us emphatically that they cannot possibly come to our aid might miraculously find it possible if we declare for Victor? I hope that's not what you're telling me, because I would hate to think that your beloved prince would try such a trick to win my loyalty."

For the first time in a long time, a hint of emotion washed over Ardan's face, though it was mostly unreadable. "Duke Hasek, please, that's not what I was suggesting in any way. Prince Victor would never use such leverage. I simply meant that there might be regimental commanders loyal to Victor who believe their current battles are more important than yours because you are neutral in the conflict. If you announced full support of Prince Victor, the fight for New Syrtis might suddenly become more important in their eyes."

George stared at Ardan for several long heartbeats and wondered for the hundredth time whether he was hearing the complete truth, or the truth as filtered by Ardan, a man unwaveringly devoted to Victor.

He felt weary, weighed down by the months of constant fighting. "I'm sorry, Ardan. I'm just not willing to do that yet."

"You've been saying that for a long time, Duke Hasek."

"And for now, I'll keep saying it."

"Then, I don't believe you'll have any reinforcements. General Amelio will surely assault Saso within the next two months—perhaps three, if the weather is kind to us—and you'll have to defend with what you have. I hope it's enough."

George hated Ardan just then, even though he knew he only spoke the truth. Looking around, he could see generals' aides, warrant officers, and comm techs all listening in but trying not to meet his eyes, the despair of the moment too much for them. Then, he turned to Deborah. Something moved in her eyes, and again he felt a warm strength passing from her to him.

He looked back at Ardan. "I hope so, too, Ardan. But we'll survive this, and I'll tell you why. It's because we've got something the invaders do not. Not only do we have right on our side in defending ourselves from attack, but we love the soil of the world we're protecting. General Amelio and his troops can lay claim to neither, and in the end, that will defeat them."

Around him, George thought he saw his people sitting up straighter and even smiling with more confidence than they'd showed for some time. They took courage from his words. He only hoped he believed them as much as they did.

24

Our top news story tonight is the cessation of hostilities on the world of Wernke, which has been bitterly contested since late 3062 by two sister regiments, the Twentieth and the Twenty-second Avalon Hussars.

The destruction of the Twentieth, staunch Victor loyalists, leaves the Archon-Princess in control of a critical 'Mech-producing world. Having lost a number of important 'Mech producers in recent years, including Nanking, Coventry, and most devastating of all, Tikonov, control of Wernke is critical for the Archon-Princess' future ability to wage war against forces loyal to Prince Victor.

—From *Headline News*, Federated News Services, Robinson, Federated Suns, 1 April 3066

Morgan Hasek-Davion Memorial Park
Mawrydogg Glacier, New Syrtis
Capellan March
Federated Suns
1 April 3066

"**S**top!" Grayson cried out over the general frequency. "Stop the fighting!" But it was no use. No use at all. The fact that the Ridgebrook CMM had chosen the Morgan Hasek Memorial Park for its escape route had ignited a berserker rage in his men that nothing could stop; he'd been trying for fifteen minutes.

His *Templar* rocked back as a *Cestus* blasted away almost a ton of armor from his *Templar*'s upper-right torso with a shot from its gauss rifle. He back-pedaled to keep his balance, then rotated to return fire with his Streak short-range missile four-packs. He was still unwilling to unleash his full weapons load for fear of collateral damage to the park. Eight bright flames cut the twilight, their contrails quickly streaming away in the perpetual wind before explod-ing all across the *Cestus*'s torso. The ungainly, hunched-over 'Mech stumbled, smashing a sculp-tured ice unicorn under its huge metal foot as it did.

"NO!" Grayson yelled at the top of his lungs. Tears of anguish started in his eyes, and great gasping sobs threatened to overtake him. "Please, not here. We'll disengage . . ." But he knew that was not true. In their righteous anger, his Fusiliers were destroying the very thing they sought to protect. It was mad-ness.

Off to his left, Jonathan Tomlinson stood his ground in his *JagerMech*, firing continuously, the thunder of his dual ultra autocannons echoing across the frozen plain. He seemed not to care that he had stepped on and destroyed a statue of a woman with a babe at her breast.

Further on, Grayson could see Leftenant Jack Man-tas's *Banshee*, its PPCs firing with abandon, exploding multiple sculptures all at once. A star surrounded by seven planets was vaporized in an instant, as though the icy sun had suddenly achieved reality and obliterated itself along with its solar system in the colossal flare of a supernova. A smoke jaguar fighting a valiant but ultimately hopeless battle against a lion vanished as surely as the Clan that had inspired the piece. A giant gladiator pinning a Chinese dragon to the ground sublimated as quickly as the changing fortunes of the Capellan state. Grayson could hardly bear to look.

Duel ruby beams split the air and cored into his right and left legs, bubbling another ton of armor off his *Templar*. Walking backward in the vain hope of drawing the *Cestus* away from the ice sculptures, Grayson lined up a shot with his pair of extended-range medium lasers and let fly. Thanks to his careful aim and his advanced targeting computer, both shots found their mark over the center torso. Trying not to further harm the park, he was doing only half the damage of his opponent. His concern was probably ludicrous, like someone trying not to spill his canteen into a flood sweeping through his hometown. Just another drop in the ocean, he thought.

A full barrage from the *Cestus* brought him back to the fight, the dual large lasers and gauss rifle all finding their mark on his *Templar*. The transfer of kinetic energy, combined with the loss of almost two tons of armor and the icy footing, finally knocked him off balance. The keening of the gyro housed beneath his cockpit let him know that gravity had won this round.

The *Templar* slammed onto its back, slamming Grayson's helmeted head painfully off his command chair. Breathing heavily, realizing that his *Templar* was as dead as any tortoise if it stayed on its back, he tried to roll over and regain his footing. The task was made a lot more arduous because he didn't want to use his gun-barrel arms. Packing them with snow would destroy them as surely as any weapons hit if he fired them in that condition. The *Cestus* continued to worry his armor with additional energy strikes against his flank, and Grayson's ire grew with each blast.

By the time he had the *Templar* back up to its eleven-meter height, his anger got the best of him. He waited an instant for his reticle to burn gold before clenching his joysticks in both fists and firing every weapon at his disposal. Four extended-range medium lasers, twin Streak missile four-packs, and dual type-five autocannons lashed out at the *Cestus*. As before, the Streaks all locked onto their target and corkscrewed in to devastating effect. The precision autocannon ammunition and the *Templar*'s targeting computer kept both metal streams on target, eating away like a fungus at the crystalline armor. Only two lasers found their mark. The other two flashed within a finger of the *Cestus*, hitting further back into the park.

A distant part of Grayson's mind watched as both lasers lashed at other ice sculptures. The first beam sliced across a magnificent ice tree that must have stood twenty meters high. Chopping through the base, the flash of light felled the tree as surely as any woodsman's ax, and the tree crashed down, flattening even more sculptures. To Grayson's utter horror, the second laser flashed toward the very center of the park, where an untouched *Daishi* crouched protectively over Morgan's tomb. The beam appeared to pass through the ice 'Mech's right-arm shoulder joint. As the *Templar*'s full weapons load-out cycled back into ready status and unleashed another barrage, Grayson almost sighed with relief when the *Daishi* at first seemed unharmed. Then, like a wall of snow toppling as it became an avalanche, the arm slowly began to twist down and out, ice shards exploding like spent fireworks in the bright sunshine.

Grayson's second volley scored along the same lines as the first, twin laser beams punching through the *Cestus*'s center torso. The sudden spike on his IR screen indicated that he'd struck the other 'Mech's engine. As more shots followed the energy into those holes, the *Cestus* suddenly froze as gouts of flame began to shoot out of the gouge in its armor. In surreal unison, the arm of the *Daishi* finally tore free as the energy trapped in the *Cestus*'s fusion engine escaped its bounds and engulfed its jailer. Exploding outward, it incinerated the entire machine in an instant. No ejection seat made it away from the explosion. The ice-arm crashed to the ground, shattering into a million pieces.

Shaking, Grayson began to weep. Though he'd fought countless battles in the last few months, he'd killed only three MechWarriors, all of them Lyrans. The *Cestus*'s MechWarrior had fought every bit as hard as Grayson, convinced he was in the right. He was a Davion, a soldier from the same House as Grayson, and Grayson had killed him. Worst of all, his errant shot had defaced the ultimate sculpture of the Memorial Park. He might as well have spit on the grave of the Federated Suns' greatest hero.

He began to laugh, the sound tinged with hysteria. "All the king's horses and all the kings men . . ." he murmured. Until this moment, he'd hoped that somehow the wounds of the civil war could be healed. That even after years of fighting and thousands of deaths, the leaders and the people of the greatest star empire since the Star League could and would find common ground to unite once more. That, like a phoenix, it would rise from the ashes of this great mistake and become more magnificent than ever before.

No more. The hope had shattered just as surely as the sculptured arm of the *Daishi*. It had been no more substantial than a dream, and Grayson saw it for what it was—denial on a grand scale. He could not hide behind his illusions anymore. The truth was as bitter as the wind of New Syrtis. No matter how long, no matter how hard they tried, they could never put Humpty together again.

25

Tonight, President Grover Shraplen's press secretary announced that the complete destruction of the mercenary unit DeMaestri's Sluggers of the Fighting Urukhai was warranted and necessary. He stated that the unit entered the Hyades Cluster and began an immediate high-speed burn toward the planet Taurus. When they ignored repeated warnings to stop for boarding, President Shraplen felt compelled to defend the citizens of the Concordat against a possible invasion by a mercenary unit in the employ of the Federated Commonwealth. He authorized the Fourth Taurian Air Division of the Taurian Guard to act at their discretion. As all enemies of the Taurian Concordat have learned over the centuries, attacking Taurus means almost certain death, and the Sluggers met theirs in the depths of cold space.

Sources close to the mercenary unit say that the Sluggers did broadcast their intentions, stating that they had abandoned their post on Lothair, where they believed their position was untenable, and that they wished to offer their services to the Concordat. President Shraplen has offered no further comment.

—From *News at Six*, Taurus Broadcasting Company, Taurus, Taurian Concordat, 25 April 3066

Bowerton Glacier, New Syrtis
Capellan March
Federated Suns
26 April 3066

Standing in the ready room of the *Proletariat*, General Victor Amelio smiled for what felt like the first time in weeks. Spread before him was a holographic map. It showed Saso and the Cave at the center of a circle with a radius of two hundred-fifty kilometers. At the very edge of the circle was a large blue triangle representing his DropShip. Fully surrounding Saso, other smaller blue triangles showed brightly against the white of the map. The closest triangle, representing First Battalion of his own Guards, was just over a hundred kilometers from the city.

Yellow circles also dotted the map, representing all the known locations of enemy forces. Two yellow dots faced his First Battalion, and he knew they would make his men pay dearly for every step forward. The important thing was that he was within striking distance of the capitol. After so many months and so many losses, he had finally linked up his men in a full siege around the city, with his command DropShip present to oversee this final move. It was only a matter of time. Yes, he had every right to smile.

"General," Major General Emeline Jones said, approaching from the access way. The months of fighting had worn down her once proud carriage, and her shoulders slumped as though the weight of the newly thickened strip on her epaulette was more than she could bear. Of course, not many tankers in a militia unit ever found themselves raised to the exalted rank of commander of an entire RCT. Of course, there wasn't much left of the RCT at this point, which was why he hadn't even blinked at making the field promotion. It was good for morale, and Amelio didn't think she could screw things up too badly.

"Yes, General," he said.

"I've just come from Communications with the latest communiqués. It appears that all of our troops are in position."

"What about supplies?"

"The final dispatch was from your Third Battalion. They say two of their Karnov transports crashed in a severe overnight storm, so they've replaced only half of their consumables. But they're still confident they can maintain a forward drive for at least seven days."

"Excellent. We can divert additional stores to them by that time. What about the defenders? Have we additional confirmation of their deployment?"

"Not yet."

Amelio frowned slightly. Though he was confident of his intel, he would have liked an update. His last report was almost three weeks old. That was why he'd sent out a half-dozen scouts a week ago to reconnoiter Saso. With the continual cloud cover, it was impossible to drop a satellite into orbit for a clearer view, and the Spotter plane he'd sent on a high fly-by had been destroyed even before it was within visual of the city. Turning back to the holotable, he placed both hands firmly on the lip and leaned over, staring intently at the city. Have I finally cornered you, George? he asked silently.

Then, it dawned on him that he'd stopped referring to the duke as, well, the duke. He wasn't sure when it had happened, and it bothered him a little. Regardless of his orders, regardless of how much the duke had defied the Archon-Princess, George Hasek was still a duke. In a feudal society where a man like Amelio usually owed such men complete fealty, he'd needed to find some way to distance himself, to rationalize what he was doing. He chuckled to himself. Here he was, a general in command of an entire planetary invasion force, and he was still thinking like any Joe farmer from the backwoods.

"General," Jones said, interrupting his thoughts. Turning, he found her holding out the batch of messages with one hand. He reached for them, then set them down on the table without reading them.

"How long until we reach Saso?" he asked. Jones looked surprised, then quickly tried to hide it from him. He understood that she was startled to have him asking her opinion. It didn't mean he'd give it a second's consideration, but she couldn't know that.

"There are a lot of factors, General. As last night can attest, the weather is always a wild card. Not to mention that the defenders are sometimes pushovers and sometimes they can be very tenacious. Even—"

"I'm perfectly aware of that," he said firmly. "All things considered, how long?"

Jones studied the map while Amelio surreptitiously studied her face. For the first time, he noticed that she was not unattractive. Except for the some-what deflated look about her, she might even have been pretty. He could almost see the struggle work its way across her face; she even hunched her shoulders slightly as though to ward off a blow. So, it was worse than he imagined, he thought with an internal sigh. She was almost completely broken. Perhaps he would remove her before the final push began.

"Three weeks," she said finally, her voice strained as though the answer was being tortured out of her.

He raised an eyebrow in surprise. "Three weeks. Pretty ambitious, don't you think?"

She flinched visibly at his rebuke, confirming his assessment. "You asked my opinion and, all things considered, I believe we can reach the outskirts of the city in three weeks. We're having problems with supplies, General, but I think the defenders may be, too. We've seized a lot of whatever they had, and they probably weren't able to stockpile much with so many of the duke's regiments on other worlds needing supplies more than they did."

As she continued to speak, her voice gained more strength and her shoulders straightened a little. Maybe he'd been wrong about her, Amelio thought. She still seemed to have some fight in her. "I believe they're running extremely low on expendable ammu-nition. Witness the latest push by your Second Battal-ion against the Legion. It was only a probe, and yet they fell back, despite the fact that they had the superior position, if not numbers. So, I believe they're hoarding their ammunition, waiting for our final as-sault on the city.

"Of course, even if it is three weeks till we reach the outskirts of the city, that doesn't mean we can take it in that time. If I'm right, they'll give ground in order to pull our forces closer, to concentrate them more. Then, when we think we have them, they'll strike back, hoping to break our lines, to push us back. Maybe to even break our backs with a counter-offensive. At least, that's what I would do if I was in their position." She turned and looked him directly in the eye, as though daring him to contradict her. Well, well, well. A lot more spine than he'd thought.

"A good assessment, Major General," he said. "In fact, very close to my own thoughts. At this point, it does not matter that our scouts have not returned, though I want you to follow up on that." He turned to stare at the holotable one last time. "The enemy are on their last legs, General. Even if they do have one or two gasps left, they're the gasps of a dying man. By the end of May, I expect to sit on George's throne while he kneels before me and swears allegiance to the Archon-Princess."

As he finished speaking, Amelio suddenly wondered what he would do if the duke refused. Throw him in jail? Execute him? He shuddered slightly as his upbringing once more reared its ugly head. No, he thought, he could never bring himself to do anything like that. Better to send him to New Avalon.

As he turned away from the table, Amelio smiled again. He couldn't help thinking it might almost be more merciful to take George's head than to deliver him into the hands of the Archon-Princess.

26

Less than four months have passed since the arrival of the Nineteenth Arcturan Guards and the Fifth Donegal Guards RCT on New Avalon, and yet the spectacle of another parade can still draw the masses like beetles to dung. This time, the throngs mindlessly applauded the display of the Seventeenth Avalon Hussars RCT. Standing on the reception podium in his colorful rags, General Kev Evans gave a rousing speech that had the cows frothing and lowing for long minutes.

Of course, no mention was made of the Seventeenth's traitorous actions in launching an unsanctioned attack against the Combine world of An Ting, or the fact that the Dragon banner now flies over Davion worlds because of such actions. No, as long as the Hussars remain loyal to the Archon and are willing to shed their blood in her defense, she doesn't care about anything else.

Then again, with forces loyal to Victor making their way toward New Avalon, is it any wonder? Does she yet see the writing on the wall? Do the pain and suffering of millions because of her rapacious rule finally haunt her at night? The next time I walk the streets and cheer will be when her head is mounted on the walls of the Royal Palace!

—Pirate broadcast by Death to the Archon, New Avalon, Federated Suns, 14 May 3066

University of Saso
Saso, New Syrtis
Capellan March
Federated Suns
14 May 3066

The library building literally exploded outward, a brick and mortar volcano spewing a storm of what had once been thousands of books into the snow-blown atmosphere.

"Uh, don't know about you, Grayson, but that artillery is getting too close for comfort," Jonathan announced; he could never resist making the most absurd understatements in the midst of a desperate fight. Any closer and pieces of him and Grayson would be strewn across the snowy streets instead of the torn and shredded pages of books.

"Well, if you wouldn't—" Grayson broke off in mid-sentence as a shape loomed out of the literary blizzard. "What the . . ." he began as emerald darts and ruby shafts came at him, instantly setting fire to some paper in the air. The swirling wind fanned the flames that danced to and fro as they scored against his 'Mech. He swore as his damage schematic lit up like a Christmas tree. He hadn't fully replaced his armor from the last battle, and the accursed lasers had found their mark as though hunting specifically for his critical wounds. As the attacking shape fully resolved itself into a 'Mech, he swore again, realizing that it was not an artillery strike but this machine that had destroyed part of the library. It was walking through the walls to get at him . . . and what a 'Mech.

Weighing in at ninety tons, the *Highlander* was by no means the largest or heaviest 'Mech in production, but it was still one of the most potent designs ever to stride across the battlefield. Dating from the Star League and only recently under manufacture once more, its boxy torso, flat, hooded head, and thick limbs exuded power, not to mention the maw of a giant gauss rifle at the end of its right arm.

As Grayson brought his *Templar*'s weapons on-line, the *Highlander* raised its right arm toward Jonathan's *JagerMech*, firing not the gauss round Grayson expected but a stream of depleted-uranium shells. At this range, the shot was right on target, carving a swath of destruction from the *JagerMech*'s right torso to its right arm. It tore the arm clean off, and the double-barreled appendage whirled through the air to crash through a hover car unlucky enough to be parked along this street.

Not that the owner was likely to care at this point, Grayson thought as he chewed at the *Highlander*'s armor with his own autocannon. Most of the city's inhabitants had long since been evacuated. Staring at the 'Mech through his view screen, he thought it looked newly repaired, and its armor was thick indeed. It was obviously not the standard model. From the horrific destruction and the pattern of damage wreaked on the *JagerMech*, he guessed that the *Highlander* mounted an ultra type-twenty autocannon in place of the usual gauss rifle. The weapon would be appallingly effective at this range, able to tear through armor anywhere on his *Templar*.

As he began to back up, hoping to put distance between himself and the *Highlander*, he heard the warning of enemy target-lock, followed by a storm of short-range missiles coming at him. Damn, he thought. How many Streak missiles did that thing mount? He might actually be outgunned, perhaps considerably so.

Still moving backward down the street, he brought up both his autocannon barrels and unleashed another long, rolling barrage. Seemingly unconcerned, the *Highlander* simply lifted its right arm in the direction of Grayson's XO again.

"Jonathan! Eject!" No way could the already damaged *JagerMech* stand up to another such beating. Apparently, even Jonathan realized that sarcasm was inappropriate right now, and silenced reigned on the channel as the top of his 'Mech blew away. As the stream of death from the *Highlander* systematically caved in the right side of the machine and bored inward, Jonathan's command chair rocketed out of the doomed *JagerMech* on jets. He arced over several streets before finally deploying his parachute. Grayson hoped Jon hadn't been knocked unconscious on landing, or he would probably freeze to death.

Knowing he was expending his armor-piercing ammunition at a terrific rate—ammo he wouldn't be able to replenish—he opened up a third time with his twin autocannon. He also toggled his quad extended-range medium lasers and Streak short-range missiles.

With the *JagerMech* finished off, the *Highlander* turned just in time to take the brunt of Grayson's fire even as it launched an assault of its own.

The very air burned and writhed with twisting streams of lead, pulsing jade darts, flashing crimson beams, flickering flames, and expanding contrails—the colossal destructive power of two giant war machines unleashed.

Explosions flared and engulfed Grayson's *Templar*, which stumbled and fell forward. Warning lights added their glow to the visual overload, and alarms joined the unending cacophony. He was stunned into insensibility as his mind simply shut down for a moment.

"Sir! Grayson! Addison! Are you there?" The shouting felt like someone beating incessantly on his head with mallets, trying to use it as a timpani. Coming back to his surroundings as the pain began to lessen, he realized he was hanging face down, the restraint harness of his command chair the only thing keeping him from dropping onto his console. He slowly readjusted his neurohelmet, which had slid askew in the fall of his *Templar*, and got his machine back onto its feet. He tried to speak softly because his head still thrummed with the echo of a hard blow, but his voice-activated mic would not pick up. With an effort of will, he spoke louder. "Yes, I'm here, if barely. Subaltern Tonkovic . . . Adela, is that you?"

"Yes, sir."

Grayson suddenly remembered the terrible fight

he'd been in and quickly scanned the street, but the *Highlander* was nowhere in sight. "Adela, the *Highlander*, where . . ."

"We managed to push him back for now, sir." As Adela spoke, Addison realized it wasn't only her *Quickdraw* behind him. He saw Subaltern Darrey's *Axman* and Subaltern Holtzman's *Cataphract* as well. "Sir, they've pushed through in this entire sector. We only forced the *Highlander* into a retreat temporarily. He'll be back, probably with reinforcements. We've got to pull back before we're overrun ourselves."

Grayson thought for a moment, then said woodenly, "You're right, Adela. Pull back." He felt almost hollow as the ad-hoc lance began to make its way deeper into the city. Now that he was listening for it, his external mikes picked up the sounds of fighting—sounds that seemed disturbingly close. Occasionally, he could even see the blinding flash of an explosion from several streets away.

He'd blacked out while fighting the *Highlander*, and he was ashamed of it. Ever since the battle at the Memorial, where he'd lost some indefinable spark, he'd been fighting almost mechanically. In every engagement since then, he'd felt out of sync with his *Templar*, almost as though his neurohelmet's brainwave setting no longer matched his own. As though he were a different person than before. Even so, this time was the worst. To have actually zoned out . . . it was sickening.

Trudging through wind-blown streets, the sounds of fighting reminding him that the enemy had managed to penetrate to Saso even after the duke's men had put up six months of determined defense, he realized that he'd died that day at the Memorial. His spirit had been extinguished, and his body had yet to realize it. Today, though, his body would finally catch up. Today was his day to die.

27

Is there anyone alive out there? This is Jason Dilabio broadcasting from Saso at 224th Street and 74th Avenue, and I've not seen another living citizen for most of three days, though I've been making forays into nearby neighborhoods. All I see are blasted, empty buildings, the furtive movements of armed soldiers, and the tremors heralding the approach of a 'Mech. I make myself scarce then, so I've been lucky enough not to actually see one yet.

But the bodies? God, it's awful. Just saw a woman holding her baby. Looks like debris from the building she was walking past fell on her, caving in her head—probably a missed 'Mech shot that broke off the façade. Looks like she managed to cradle the baby in her arms when she fell, as I couldn't see any marks on the child . . . It froze to death.

What have we become? We're crazed animals killing each other, and for what? For a ruler a hundred light years away who's never met my mother now dead, or shopped at what used to be Jerry's Market down the street, or attended The Freeze, the local dance club, or even set foot on our planet!

My father fought and died for the First Prince in the Fourth War, because he believed that his liege lord had a better vision for our tomorrow. I weep

with joy that my father did not live to see what
that vision has become.
—Pirate broadcast from Saso, New Syrtis, Federated Suns,
   16 May 3066

Industrial Center
Saso, New Syrtis
Capellan March
Federated Suns
16 May 3066

The giant fist, as big as an ultra-compact hover car,
reared back and then smashed into the *Enforcer's*
head, pulverizing its weak armor and pulping the
enemy MechWarrior instantly. The *Enforcer* slowly
began to crumple backward like a falling tree, some
red-smeared wires from its head still entangled with
the *Hatamoto-Chi's* fist. It crashed into the north wall
of the smelting plant it had occupied in Saso's industrial center, tearing at the foundation and collapsing
an entire section of the building's walls.

Colonel Chad Dean did not even smile in satisfaction at the death of another Lyran. That would have
equated them with humans. It felt more like an exter-
mination, a ridding the Inner Sphere of a pestilence.
If it was possible, his detachment only increased. This
was not a 'Mech battle to defend Saso against an
enemy invader. This was mortal combat against an
infestation, and he was the harbinger of the phage's
doom.

"Colonel, do you copy?" Captain Kelly Marc said,
his voice filling Chad's ears with the first human

noise in what seemed like a long time. A quick glance at his chronometer showed that he'd been exterminating solo for almost forty minutes. Three more kill marks on the inside of his cockpit, he thought absently while opening the channel to respond.

"Aye, Marc, I copy. What's the sitrep?"

"I've got Second Assault pinning the center along Aleksandr Boulevard, while Force Alpha and Recon Blue have moved into position to the west along Chauser Avenue, ready to pinwheel forward to the right." An easy laugh followed. "Seems like you were right again, Colonel. Push into their teeth when they least expect it, and you'll take them by surprise every time."

Chad nodded to himself. "It's as old as the hills, but the axiom holds true. Especially when they think we're almost out of supplies and ammo." No need to voice the obvious; they *were* almost out of supplies and ammunition. "Where's the rest of First Command?" he asked.

"Can't raise 'em, Colonel. I hate to say it, but I think Jason and Sandy may have bought it."

"Just one more debt to strip from their blue hides," Chad said, without emotion. There was no immediate response. After all their years together, his men knew him well enough, especially his XO. Nothing could touch him when he was in this mood. Everything was outside: pain, emotion . . . conscience. At this point, when it came to the Lyrans, he was ice—cold and hard as aligned-crystal steel.

He glanced at his tactical screen, quickly keying in the sitrep from his XO, toggling through several screens to update them. Then, he said, "So, have we actually pushed them back toward the city limits or just stalled them? And where are the Fusiliers? There's no way we can hold the Guards without some reinforcement."

"I haven't been able to raise them," Marc said. "Not surprising, considering all this damn metal. I did tell you I hate fighting in a city, right?" The accompanying laugh had a cynical bite, unusual for Chad's XO. Then again, when your unit had taken over fifty percent losses, what could you expect? "Anyway, toss in the damn storm front coming in with the jamming from the Guards all over the place, and I'm sure the Fusiliers have their hands full, and well . . . I'm just not surprised. With the losses we've taken . . . you're right. We'll never be able to hold a sustained offensive against their numbers. Surprise is the only thing we've got going right now."

A smile almost tugged at Chad's lips. He knew his XO had left out the other part of the equation that was allowing a unit down to less than a battalion to not only stall but apparently to drive back almost twice their numbers.

Hate.

Not something his XO wanted to dwell on too much right now.

Of course, some might say that hate was driving the Guards as well, but theirs was a hot hate and mostly directed at the Fusiliers. The Legion's hate, and particularly their commander's, was a cold thing. Something banked and tended over long years. Something never allowed to flare, for it might extinguish itself. Better to keep it burning cold, like a neutron star in the depths of the galaxy. Then, it was more powerful than any flaring, white-hot supernova, sending out streams of high-intensity X-rays to shower the galaxy for untold millennia. What was the old adage . . . Revenge was a dish best served cold? A smile finally dragged its way into existence, a look that would have terrified most men.

Checking his data readouts once more, Chad said, "It doesn't matter, Marc. I know Grayson, and he'll find us, no matter what. And even if he isn't able to disengage and reinforce, we're still moving forward. We've got the initiative here, and we'd be fools to lose it."

There was a momentary pause before Marc responded in a tone of resigned acceptance. "Aye, Colonel. I had a feeling you'd say that. We just need Third Assault and Command Second to reach Cheshire Street, then we'll be in a position to pinwheel both sides forward."

"When will they be in position?"

"Captain Jefferson said another fifteen minutes."

Chad didn't get a chance to say anything more as proximity alarms filled the cockpit with their wail, lighting up his console like a hooker tricked out for a night in Solaris City. His *Hatamoto-Chi* was already moving, its torso twisting in the direction his targeting acquisition had already lit up. Punching up magnification, he saw that an *Assassin* had limped through a breach in a building wall a scant seventy meters away. A quick visual showed its left arm completely torn away, and massive rents in the machine's armor ran from its gimpy left leg all the way up to the right arm. The *Assassin* seemed not even to notice the assault 'Mech that outweighed it two-to-one drawing a bead with its weapons. Most of its sensors must be fried, Chad thought.

Had this been a MechWarrior from any other House—or even the Clans, for that matter—he would have spared the warrior by either giving him the chance to surrender or by tearing off the 'Mech's legs to incapacitate it. Without a moment's hesitation, he pulled the trigger on both joysticks, launching a full salvo at the enemy 'Mech.

Heat boiled up from under his feet, creating currents that actually blew his long, wet hair across his back. His twin extended-range PPCs, his medium lasers, and his dual Streak six short-range missile packs sent their combined fire at the hapless machine. Even in perfect condition, the *Assassin* would have been hard pressed to survive the onslaught. Taking mortal damage, the 'Mech literally disintegrated in front of Chad's eyes, his energy beams vaporizing armor into metallic clouds and the Streak missiles blasting what little remained into a cascading metal-fall. Though the fail-safes on the *Assassin*'s fusion engine kept it from exploding, it was almost as vaporized as if it had exploded, and the MechWarrior never knew what hit him.

"Colonel, some trouble?" Marc asked, hearing the sounds of Chad's weapons fire over the comm channel.

"None whatsoever." Chad moved toward the hole in the wall the *Assassin* had passed through.

"Good, because Jefferson's group is in position ahead of schedule."

"Excellent. Looks like it's time to smear a little more blue onto the ferrocrete, eh, Marc?"

"Aye, Colonel. Let's just hope Colonel Addison finds us soon, or this might be one of the shortest offensives of our career."

"Ha!" Chad barked, without the least trace of humor in the sound. "Then, let's make it count, shall we?"

The Vanguard Legion began to advance forward.

28

The bloody conflict for Cavanaugh II has ended. In one of the largest battles to date in the Alliance, no less than six military units were involved in the fighting: the Penobscott CTM (destroyed during the sixth wave), the Seventh and Tenth Lyran Regulars, the Second Crucis Lancers RCT, and most surprising of all, the 182nd Division of ComStar's Eighth Army, who followed the lead of their sister unit, the 244th Division, in declaring for Prince Victor.

Three days ago, in an action that pundits are calling a brilliant political move, General Richard Steiner negotiated a cease-fire that resulted in the surrender of the Seventh and Tenth Lyran Regulars. Though they will maintain control of their assets, they have ceded complete control of Cavanaugh II to Prince Victor.

Though General Steiner has a history of building his own power base, for him to relinquish his support of the Archon-Princess is a blow to the Archon's power in the Alliance.

—From *Headline News*, Donegal Broadcasting Company, Donegal, Lyran Alliance, 15 May 3066

Industrial Center
Saso, New Syrtis
Capellan March
Federated Suns
16 May 3066

A good day to die. The thought kept echoing in Grayson's mind, as though on a repeating loop. It was an endless wave of despair that washed incessantly against the sand castle of his will to live, ever eroding. He couldn't shake it off.

After his disastrous encounter with the *Highlander*, the Fusiliers under his immediate command had fallen back across eight blocks of the city, attempting to close ranks enough to finally stall the offensive. Yet, the invaders seemed limitless, a steady, crushing stream of 'Mechs smashing against the Fusilier bulwark. At one point, he lost seven 'Mechs in less than five minutes. That was when he knew his Fusiliers were past their CLG, and another section of castle washed into the swirling black foam.

CLG stood for Combat Loss Grouping and was an old term in MechWarrior circles. Basically, it was a fancy phrase for when a 'Mech or unit's cumulative damage had reached critical levels. A 'Mech battle might continue for what felt like an eternity, with no appreciable loss of forces on either side. Then, at a specific point, warriors on both sides would start dropping like flies. That was CLG. Not only would a 'Mech reach a critical level of damage at some point, but if all 'Mechs in a unit have been fighting for the same duration, they will tend to reach CLG at almost the same time.

That was what occurred when Grayson lost seven 'Mechs in a mere handful of minutes. The damage to his unit had reached CLG, and now it seemed like every gauss slug, every missile barrage, every fusillade of laser fire from the enemy downed one of his own. At that moment, he felt like he couldn't breathe, as though the waves in his mind had materialized as actual water filling up his cockpit, suffocating him. Only the needs of his unit kept him going.

Then, all of a sudden, the enemy attacks decreased. Within fifteen minutes, they ceased altogether, leaving the burning heaps of their fallen comrades stacked up like cordwood. Grayson shuddered to see so many of his own men and women in the same condition.

When another half-hour passed with no new attacks, he decided that the enemy had pulled back to reinforce a push into another section of the city. According to his information, the only other drive in the area was being held off by the Vanguard Legion. Between the Legion's hatred and its skill, Grayson didn't think the Guards could have pushed past them yet. If the Legion had managed to stall the enemy drive in their part of the battle, perhaps the attackers had been reassigned to strike at the flank of the Legion defense, to cut them in half and then shatter them.

Grayson decided he'd better find out. Leaving a skeleton defense at his current perimeter—enough to hold off a new onslaught until the bulk of his remaining Fusiliers could arrive—he'd taken his unit in search of the Legion. Twenty long minutes had passed before his external mikes picked up the sounds of fierce fighting.

"Colonel, looks like we've found them," said Leftenant Dejan, commander of Recon Lance. "Um, sir, you better come quick." His voice was filled with urgency, and Grayson hurried his *Templar* forward.

Continuing another five minutes through several streets to reach his outrider, he realized that the earlier sounds of fighting had fallen off, as though the Legion had pushed the enemy back or else the attackers had retreated once more. He wondered whether it was part of some elaborate trick to lure the bulk of the Fusiliers away from their previous defensive zone. By appearing to attack the Legion with the majority of their forces, the enemy could wheel at the last moment to slam back through the skeletal defense Grayson had left behind. It was a real worry, and one he'd just opened up a commline to investigate when his *Templar* rounded the corner into a city park. The sizzle of a single extended-range particle projector cannon drove all such thoughts from his mind.

In horror, he watched as the PPC ate through the remaining armor of an *Orion*'s head, and the headless 'Mech crumpled to the ground. It wasn't that Grayson had never seen such a death. He must have seen sights like this a hundred times in his years on the battlefield. What made this one different was that six Legion 'Mechs—and five Fusiliers, he noticed to his disgust—stood in a circle with their weapons trained on three Lyran 'Mechs in their midst. From what Grayson could see, the *Hatamoto-Chi*, piloted by Colonel Chad Dean himself, had just executed the Lyran MechWarrior. The scene became even more surreal as the *Hatamoto-Chi* calmly walked up to the next 'Mech, placed its right arm-mounted PPC close to the *Falconer*'s head and discharged at point-blank range. The *Falconer* joined its companion in slumped repose on the muddy grass of the park.

Anger erupted in Grayson, exploding up from the core of his soul as though a fusion reactor had been unleashed inside him. Weeks of malaise and brooding were washed away in an instant, and the righteous indignation he'd felt for so long over the hate and brutality of this civil war burned hotter than ever. As the *Hatamoto-Chi* began to move toward the second-to-last 'Mech, he opened up a general frequency.

"What the hell are you doing!" he yelled as he brought his *Templar* into the park, still some forty meters from the Lyran *Banshee* and the *Salamander* awaiting their fate. "This isn't war. This is an execution. By what right do you exact such justice, Chad? What right do any of you have?"

The *Hatamoto-Chi* stopped and, in a very human gesture, slowly rotated its head and upper torso to face Grayson's *Templar*. "By what right, you ask?" Chad said. "By right of the war they've waged against us. Did we attack them, Grayson? Did we kill their troops or their civilians? In almost three years of fighting, the duke could have ordered us to attack any number of targets and never once did we even board a DropShip, much less probe the aerospace defenses of a near planet that contained Katherine supporters. And yet here they are, raping, pillaging, plundering. How many men have you lost to them, Grayson? How many civilians have you seen slaughtered over the last half-year? I don't know about you, but I've seen the villages they passed through. I've seen the remains of burned bodies. Come, tell me why I don't have the right to execute these criminals for their crimes."

Dead silence filled the line, and no one moved. Even the wind had died down, as though waiting for Grayson's response.

What made it so crazy was that Chad was right about a lot of it. Grayson had seen villages almost razed to the ground. He had seen civilians killed before his eyes by enemy fire. And look at his Fusiliers—his own battalion had taken over fifty percent losses. Stacked up like that, the arguments made sense, and the calm way Chad had delivered them also carried weight. But it was all wrong, all skewed. He had to make them see.

"You're right, Chad. Almost everything you say is true." Grayson tried to strip the rage from his voice, to sound as reasonable and convincing as Chad had before the other soldiers, but it wasn't easy. He took several breaths to calm himself and began again. "No, we didn't attack any other world, but almost every unit under the duke's command—except for those on New Syrtis—has been fighting troops loyal to Katherine from the beginning. Yes, some of them may have gone rogue, but if you were Katherine, could you really sit back and believe that those units didn't have at least tacit approval from the duke? If he was no threat to her, why did he not provide support for her or at least declare the units under his nominal command as rogue?"

"Are you saying you support Katherine?" Chad asked quietly, a preternatural calm to his voice. Grayson watched as the *Hatamoto-Chi* turned slowly to face him full on, and it suddenly dawned on him that there might be only one way out of this situation. A way that he might not survive. Perhaps this was why he'd been so sure that today he would die.

"That's not what I'm saying, and you know it. Haven't I been fighting these invaders, too? What I *am* saying is that you have to see it from her point of view. From the point of view of the units loyal to her. The duke may not have attacked them outright, but in all this time, he's never once offered any sign that he supports Katherine. As such, why shouldn't she try to dispose of him?"

An almost imperceptible move by Chad's *Hatamoto-Chi* set Grayson's heart racing. Would Chad really attack him? Would his hate for anything Lyran actually drive him to fire because Grayson was trying to make him see the other side? With a sick feeling, he knew it was a distinct possibility. Could he bring himself to fire back? And if they did fight, would he survive? Chad was a superb MechWarrior, and his *Hatamoto-Chi* was a slightly better machine than the *Templar*. They'd both long ago reached their own CLG, so any combat would be very quick and very deadly.

"Chad, listen to me," he said. "You talked about

the civilians they killed. Some of it was deliberate. I'm not denying that. But a lot of the deaths were unintentional, caused by stray fire. Can you honestly tell me that you've not killed any civilians accidentally during all this time?"

He waited for Chad to respond. When he didn't, Grayson went on talking. "I thought not. Much to my shame, I know some have died even as I was attempting to keep them safe. That is sometimes the price of war, but the price you're demanding is too high. Too much to pay. You accuse the Lyrans of becoming monsters, and yet what do we become if we execute them in cold blood? Maybe you'll tell me that sometimes you have to become an animal to stop one, but I call that a lie."

Without raising his 'Mech's arms, he slowly maneuvered his *Templar* in a full circle, as though to look each MechWarrior directly in the eye. "We don't have to stoop to their level to stop them. We can remain human. We can remain true to ourselves and our beliefs and still defeat them. Can't you see that?" Again, he waited for Chad to answer.

No one moved. No one spoke. Perhaps he had reached them, Grayson thought. Perhaps they were beginning to understand the line they'd crossed and wondering how to extricate themselves.

Then, the *Hatamoto-Chi* moved, and Grayson heard Chad say, "No," as he raised his right-arm extended-range PPC.

Grayson flinched back into his command couch, afraid his friend was going to fire on him. Only at the last second did the arm swing toward the Lyran *Salamander*.

"Stop!" he screamed, knowing he was already too late. Azure energy burned the Lyran MechWarrior's life away.

Chad was already turning his *Hatamoto-Chi* toward the remaining *Banshee*. As the 'Mech's right arm swung into place, Grayson was in anguish even as he brought up his own weapons. In a dark corner of his mind, he'd hoped that Chad would fire the first shot, making it all so much easier. But he hadn't, and the pivotal decision was Grayson's. There was only one outcome.

Both autocannons cut the air, chopping into the *Hatamoto-Chi*'s right arm, spoiling its shot, which smashed into a building. And Grayson's CLG estimate was right on target. The stream of shells tore the arm clean off his friend's 'Mech.

Like a holovid with a glitch in it, the entire scene froze once more, everyone stunned by Grayson's actions. After several heartbeats that thumped in his ears loud enough to drown out every other sound, a soft voice spoke in his ear. "I'm sorry you did that, Grayson."

The *Hatamoto-Chi* moved forward quickly at an oblique angle to Grayson's *Templar*. Its torso twisted as Chad cut loose with his twin Streak six-packs, his paired extended-range particle projector cannon, and his medium laser. They all found their mark, the energy beams sloughing off armor in molten rivulets while the short-range missiles blasted through the holes that appeared underneath the trails of liquid metal. Lights flashed all across his damage schematic while he throttled the *Templar* backward and unleashed his own whirlwind of destruction.

Grayson felt no satisfaction at seeing the blasted armor that flew away from the *Hatamoto-Chi* or the craters that remained. Chad was his friend, but even friendship had to be weighed against wrongdoing. Though a part of him was dying—perhaps the death he'd felt coming for some time—he continued the furious duel. He didn't intend to kill Chad, but if it came to that, so be it. Some things were beyond price. Some things were beyond compromise. If he didn't try to stop this atrocity, he'd become everything he hated about this war. He'd have sold his soul.

As his *Templar*'s right arm was sheared off at the shoulder, he realized how close he'd come to doing just that. By looking the other way—just like his duke—he'd given tacit approval to the barbarism his troops had heaped on the enemy in the past months. It simply did not matter that the invaders were doing the same. Two wrongs did not make a right.

As the two 'Mechs circled each other, not one of the surrounding MechWarriors so much as opened up a commline to stop the fight, much less brought their own weapons to bear on either opponent. Perhaps this was their way of extricating themselves, Grayson thought. Letting him and Chad decide their future.

As quickly as it had begun, it was over. Grayson's extended-range lasers cored into the *Hatamoto-Chi*'s head, and the 'Mech fell backward. It wasn't the lifeless fall of a dead MechWarrior, but the spasmodic jerk of a wounded pilot. Grayson had no idea how injured Chad was, but after twenty seconds, he knew the 'Mech would not regain its feet anytime soon.

For a moment, he did nothing. Looking around him at the silent assemblage of MechWarriors, he finally opened a channel.

"This is over now," he said, feeling a weariness greater than any he'd known in his entire life. "Get a medic to Chad immediately."

He'd stopped it. He'd saved himself, but he wondered whether the price was worth it. His mind was too tired and confused to know anymore. For now, he slowly powered down his 'Mech and wept in darkness.

29

We, the People for Unity, want this senseless fighting to stop. We have been ruled by the Davion and Steiner dynasties for centuries and, unlike some of our more radical brethren, we see no need to change that. What has made us great for hundreds of years will continue to uphold us once this horror is done.

Nevertheless, Archon-Princess Katherine Steiner-Davion and Prince Victor Steiner-Davion have both proven they are unfit to rule. Though young, Duchess Yvonne Steiner-Davion has shown that the blood of her mother and father runs true in her veins. She should be allowed to re-ascend the throne of New Avalon. As for the throne of Tharkad, only Duke Peter has a right to it now that Arthur is dead. But where is Peter Steiner-Davion? It is time for him to come forward from whatever seclusion has shrouded him in these last years. Time for him to assume the throne on Tharkad, and end this terrible war forever!

—Pirate broadcast by the People for Unity, Donegal Broadcasting Company, Tharkad, Lyran Alliance, 16 May 3066

Industrial Center
Saso, New Syrtis
Capellan March
Federated Suns
16 May 3066

Hauptmann General Victor Amelio slowly realized that he was not going to die.

He sat in a pool of his own sweat, which poured down his face and in rivulets down his back. Yet, his *Banshee* had been powered down for almost five minutes, so it wasn't the heat of the fusion reactor that had him sweating. It was fear. Fear and horror at hearing the sounds of his command lance being executed around him like common criminals while he awaited his turn.

At first, it took him several long seconds to understand why he heard the sound of a single PPC discharge and a 'Mech crashing to the ground after his lance had surrendered. It wasn't until a second MechWarrior under his command died that he realized what was happening. He rushed to restart his 'Mech, then stopped the frantic movements of his fingers. A full company of enemy 'Mechs surrounded him. Even if he started up his *Banshee* again, he would die as surely as his men already executed. For the briefest instant, he thought of trying to reason with the enemy, but with his 'Mech powered down, he had no way to communicate. In the end, all he could do was wait for the end to come. And he had never been good at waiting.

It was all his fault. He was a general, for god's

sake, he berated himself while waiting for the headman's axe. Generals weren't supposed to fight on the front lines, but he hadn't been able to resist the desire to lead his men in battle after so long on this frozen hellhole. He'd mounted his *Banshee*, which he hadn't piloted in half a decade, to lead one of the prongs into the very heart of Saso. Having taken almost the whole planet, having utterly destroyed the New Syrtis CMM and decimated the Davion Light Guards, he'd succeeded in driving directly on Saso. What MechWarrior wouldn't have burned to be in the thick of the fighting again?

Reports coming in told him his forces had succeeded in pushing the defenders back, but it had been his accursed luck to attack the section of Saso defended by the Vanguard Legion. Not only had they stalled him, they had actually driven him back. He'd been forced to recall troops from a successful strike against the Fusiliers to help him turn back the Legion's counter-offensive.

In the end, it had availed him nothing. First, he'd lost almost an entire battalion against the Legion, and then his command lance had been surrounded and outnumbered three-to-one. With his ammunition almost exhausted and his armor at less than forty percent, he'd surrendered while radioing his remaining troops to pull back, regroup, and try for a push toward his position at a later time. He'd hoped that his surrender would give the enemy a false sense of victory that he could exploit. Then the horror had begun, and for the first time in many, many years, he'd felt completely out of control of a situation. One that would end in his death.

Suddenly, all went silent around him. Unable to stand not knowing what was happening, even if it meant his death, he brought his 'Mech back on line just in time to see Cadet Jeanpierre Nyanue's death as a *Hatamoto-Chi* tore the *Salamander*'s head off with its PPC. Then, he watched in wonder as a fight began between what he assumed was the leader of the Vanguard Legion and a Fusiliers warrior.

The fight ended with victory for the Fusilier. "This is over now," the enemy warrior said on an open channel, and Amelio realized he'd been wrong. He would not die today. Perhaps the other warrior was referring to the macabre execution, but Amelio sensed it was more than that. The battle was over. The invasion of the planet was over.

With the shadow of death still hanging over him, he knew it was time to stop the madness. Even if by some lunacy he had wanted to continue prosecuting the assault, he might not have the resources to do so. In less than twenty-four hours, his own command had been reduced by half. Even if the defenders were similarly hurt and Amelio could win with one final push, it would be a Pyrrhic victory—one he was not willing to take. This would be the end of his military career—perhaps even the end of his life when the Archon learned what he had done—but he took heart from the courage of the Fusilier warrior who had stopped the executions.

He opened a general link and said, "This is Hauptmann General Victor Amelio, commanding officer of all attacking forces on planet. Under my own authority and in the name of Archon-Princess Katherine Steiner-Davion, I surrender. All forces under my command are to immediately cease fire. In exactly thirty minutes, any unit previously under my command that has not ceased aggressive action against the defending forces will be considered a rogue unit."

He paused, suddenly choked with emotion. In his entire career, he'd never been forced to surrender so completely. Though he believed it was the correct course of action to save the lives of the men left to him, it still galled. He took a breath, then forged on. "Duke George Hasek, I give my forces into your hands with the understanding that the Ares Conventions are in full force. Take care of my men."

30

Our top news story is the complete cessation of hostilities on New Syrtis, with forces loyal to Duke George Hasek still in control of the planet. From the original combined attack-force of the Eleventh Avalon Hussars RCT, the Fourth Donegal Guards RCT, and the Ridgebrook CMM, only remnants of the Fourth are left. They are lifting off planet as we speak, leaving the blasted remains of two enemy RCTs littering the snowy landscape.

In a public statement released today, Duke Hasek is calling the defenders of New Syrtis heroes who answered the call of duty above and beyond all expectations, incurring a debt he hopes to spend the rest of his life repaying. He also singled out the Vanguard Legion and their commander Colonel Chad Dean for particular praise, noting that it was their counter-attack into the teeth of the Fourth Donegal Guards RCT that stalled the assault on Saso, finally ending the conflict. Our sources report that the Vanguard Legion has been secluded on the Jason Hasek Proving Grounds for the last week, with all attempts to gain access denied by Fusilier personnel. It is rumored that they are preparing to lift off planet, which is a strange response to Duke Hasek's praise.

Regardless, the day we have all yearned for has finally arrived, and we can only hope and pray that the peace begun here will spread to the rest of the Federated Commonwealth.

—From *Headline News*, Federated News Services, New Syrtis, Federated Suns, 23 May 3066

The Cave
Saso, New Syrtis
Capellan March
Federated Suns
24 May 3066

"**C**an it really be over?" George Hasek asked as he looked at the tired faces of the men and women standing around him in the Cave.

No one spoke for a moment as several technicians and comm techs continued to busily tap away at their console keyboards. Finally, Jessica Quarles, commander of the Davion Light Guards, looked up from the station where she'd been reading data over a warrant officer's shoulder. "Yes, sir. We have confirmed that the last DropShip has just lifted off planet."

George thought she looked like hell, like someone who'd been beaten with a baseball bat, leaving sickly blue-green bruises just under the skin that were only now starting to fade. That was exactly what the Eleventh Lyran Guards had done to her Light Guard—at least metaphorically—and she'd felt every blow. Glancing around, he thought everyone else looked just as bad, like refuges from some natural disaster, the haunted look of what they had seen in their eyes. He glanced down at his gloved left hand and clenched the prosthetic angrily. This fight had scarred them all.

A comm tech's voice broke into his thoughts. "My

lord, excuse me, but we've just received a priority transmission." From the way the man fidgeted, George thought the news must be bad. It had to be Katherine. What had she done now?

"Let me see it," he said.

The man moved toward a private message-viewer so George could read the message in private, then decide whether to share with the others. The comm tech nervously inserted the disk and activated the viewer, then moved aside to let George take his place.

George wondered if he was imagining the look of relief on the man's face, probably because he'd escaped without a reprimand. Prone to dark moods and outbursts these days, George knew he hadn't been the same since the attack on his life. He only seemed to feel like his old self when Deborah was near. Oh, how his dear mother had railed against him when he'd told her he'd chosen a wife. "You wanted an heir to the throne, Mother," he'd commented dryly. "You'll have one in less than a year." He wondered if she'd ever speak to him again.

He rubbed at his forehead, trying to bring his thoughts back to the message. The battle for New Syrtis was over, but others were still raging all across his Capellan March, and this communication might deal with any of those.

The viewer flashed briefly, then a holomessage flared into existence. It showed a man with close-cropped black hair and a dark complexion, wearing a Federated Suns uniform. George recognized him immediately, and his mind raced, trying to figure out why he was sending him a message.

"This is a priority message Alpha-Zulu-Zulu-Sierra for Duke George Hasek only," the man said. The screen went blank for several long seconds, waiting for the voice-activation code from the duke.

"Baker-Zeta-Absolution," George said, and the viewer lit up again and activated.

"My Duke, this is Major General Oscar Carlson, commanding officer of the Second Ceti Hussars Regimental Combat Team. Having finally secured my unit's previous posting, we've come in response to your summons for aid. We are here to lift the siege on New Syrtis, and then we will continue on to help the Prince remove Katherine from power. We've already begun a fast burn toward the planet, and estimate our arrival in less than four days. We should begin immediate coordination of all on-planet force deployment information, so my Hussars can be used to their utmost. I respectfully await your communiqué." After a final salute from Carlson, the screen went dark.

George stared at the private viewer as though it had sprouted five heads, all of them looking like Aleksandr Kerensky sticking out his tongue like a pouting three-year-old.

A silent laugh built up inside him. It started low in the pit of his stomach and grew until it shook his entire body. Bending over in his seat, he continued to convulse while trying not to laugh out loud until he could no longer tell whether the tears rolling down his face were from mirth or whether he'd begun to weep.

"Sire. My Duke, are you well?" someone asked from

behind him. George raised his hand to say he was okay. Dashing the tears from his eyes, he summoned the strength that had fortified him through six terrible months of fighting on his homeworld. He stood up and walked slowly back toward the main conference table in the center of the Cave, then leaned heavily against the edge as though he would collapse without its support.

After an uncomfortable stretch of silence, he got control of his voice and began to speak. "Well, it would seem that my call for aid several months ago has finally been answered. That was Major General Carlson and his Second Ceti Hussars. They're inbound even now."

He stopped as he felt another bout of black humor about to erupt. What irony, he thought. After all this time, one of his units had finally answered his call. Except that now there was no siege to lift, and the unit was only stopping on its way to join Victor. That a unit under his command was "stopping along the way" to lift a siege of their liege lord's homeworld after the siege was broken made him want to scream in frustration. "They say they're here to save us on their way to take back New Avalon."

From the look on Deborah's face, he knew what she thought of their not-so-timely arrival or their arrogant assumptions. Jessica Quarles, on the other hand, seemed to light up for the first time in many weeks. Perhaps the mention of Victor Davion and a drive to unseat Katherine touched her pride in her unit's history. The Light Guards were members of the Davion Brigade of Guards, after all. Even after the years she'd faithfully served under George, he'd lost her with only a few words. Such was the pull of the Davion line on those who'd sworn oaths to them. To the question of why his own fealty was not bound so tightly, he had no answer.

As he looked around at the other officers and staff in the room, their reactions fell somewhere between those two extremes, though most seemed put off by the irony of the situation and the arrogance of the Ceti Hussars. Significantly, Ardan Sortek was not present.

Turning, he noticed that the comm tech who'd given him the message was again at his elbow, waiting for something. George was about to order the man away when he realized he was waiting for a response. Tired to his bones, vexed that this annoyance came during what should have been a celebration of the liberation of New Syrtis, he said, "Tell Major General Carlson that we'd be happy to receive a visit from the Second Ceti Hussars. Have them ground directly at the Saso Spaceport."

Epilogue

REPORTER: So, Mr. Lewis, it seems that the major conflicts that have been flaring these long years have finally begun to wind down. Can we hope that this means the end might finally be in sight?

LEWIS: I only wish that were true. There are two reasons why most conflicts have either ceased or are in their final stages throughout both the Lyran Alliance and our own Federated Commonwealth. First, there are simply no more forces to assign to those conflicts, and so they have been won or lost by ones loyal to either the Archon-Princess or Prince Victor. From Cavanaugh II to Dalkeith, Hesperus II to Tikonov, and Kathil to New Syrtis, most of the significant battles to date have finally wound down because of attrition on both sides. For the battles still underway, the side that has taken the least damage on any given planet will soon be in control of their world. The second reason is the coming battle for New Avalon. Over the last year, the Archon-Princess has achieved a massive troop build-up, which my sources last reported at nine regiments—most of them regimental combat teams. Prince Victor has had no choice but to strip as many units as he can from every theater of the war as he begins the long march to finally unseat his sister. I have no doubt that this will be the largest single battle to occur in centuries, even surpassing the assault of all eight Crucis Lancers RCT on Tikonov during the Fourth Succession War.

REPORTER: Is there any hope that the Archon-Princess might abdicate?

LEWIS: Do I really need to answer that?

REPORTER: Apart from the horrific battle you predict for New Avalon, can the rest of the Commonwealth and Alliance prepare to breathe a sigh of relief?

LEWIS: Except for Tharkad.

REPORTER: Tharkad! But why?

LEWIS: Because the Estate General is still loyal to the Archon-Princess. More important, General of the Armies Nondi Steiner and the forces under her command are loyal as well. Though it will be nowhere near the size of the conflict brewing on New Avalon, Tharkad will be the other pivotal battle as we move into the final throes of the civil war. In less than a year, the smoke will finally clear and a victor, be it Archon-Princess or Prince, will finally emerge from the ashes.

> —Interview with military analyst Geoffrey Lewis, *Conflict*, Federated News Services, Robinson, Federated Suns, 28 May 3066

Hasek Ancestral Palace
Saso, New Syrtis
Capellan March
Federated Suns
29 May 3066

The Hall of Audience stood resplendent in the full colors of the Federated Suns and the Capellan March, along with the ancestral colors of the Hasek household. The walls were hung with numerous other dark blue pennants highlighted with red and light blue to celebrate the arrival of the Second Ceti Hussars. Gaily attired servants and soldiers lined the walls, and the whole place had an air of merriment and celebration. Yet, a dark undercurrent ran through the crowd, an echo of the blasted hulks of buildings and dead bodies spread across Saso.

For a moment, George Hasek almost felt sorry for the commander of the Second Ceti Hussars. He seemed at a loss for words, looking around him and perhaps finally catching on to the emotional vibe of the throng. A fleeting look of alarm showed on his face as he realized that he was not the honored guest he seemed to be and that his six honor guards were very few against such numbers. The doors were a long way off.

As the thrum of voices rose, echoing off the walls, Ardan Sortek stepped from the crowd and approached the front of the Hall, his polished boots tapping sharply on the marble floor. Watching him, George was not surprised that Ardan was coming to this man's rescue. After all these months, after all the years of friendship to the Hasek family, Ardan was a Davion man to his soul. For a moment, George felt sorrowful, realizing that he would probably never see Ardan alive again. What's more, they would not part as the affectionate friends they should have been. The fine line of their loyalties divided them as surely as the gulf between worlds was impossible to traverse without a JumpShip. Would that we'd found a JumpShip to bridge our differences, George thought with melancholy.

"My Duke, what are you saying?" Ardan asked, his voice calm but solicitous. For some reason, it made George remember a long-ago comment by his father that his friend Ardan Sortek made the perfect politician because he hated everything he did in the name of politics. Seeing Ardan now, so deft at producing the perfect reconciliatory manner, George thought his father was wrong. No one this good could hate their work.

"I'm sure I made myself clear, Ardan," he said, his own voice equally congenial. Though he'd had a moment of wanting to stand up and slap the arrogant look off Carlson's face, he would not let emotion rule him. This would be a matter of reason, of thoughtful action. There would be no accusations of impropriety at a later date. He had no doubt that history was in the making and that, for good or ill, he was at the center of it. Decades or centuries from now, imbecilic old men with no military experience who dared call themselves historians would look back on this time and decide whether his actions had strengthened the Federated Suns or weakened it. At the moment, he was following the course of action that his loyalties, as well as his own heart and mind, demanded of him.

"I thank the general for coming to our aid, belated though it may be," he continued, keeping sarcasm to a minimum, "but he is free to depart as quickly as possible to pursue his unit's desire to join Victor Davion in his march on New Avalon."

"But, my lord, should that not be your agenda as well? A usurper sits on the throne of New Avalon, and it is time the realm was again in the hands of its rightful ruler."

George nodded. "I haven't heard the name Yvonne mentioned in all the time you've been on planet, Ardan."

Annoyance flashed in Ardan's eyes, telling George that he'd scored a point. If Ardan was going to force his hand, then he would force Ardan's in return. "There is a reason I have not mentioned Yvonne, my lord. At the time Katherine took the throne away from her, Yvonne was only acting regent in Victor's absence. As Victor intends to remove Katherine, should you not support him now?"

"Is he going to remove her, or is he going to reestablish his claim to the throne?" George asked. The hall had gone silent, and his words seemed to reverberate beyond the walls of this great hall. What was happening here would spin outward from New Syrtis to affect every world of the Federated Suns and perhaps even the whole Inner Sphere.

Ardan hesitated slightly, but he covered it well. "Victor has stated many times that his only purpose is to remove an unfit ruler from the throne. Perhaps now that Yvonne has had time to mature, he will bestow on her the honor of reassuming the throne. Regardless, I ask again, my Duke, shouldn't you provide support for such an endeavor? Shouldn't you directly assist in removing the person who ordered the attack on your own capital world?"

George stared at Ardan, then looked at General Carlson, and finally allowed his gaze to wander across the throng gathered around him in the Hall of Audience. His people. Though he detected anxiety or fear on a few faces, most seemed to listen with calm acceptance. Having survived a devastating, six-month-long attack, they still trusted him to lead. Trusted him and believed in him enough to wait patiently for whatever he decided. Though he'd known it would be like this, their faith almost moved him to tears. Looming behind him, he felt the shadow of his father and the weight of responsibility for the people of the Capellan March.

"No," he said, his voice thick with emotion. "I should not."

General Carlson shook his head as though unable to believe his ears, and Ardan's eyes widened slightly, the only indication that George's words had taken him by surprise.

"My lord, no?" he said. "I apologize for showing the ignorance of a common man, but how can your cause not coincide with that of Prince Victor's in wanting to remove Katherine?"

George leaned back, more relaxed then he'd been in some time. The words had been spoken, the gauntlet cast onto the marble floor. Now it was time to finish this and get on with securing his March. "I never said I didn't support removing Katherine from the throne. What I said was that I would not directly support Victor in that bid."

"But how can those be different?"

"Very easily, my good Ardan. Yes, we've finally driven Katherine's troops from New Syrtis, but there are dozens of worlds under my stewardship that are still at war. Should I race off to New Avalon when my own house is not yet in order?"

He leaned forward and placed his left hand on his leg, an ever-present reminder of what he'd already sacrificed to defend his people. "I must care for my realm first, Ardan—my people first. My loyalties and duties are to them first, then to the rest of the Federated Suns. Perhaps that is something that Victor has forgotten. In his drive to eliminate the Clan threat, he overlooked the simple fact that he is *our* First Prince, not the Prince of the Inner Sphere. If he'd remembered that, perhaps none of this would have happened. Nevertheless, *I* remember it, and my first loyalty is here.''

The hall was stunned silent by his words. Not only had George publicly rebuked Victor for his actions, but he left no doubt that his loyalty to New Avalon had been severely strained. He had just woven a new skein in history, and it would grow to cover the entire Federated Suns. For the first time in almost half a millennia, the Prince of a Federated Suns March was taking back the power that made him a first among equals to the First Prince on New Avalon. Whether his beloved realm would be strong enough to survive such a weakening of central authority, George did not know. But he believed—he had to believe—that it would be. The history of the Suns had proven that its people were resilient. Events like the one he was setting in motion would come and go, leaving them stronger for the tempering.

''I thank you for your companionship and aid during this time, Ardan,'' he said, ''but I believe your visit has come to an end. Depart with the Hussars to free New Avalon. I'm sure what's left of the Light Guards would also be happy to accompany you. Perhaps when my own realm is in order, we may one day meet again.''

About the Author

Randall N. Bills began his writing career in the adventure-gaming industry, where he spent five years working full-time for FASA Corporation, specifically on their BattleTech® line. After publishing several scenario books and sourcebooks for both BattleTech® and Shadowrun®, he moved to novels and to on-line serial fiction. This is Randall's second BattleTech® novel after *Path of Glory*.

He recently moved to the Pacific Northwest to pursue full-time writing, including novels and freelance game development. He lives with his wife Tara, son Bryn, and an eight-foot red-tailed boa called Jak o' the Shadows.